Daisy Lansing's ability to transfer images from people's thoughts onto paper was a novelty she used to trot out to amuse her friends. But when her "entranced drawing" begins to cause serious trouble for her guardians, she is banished to the country and forced to marry a man twice her age. After the joyless wedding, Daisy is determined to bury forever the strange skill that upended her life. However, she soon finds herself a widow and in dire financial straits. Suddenly, her curse may be her one chance at true independence.

Jackson Gallway's reputation as a rogue has far surpassed his success as a lawyer. In the wake of yet another scandal, he decides to head west. But before he can escape Misty Lake, Jax makes a promise to find an elusive killer. When he encounters a lovely young artist with an unusual talent that could help him in his search, what he finds is something neither of them can escape . . .

Books by Thomasine Rappold

The Sole Survivor Series
The Lady Who Lived Again
The Lady Who Saw Too Much
The Lady Who Drew Me In

Published by Kensington Publishing Corporation

The Lady Who Drew Me In

A Sole Survivor Novel

Thomasine Rappold

LYRICAL PRESS
Kensington Publishing Corp.
www.kensingtonbooks.com

First Electronic Edition: December 2016
eISBN-13: 978-1-61650-995-8
eISBN-10 1-61650-995-3

First Print Edition: December 2016
ISBN-13: 978-1-61650-996-5
ISBN-10: 1-61650-996-1

Printed in the United States of America

For my daughters, Carlie and Andrea, whose kindness, independence, and strength make me smile every day.

Acknowledgements

As always, thank you to my agent, Stefanie Lieberman; my editor, Paige Christian; Kimberly Richardson, Michelle Forde, Lauren Jernigan, and the rest of the team at Kensington/Lyrical for all the hard work you do to make me look good. Thank you to the Capital Region Romance Writers and my critique partners (the BFS), for being there through the crazy ups and downs, and for all the laughs in between. Special thanks to my family, friends, and readers, for the ongoing support. Much love to you all.

Chapter 1

Misty Lake, New York, 1885

The man was controlling her from six feet under. Daisy Lansing stared up at the portrait of her late husband, so angered by his betrayal she could scream. *Monthly allowance, my foot.*

With a sigh, she slumped into the high-back chair behind the large desk, fighting back tears. All his promises, all these years… He'd lied, and then he'd died, taking the independence she'd thought would finally be hers along with him. Not to mention her dream of opening a day home for working-class children. The crushing reality weighed on her shoulders, tightening her neck muscles into knots.

She glanced to the large bay window, watching her latest financial prospect scurry to his carriage, then speed away in a cloud of dust. Failed attempts to secure an investor for her plans for the home were mounting as high as the stacks of neglected paperwork on the desk in front of her. Completing her latest painting had taken its toll. And she'd yet to be paid for the blasted thing.

She checked the hour on the gold watch around her neck. Her appointment with William Markelson was at three o'clock, so she had only minutes to brace herself for more bad news. Rubbing her temples, she soothed the budding throb of a headache. At the sound of a woman's laughter outside, Daisy glanced to the window. Felice Pettington.

Daisy shot to her feet. "It's about time," she mumbled, scooting around the desk for a closer view. Misty Lake's most celebrated summer guest strolled up the walkway, blond spit curls bobbing beneath her stylish bonnet as she slathered her charms on the tall man at her side.

And who do we have here?

Daisy craned her neck toward the window. The pretty heiress nestled against her handsome escort, her gloved hands like twin boa constrictors coiled around his arm. Curious as to whom the woman had snared to join her on the impromptu visit, Daisy hurried out to the porch.

Felice's sweeping yellow skirts brushed the blooming shrubs flanking the stone walk, stirring petals and the scent of rhododendrons through the air. Her mousy maid followed in the flurry.

"Yoo-hoo!" Felice unfurled her grip on the man just enough to wave her gloved fingers. "This is Mr. Gallway." She leaned toward the man's impressive shoulder, batting her lashes as they stepped up to the porch. "Mr. Gallway is from Troy."

Daisy's heart lurched, as it always did, at the mention of Troy. Even after all this time, the painful memories of her past in the city hadn't faded a whit.

Felice smiled smugly. "He's an attorney."

Daisy took a deep breath. Of all the lawyers Felice might have cajoled to browbeat Daisy on her behalf, the woman had enlisted a relative of Daisy's closest friend. Tessa Gallway had gushed that her rakish brother-in-law was handsome, but the simple description hardly did him justice.

Daisy gave a slow nod, her aversion to lawyers suffering a brief lapse as she studied him closer. Layers of wavy black hair matched his thick brows and the sideburns that led to his jaw. His sapphire eyes sparkled in the sunlight.

And his mouth. Good Heavens, his mouth. Daisy swallowed hard, awed by her response to the man. He was nothing like she'd imagined, yet everything portrayed in the gossip. A notorious rogue intent on skirting marriage and sowing a silo's worth of oats in the process.

His smile widened, as though he'd heard Daisy's unspoken assessment and expected no less. More likely he was simply too arrogant to care.

"You can wait for me here, Myrtle." Felice waved her maid toward one of the rocking chairs on the porch.

Daisy ushered them inside, and then led them down the hall to the library. After all this time, the scent of Lawry's final cigar still clung to the paneled walls. The familiar smell she'd relished so fondly after his death affected her differently now. How could he do this to her?

Blinking back tears, she returned her focus to her guests. Felice batted her lashes, then proceeded with a formal introduction. Extending an arm toward Daisy, she said, "Mr. Jackson Gallway, I present the Widow Lansing."

Daisy cringed.

Felice smiled.

Jackson Gallway stepped forward, his eyes wide. "You're the Widow Lansing?"

Daisy frowned. "I am Daisy Lansing, yes."

He gave her a thorough once-over. "You're much younger than I expected."

The blunt confession surprised her. Not that she blamed him for his presumption she was a wrinkled old prune. She'd married a man thirty years her senior and was used to the reactions she'd garnered during introductions. Surprise, suspicion, disgust—she'd seen them all. Since Lawry's death ten months ago, she'd become known as the Widow Lansing and, like it or not, the title carried an image.

"It's good to finally meet you," she replied honestly. At the inquisitive arch of his brow, she explained, "Your brother's wife is my dearest friend."

"Ah," he said with a nod. "Any friend of Tessa's ..."

Reaching for her hand, he smiled, the effect of which she couldn't ignore. His confident grip said he'd done this before—charmed women senseless with barely a word. And still she felt flattered. Clasping her fingers, he stared down at her, and she marveled at the unique shade of his eyes.

Had she imagined the flash of desire that sparkled inside them? After all, it had been ages since a man had touched her. Although she hadn't particularly missed marital relations, abstinence, it seemed suddenly, had made her body grow fonder.

"It's a pleasure, Mrs. Lansing." The sound of his voice was as smooth as the skin on his freshly shaven face. The perfect form of his lips steered her mind down a path it hadn't wandered in years. Her pulse quickened.

"Daisy," she uttered, sounding more like a smitten school girl than a twenty-four-year-old widow.

Several long moments passed, and every nerve in her body tingled beneath the heat in his eyes. Her mouth went bone dry.

"Ahem." Felice took an imposing step forward. "I came to settle this business of the portrait."

Daisy took a deep breath. "And you needed a lawyer to assist?"

"I am not her attorney, Mrs. Lansing. I am merely her escort."

Daisy eyed him warily. *Escort, my foot.* She knew all about Felice's string of admirers from the city. The woman's visit to the Misty Lake Hotel across the lake was the talk of the town. As were her suitors—men who tripped over themselves to alleviate her boredom.

Jackson Gallway seemed a potent cure for the doldrums. The thought made Daisy flush. From what she'd heard of him, he'd had plenty of practice entertaining women. Tessa's husband was pressing him to settle down, though. Who better for the wayward lawyer to settle down on than a beautiful heiress?

Daisy shook off her irritating envy. When had her focus turned from Felice to the wretched woman's *escort*?

"Please sit." Daisy motioned toward the Grecian sofa in the center of the room.

Gallway waited until both women were seated before joining Felice on the sofa. Felice adjusted her ample skirts, inching casually toward him. Daisy settled into the chair across from the pair, rolling her eyes at the woman's blatant flirtations.

"As I made clear in my notes to you, Felice, your portrait is ready, and payment is now due."

"That's precisely why I came to see you. I've changed my mind about the painting."

"But the work is complete."

Felice shrugged.

"Let me remind you," Daisy said. "I had no wish to paint you until you insisted your payment would be well worth my trouble."

Felice tossed her head, unaffected. "I no longer wish to purchase another portrait of myself."

Daisy clenched her teeth. The heat of anger rushed to her cheeks. "I don't give a fig what you do or do not wish. I spent nine days painting this piece. From memory, I might add, since you couldn't be bothered to pose for longer than half an hour."

"Half an hour?" Gallway cocked a brow, pointing with a nod of his chin toward the portrait on the easel by the window. "You painted that portrait from a pose you sketched in less than an hour?"

Daisy straightened, puffing her chest. "I have an exceptional memory."

"Exceptional, indeed," he uttered.

Felice huffed. "Be that as it may, these things happen. I hope my visit today puts an end to your incessant demands for payment."

Daisy took a deep breath, glancing to the man at Felice's side. He sat silently, an expectant look on his handsome face. He awaited Daisy's response, her inevitable defeat, as though his mere presence ensured it. Blasted lawyers.

Daisy turned to Felice. "You are absolutely certain that you do not want the piece?"

"Quite certain," she snapped. She primped at her curls. "It hardly flatters me."

Daisy took a deep breath. "Very well then." She mustered her most diplomatic tone. "Since you refuse to pay me for my work, I am forced to find someone who will."

Felice narrowed her eyes. "What do you mean?"

"I shall seek another buyer," Daisy said.

The woman's perfectly groomed brows shot up in surprise. "Another buyer?"

"That's right."

"But who—"

"I've heard of a businessman in Texas who is currently shopping for just such a piece." Daisy stretched her arm toward the easel, presenting the work in a show of admiration. "He's enamored with the idea of displaying a portrait of a genuine heiress above the bar in his saloon."

Felice gasped. "His saloon? My portrait?"

"My portrait," Daisy reminded her. "I will be compensated for my services one way or another."

Felice's eyes bulged.

Daisy's heart pounded a battle sound in her ears. She fired a glance at the lawyer. He sat, riveted in silence, his fine mouth pursed tight. The surprising possibility he would remain that way fueled her confidence.

"Of course, I'll have to alter the painting," Daisy continued. "Lower the neckline of the gown, enhance the décolletage."

"You can't do that!" Felice spun her head from Daisy to Gallway and back so fast her bonnet slid askew. She adjusted the cockeyed thing quickly, chest heaving.

"It's my painting, and I can do with it whatever I please. Anyone with a brain will tell you that." Daisy turned to Gallway. He disputed nothing, proving her point. From the smile quirking his lips, it seemed he was enjoying Felice's comeuppance almost as much as Daisy.

"This is an outrage." Felice ground out each word. Her eyes were blue ice. Even her curls froze stiff. "I will not be bullied by the likes of you, Daisy Lansing. I'll see to it you never open that day home for those guttersnipes."

"They are not guttersnipes, Felice. They are children. Good children. But I will speak no further on a topic that is well beyond your emotional capabilities as a human being."

"Hmph!" Felice turned toward the lawyer. "Do something," she demanded. "Tell this—this—person, that I will report her to the authorities. That—"

"The price for the painting has doubled," Daisy announced.

"What?" Felice shot to her feet.

Daisy straightened her spine. "Ante up, Felice, or your likeness is on the next train bound for the Yellow Rose Saloon and Gaming Parlor."

The woman gaped.

Gallway coughed.

"Criminal!" Felice screeched.

The woman's undoing filled Daisy with a satisfaction so strong she had to bite her lip against smiling. She shrugged. "I've done nothing illegal. Have I, Mr. Gallway?"

He shook his head, coughing some more. "Mrs. Lansing is well within her rights," he sputtered, composing himself. "Possession and all."

"But—"

"The law is the law." His solemn words contradicted the gleam of amusement in his eyes.

"You don't know everything, Jackson Gallway. This matter is far from settled."

"Pursue it, if you must." He stood, his voice rising in the volume and formality so common among lawyers. "But consider the publicity. Settle your debt with Mrs. Lansing, and enjoy your new portrait." He glanced to Daisy. "Remarkable work."

His admiration seemed genuine, and she gobbled it up like a woman starved. If he noticed her pathetic reaction, he didn't show it. He merely took a deep breath and turned to Felice.

"If you will pardon us, I have some important business of my own to discuss with Mrs. Lansing."

This news surprised Daisy as much as it insulted Felice. The woman adjusted her bonnet, then gave a stiff fluff of her skirts, composing herself as she swished toward the door. She tossed a flippant wave behind her. "Have the thing wrapped. My coachman will stop for it tomorrow. He'll deliver your payment as well," she called over her shoulder as though she were the victor of the dispute. She disappeared from the room.

"Well done." Jackson turned to Daisy. "Very well done." He laughed, shaking his dark head.

"She deserved it," Daisy said, enjoying the sound of his laughter. The man was a charmer, she'd give him that. How had she not met him before now? She'd spent enough time with Tessa at the Gallway mansion to know the servants by name, and yet her path had never crossed his. Until now.

"What can I do for you, Mr. Gallway?" she asked, gesturing him back to his seat.

He stretched his long legs and settled into the sofa, which suddenly seemed too small to contain his broad frame. She let her gaze drop to his shoulders, his waist, and his powerful thighs.

"William Markelson sent me."

"Yes," she said, springing back to attention. "I've been awaiting word from him on the matter of my late husband's will."

"I've come to inform you that Markelson refused your request to review the document."

Her heart sank. "He will not even look at it, then?"

"No. Your husband was a revered attorney, and you'll be hard pressed to find anyone in his profession to challenge his will."

As she had heard from every other lawyer she'd approached on the matter.

"Your husband was quite vocal in his concerns you might be inclined to overindulge in your charitable works."

Daisy lowered her gaze. "Yes, well. Lawry never was one for overindulgence," she muttered. A blush of shame warmed her face.

"Your monthly allowance cannot be exceeded."

Daisy sighed. While she would somehow make do with the paltry sum, it would take years for her paintings to earn what she needed for the day home. She glanced toward the portrait in the stream of sunlight by the window and frowned at Felice Pettington's smug face. "I should have tripled the price."

* * * *

Jackson watched the young widow, her solemn blue eyes, the desperation in the slump of her shoulders. Perhaps she was more than the greedy schemer his associates had labeled her. She was challenging the old man's will to gain funds for her charity work, and her drive and generosity touched on his rusty conscience.

He straightened in his seat and returned to business. He sympathized with her dilemma, but after shattering her hopes for her charitable endeavors, he had a problem of his own to solve. The wheels in his mind spun with the best way to broach his forthcoming request.

"Well, thank you for delivering the message, Mr. Gallway." She stood, lifting her chin. "Unless there's anything else…"

He stood, then stepped toward her. The sweet scent of her was subdued and not fancy. As refreshing as a brisk walk in the park. "As a matter of fact, there is."

"Oh?"

She tilted her head as they returned to their seats. Shades of gold shimmered in her hair. Christ, she was pretty….

"Mr. Gallway?"

She wet her lips, and the glimpse of her pink tongue left him speechless. He shook his head, flustered.

"I need your help," he said quickly.

"My help?"

She blinked in surprise, and he found himself pleased by his role in replacing the sadness in her eyes. "Your artistic talent is evident," he said with a nod toward the painting of Felice Pettington. "But what I've heard about your other talent impresses me more."

She frowned, her face flaring with anger.

"The ability to transfer people's thoughts onto paper seems unbelievable to me," he said, "but witnesses swear your ability is real."

"It is all too real, I assure you," she snapped. "And it's an ability I no longer utilize."

"Perhaps you'd consider making an exception?"

She narrowed her eyes.

"I need to procure a sketch from a witness. Others have failed in soliciting any details from this witness—"

"No." She shook her head. "As I've stated quite clearly, I don't draw in that manner anymore."

"But you could."

"I won't." She lifted her chin. "And I won't be persuaded, so you are wasting your breath."

"And you're wasting your gift. If there's a chance you can help—"

"My gift? That *gift* ruined my life, Mr. Gallway. Not to mention the lives of several others." She tilted her head. "But you know this already, don't you?"

She had him there. Although the details were vague, the trouble she'd instigated in Troy was notorious. He couldn't blame her angry reaction. He'd had his nose rubbed in his mistakes enough times to know how she felt.

"That's all in the past," he said.

"And yet, here you are. Dredging up the sordid incident to suit your agenda." She frowned in disgust. "Blasted lawyers," she muttered as she shot to her feet. "Allow me to show you to the door."

"Please, Mrs. Lansing."

She stopped in her tracks. The tight lines of her mouth slackened at his gentle coaxing. His skill to seduce never failed, and it wouldn't fail now.

"This witness is a child," he said.

"A child?"

"His father was murdered."

She winced. "Are you speaking of Mr. Wendell?"

"I am."

"But they already caught the man who… Are you defending his killer?"

Her horrified expression bespoke her opinion on the matter, and he reined back his frustration.

"I am defending the man accused of the crime. I do not believe he is the killer. The boy may be able to help prove that. Several other vendors from the city pass that farm each week, and attaining their identities is crucial in producing other suspects."

"Or eliminating them," she pointed out.

"Either way, the boy may have seen something. Neighbors say he was out in the fields when his father was killed, but he refuses to speak of it. In the months since finding his father dead, he hasn't spoken a word. That's where you come in."

She pursed her lips, as though wresting with the dilemma. The shift in her features told him she was as distressed by the prospect of using her strange ability again as she was for the boy's situation.

"You'll be compensated, of course. I'll pay you for your time."

"I have my own money, Mr. Gallway. But my husband's cronies won't let me have it." She straightened her spine. "But if you assist with my husband's will, I'll do whatever I can to help you."

He knew she'd help regardless of his answer. There was a child involved, and that's what mattered to her now. Still, Jackson admired her attempt to use the situation to her advantage. *A woman after my own heart.*

"I'll agree to review the will for loopholes, but I won't make any promises."

"Promises are worthless," she snapped. "But we have a deal."

"The child will be difficult. As I said, he refuses to speak."

"He won't have to," she murmured.

The confidence in her quiet assertion was encouraging. While he still didn't fully believe in her fantastical ability, he'd find out soon enough.

"We'll have to travel to a farm in the Barston Mountains where the boy is staying." He held his breath. Her reputation was at risk by traveling alone with him through the woods, but there was no way around this.

"All right."

Jackson exhaled in relief. The boy held the key to Randal Morgan's freedom, and with any luck he would relinquish that key to the Widow Lansing. Jackson would have what he wanted. But at what price?

"We'll be discreet," she said. "The child needs help."

And with her words came a sinking feeling he couldn't ignore. Guilt. She didn't trust lawyers, and she didn't trust him—and with good reason.

Still, she would help. Despite her reluctance, she'd do what she could for the boy's sake, which was just as Jackson had predicted. One day of her time was worth it to her, if she could help a child. The insight into the woman and her worthy motives prompted more guilt.

Jackson stiffened against his nagging conscience. Landing that position in St. Louis hinged on this case, and the young widow was living proof that he would use anything—and anyone—to win it.

Chapter 2

Five more minutes. That's all he'd give her. Jackson sat in the driver's seat of the old buckboard he'd rented in town, gazing down the deserted road through the middle of nowhere for any sign of the Widow Lansing. Involving her was a damn foolish idea, and the longer she gave him to think about it, the more tempted he was to snap the reins and move the bucket of bolts beneath him toward the mountains without her.

As he'd discovered while investigating this case, there were no guarantees, and her assistance could put her in danger. He pushed through his reservations about dragging her into his business. He was desperate.

A moment later she appeared in the distance, her slender form moving briskly through the early-morning fog. A basket in one hand and a small case in the other had left her unable to adjust her bonnet, which the breeze of her pace had blown to the nape of her neck.

Jackson jumped down to meet her.

"Good morning," she said with a smile. A flush of exertion highlighted the sprinkle of freckles on the bridge of her nose. She looked as young as a school girl. "I'm not late, am I?"

He reached for the basket still swinging in her hand. The smell of fried chicken wafted through the checkered napkin inside. Jackson frowned. "This isn't a picnic."

Her smile faded. "I know that, Mr. Gallway. But it's a long trip. I tend to get surly when I'm hungry." She handed him the case that he assumed contained her sketching supplies. "What's your excuse?" she mumbled as she made her way to the side of the wagon and climbed aboard, unassisted.

With a shake of his head, he placed the case and the basket into the back of the wagon and hopped up to join her. The floral scent of her hair was difficult to ignore. He sat for a long moment, entranced by the smell, staring down at the reins in his hands. He couldn't go through with this. He had no right to jeopardize her safety, especially when he'd misled her about the real purpose for the trip.

He inhaled a long breath. "I've withheld from you an important detail of this case. By doing so, I've understated the—"

"Withheld? Understated?" She stared incredulously. "Lawyers," she said, shaking her head. "So what is this detail you've withheld?"

"I believe the boy witnessed the murder."

She gaped. "But you said he was out in the fields—"

"*The neighbors* said he was in the fields. They questioned him."

"And you think he's lying?"

"I think he's afraid. I think his father suspected trouble when the killer arrived at the house and told him to hide."

"To protect him."

"Yes. Which means he may have seen the killer from where he was hiding."

She winced as this registered. "He's so afraid he can't speak," she uttered.

"Now you understand my dilemma. And discretion," he said.

She nodded slowly, her gaze soft and contrite. "You're protecting him too." Her blue eyes shone with admiration, and he was struck by a sudden longing to be worthy of it.

"It's best you go home—"

"No." She straightened her spine. "If the poor child saw something, I can get it down in a sketch."

"It could be dangerous." He spoke with a fondness he'd felt for her the moment he laid eyes on her. "If I'm right…"

"You must let me try. The boy needs help."

How anyone could refuse the woman anything, he didn't know. Her eyes could melt ice. Not that he'd ever been a glacier when it came to women, but the young widow had a fire inside her.

"Besides, I know a shortcut," she said. "There's a logging trail straight through to the mountains."

He opened his mouth to protest, but the words didn't come. Like it or not, he needed her help. He snapped the reins, refusing to dwell on misgivings. He'd tried to dissuade her, what more could he do? The woman was a stubborn advocate for children. Even without a change in her late husband's will, she'd succeed with her plans for a day home, somehow. He didn't doubt it for a second.

Jackson had a job to do, too, and he couldn't afford distractions. Or another mistake. His scandalous affair in Troy had cost him more than his last position, but it could have been worse. He was lucky to be alive to regret it, and he'd never again let his weakness for the fairer sex overpower common sense.

His attraction to Daisy Lansing would be a challenge, but tonight he'd be miles away. That he might have a sketch in hand when he returned to the city would make everything worth it. Nothing mattered more than his need to clear Randal Morgan's name. And in the process, reclaim his own.

* * * *

The ride along the logging trail was rough as hell. Jackson's faith in the old buckboard dwindled with every mile, dip, and bump. Large boulders protruded through the narrow path; an overgrowth of thorny bushes scratched and clawed as they passed. Uttering a curse, he swatted furiously at another swarm of insects.

"That's Cuffy's place over there." Daisy pointed toward a small shack up ahead.

"Cuffy?"

"He works at the lumber camps. He's a giant of a man but terribly slow-witted. Always wears a cap with a set of antlers on top. Perhaps you've seen him around town?"

"I haven't had the pleasure," Jackson uttered as he eyed the shanty nestled between the tall pines. Two neat stacks of chopped firewood flanked the door, but no smoke rose from the chimney. "He lives alone out here?"

"He spends much of his time at the camps, but he calls this place home. I met him for the first time when I came out here to collect ferns."

"Ferns?"

"Barston has the best fancy ferns. Many shops in the city purchase their ferns from the local farmers, but they're free for the picking to anyone inclined to make the journey this deeply into the woods."

Jackson couldn't imagine ever being so inclined. The isolation of the forest had always made him uneasy. Trudging through the woods to hunt for game was one thing, but fancy ferns? Ridiculous.

"You strike me as someone who prefers the city to the country," she said.

Jackson swatted at a buzzing horsefly. "I prefer buildings and people to trees and insects. So yes, Mrs. Lansing, you can say I prefer the city."

His sarcasm did nothing to dim her sunny chitchat. "I find nature so peaceful."

He smacked another horsefly from his head. "There's nothing peaceful about being a feedbag for a horsefly."

Craning her neck, she peered over his shoulder. "Or a bear."

He flinched, spinning around.

She laughed at his panicked response to her joke, and he couldn't help smiling. There was something in the sound of her laughter he couldn't resist. The honest-to-goodness joy she seemed to get from everything around her. She was bright and beautiful, and he found himself wondering about the circumstances behind her marriage to Lawrence Lansing. Surely a man of Lansing's advanced age was no match for this vibrant woman. This passionate, sweet-smelling woman.

Jackson shook off his musings. What the hell was he thinking? He tugged off his hat, then ran a hand through his hair. He knew damn well what he was thinking, and it was lucky for him that she didn't. Daisy Lansing made it easy to forget his fiasco in Troy—and getting caught with his hands up the skirts of a married woman, by her husband no less, was difficult to forget.

He was relieved when they finally made their way to the edge of the forest and into a sprawling field. Jackson steered the wagon onto the narrow road, which led to some semblance of civilization. At the four corners of the small intersection sat a blacksmith shop, a general store, a church, and a tavern. Everything required to call it a town, but not much more.

"The Rhodes house is up ahead, past the saw mill." She pointed toward a large farmhouse behind a row of birch trees in the distance. Whitewashed stones lined the short drive to the house, where an elderly woman sat in a rocking chair on the porch. A small boy played at her feet.

"Are you Mrs. Rhodes?" Jackson called to the woman, who stood to scoot the child inside. She waited until the screen door slammed shut behind the boy before turning back to the wagon.

She lifted a hand to shield her eyes from the sun, a wary expression etched on her weathered face. "What's your business here, sir?"

"My name is Jackson Gallway. And this is Mrs. Lansing. We're here to see the boy."

"What for? They already caught that murdering devil who orphaned the child. Leave him be."

"It's important, Mrs. Rhodes. We want to be certain the right man is brought to justice. You want to be certain as well. For the boy's safety."

"He didn't see nothing. And he won't say nothing, either."

Jackson nodded. "I know. But we'd still like to try to talk with him."

She studied him for a long moment before her gaze settled on Daisy. "Come on in then," she said, her stern face softening a bit.

Jackson hopped from the wagon. He grabbed Daisy's case of sketching supplies and then reached to help her down. Her small hand held his firmly as he assisted her. Their eyes met, a silent exchange that unified their mission, and the strength of her grip tightened inside his palm. He ushered her up to the porch where Mrs. Rhodes stood, holding open the door.

A shaggy black cat scurried from the house, and Daisy stopped short as it whizzed by her skirt. "Thank you, Mrs. Rhodes. We'll do our utmost not to upset the child." She gave the woman a reassuring smile. "What's his name?"

"Andy."

They stepped inside, where two more cats sat like gargoyles on the deacon's bench in the foyer. Jackson harbored no fondness for felines, and seeing so many in one place was unnerving. Staring straight ahead, he did his best to ignore their keen eyes on his back as he followed the women to the parlor. A stream of sunlight poured across the faded rug in the center of the room. Lace curtains blew softly on the breeze from the open windows. Andy sat nestled against the arm of the sofa, stroking the tabby cat on his lap.

"Hello, Andy," Daisy said as she peeled off her gloves. "My name is Mrs. Lansing." She waved a glove toward Jackson. "And this is Mr. Gallway. We've come to visit with you."

The boy's timid glances moved from Daisy to Jackson before he lowered his blond head and returned his focus to the cat on his lap.

"Sit." Mrs. Rhodes gestured toward the table. "I'll get some cider." She disappeared into the kitchen.

Jackson pulled out a chair for Daisy, then took a seat across from her. Andy watched closely as Daisy placed her case on the table and opened it wide. The boy craned his neck, his eyes narrowing in a curious expression as Daisy removed a tablet of paper and a charcoal pencil, then placed them on the table in front of her. She gazed across the table at Jackson, studied him for a moment, and then started sketching.

"What are you doing?" Jackson murmured.

"I'm sketching you," she said. Her hand moved between glances at him and the sketch pad.

Jackson turned to the boy, who now stood and was moving closer. Very clever. Instead of approaching the boy directly, Daisy was luring him to her. She worked quickly, her slender wrist gliding the pencil across the page with swift, adept strokes. She used the tips of her fingers to smudge the lines into the desired effect, her lips pursed tight in concentration.

Before long Andy stood at her side, watching the sketch on the page emerge before his eyes.

Daisy held up the pad to the boy. "What do you think? Does it look like him?"

Andy smirked, and Daisy broke out laughing. Jackson watched the pair, wondering what they found so amusing.

"May I see?" he asked, feeling like the butt of some joke.

Daisy leaned toward Andy. "Should we show him?"

Her love for children was evident in her effortless talent for putting the boy at ease. With a nod, Andy smiled broadly, exposing a missing front tooth. She turned the pad toward Jackson. The sketch was a remarkable facsimile to him, except for the gigantic pair of ears protruding from his head.

Daisy and Andy absorbed Jackson's reaction, giggling harder. "I don't think he likes it, Andy," she said playfully.

The boy shook his head in answer.

Jackson leaned back in his chair, shaking his head. "Bravo, Mrs. Lansing," he said with a smile. "You've captured my likeness to a fault."

Daisy laughed, dropping the pad to the table as Mrs. Rhodes returned to the room with a tray of glasses and a pitcher of cider.

"Would you like me to sketch you, Andy?" Daisy asked as Mrs. Rhodes placed the tray on the table.

With an eager nod, Andy slid into the chair at Daisy's side.

Daisy glanced to Jackson. "Perhaps you and Mrs. Rhodes can enjoy your cider on the porch." She gestured with her eyes toward the door.

Jackson took the hint and rose from the table. "Join me, Mrs. Rhodes?"

The woman glanced to Andy. Seeing the boy was in good hands, she nodded, wiping her hands on her apron. "I'll be right outside, Andy."

"We'll let you know when we're finished," Daisy assured Mrs. Rhodes. She glanced at Jackson. "Please allow us some privacy until then."

* * * *

Daisy added a set of large ears to her sketch of Andy, too, enjoying the sound of his laughter when she showed him the finished drawing. The boy seemed completely at ease as he nodded or shook his head in response to her general chatter. While she dreaded causing him any distress, she couldn't stall any longer. In one last-ditch attempt to avoid using the cursed ability that had cost her so much, she asked, "Can you tell me what happened that day your father was shot?"

Andy's small shoulders stiffened.

Daisy sighed. "You were there, weren't you, Andy?"

He nodded, lowering his head.

Daisy drew a sharp breath against the ache in her chest. "Can you tell me about it?"

He shook his head hard.

"Or perhaps you're too afraid to talk about it?"

She couldn't blame him, and her heart filled with sorrow for what he had witnessed. A part of her wanted to leave him in peace, but she couldn't. He was a threat to the killer, and in real danger now. She had to do what she must. "If you don't want to speak about it, Andy, you don't have to. But perhaps you could think about it for a few moments instead."

He glanced up.

"Can you do that for me?" she asked. "Can you close your eyes and think about it?"

He gave a wary nod.

"Good boy." She smiled. "Now take my hand and close your eyes." She held Andy's hand between hers. "I know how difficult this must be for you. And I know it hurts to remember." She squeezed his small hand in hers. "But you are safe with Mrs. Rhodes. The man who hurt your father can't hurt you here, so you don't have to be afraid."

She slipped her hand from his, then reached for her pad and pencil. Her hands trembled as she prepared to do what she'd sworn never to do again. Closing her eyes, she staved off her own fears. The memory of the last time she'd traveled this path, the horrified faces and the scandal that followed, detoured the way. She focused harder, forging past the shame and regret and into that desolate place where it all opened wide. She emptied her mind to accept the boy's thoughts. Her fingers twitched on the page. Her tingling hand moved, ceding to the powerful force, as she let the pencil—her ability—take full control.

Andy's fear flooded through her. Submerged in the current, she plunged deeper and deeper into his memories, into the unstoppable movement of her hand and whatever images she was pulling from his mind.

Her hand finally stilled, and she opened her eyes. She'd no idea how long she'd been drawing, but Andy's wide-eyed expression told her it had been a while. She glanced down at the sketch pad.

She'd no real recollection of producing the images that had rushed through her mind. The drawing had poured onto the page of its own volition. But now the boy's horrible memories, each vivid detail of what he'd seen, chased the air from her lungs. She closed the pad quickly. "Are you all right?" she asked.

He nodded.

She gave him a moment, then opened the pad. "Is this the man you saw shoot your father?"

His gaze fixed on the page. Lifting his trembling chin, he gave a firm nod.

She smiled, drawing him into her arms. "You're a very brave little boy," she said as she reluctantly released him. "But we mustn't let anyone know about what you saw, or what occurred here today. Not yet, anyway." She took hold of his hands. "Understand?"

Andy stared up at her with frightened eyes. His lips quivered. "Will... Will he go to jail?"

Daisy swallowed hard. The hoarse words he had summoned from the depth of his fear spurred her to tears. She stared into his little face. Swelling with a fierce urge to protect him, she offered a promise she hoped Jackson could keep. "Mr. Gallway will see to it."

* * * *

Jackson sat in one of the spindle-back rocking chairs on the porch, wondering what was happening inside. The sun disappeared behind the thickening clouds in the distance. Tall birch trees swayed in the breeze. The sound of wind bells chimed through the yard.

"She likes you." Mrs. Rhodes nodded to the cat weaving between his legs.

Jackson watched as the friendly creature brushed against one ankle, then the other, purring loudly. Jackson had known several women whose advances were less subtle, and as usual, he couldn't resist. "So it seems," he said, obliging the cat with a slow stroke to its fur.

Mrs. Rhodes began talking, and to his dismay, she didn't stop. Her rambling gossip about people he didn't know droned on until his neck cramped from the constant nods he used to conceal his total lack of interest. Even the cat nestling his boot seemed bored.

Jackson couldn't wait another minute longer. He stood, interrupting Mrs. Rhodes mid-sentence. "I'll go see if they're finished," he said, walking to the door. He slipped inside the house.

He took a few steps on the carpet runner, then stopped, awed by the scene. Amid the stark silence, Daisy sat, vacant eyes open, entranced in some spell. The pencil she held flew over the page, striking this way and that, up and down, side to side.

An eerie chill ran down his spine. The instinct to call out her name and awaken her from the disturbing state was hard to resist. He retreated from the room, wishing he'd heeded Daisy's advice to remain on the porch.

He stepped outside and returned to his seat next to Mrs. Rhodes, bracing himself against the emotions roiling inside him. Whether Daisy's attempt with Andy was a success or a failure, in this moment, after witnessing the bizarre scene inside, Jackson couldn't summon the wits to care.

A few minutes later, Daisy emerged from the house. Jackson shot to his feet. She looked slightly pale, but otherwise, she seemed no worse for the wear. Jackson shifted his weight from foot to foot, lost for something to say.

"Andy is speaking," she announced.

Mrs. Rhodes pressed a hand to her chest. "Oh, thank goodness," she said. "How did you do it?"

"He was ready," Daisy said. "I merely happened to be present."

Jackson regarded her closely, admiring her modesty.

"Thank you for allowing us to visit with him, Mrs. Rhodes," Daisy said. "We'll be on our way now."

The woman tossed a nod skyward. "I think it's best you stay for supper. Those clouds mean business."

"Thank you, but I must return to the city as soon as possible," Jackson said.

"I think Mrs. Rhodes is right," Daisy said. "Perhaps we should wait it out here."

"We'll be fine." Jackson tipped his hat to Mrs. Rhodes. "Thank you, again," he said as he took Daisy's arm.

He helped Daisy into the wagon, then hopped up to the driver's seat. With a snap of the reins, he urged the horse to move, waiting until they were out of view of the house before stopping the wagon and turning to Daisy.

"What did he say? Did he see anything?"

"You were right." Her blue eyes brimmed with tears. "He saw everything." She opened her case and pulled out her sketch pad. "The poor child saw everything."

Jackson took a deep breath.

"This is the man he saw shoot his father." Daisy handed Jackson the pad.

He glanced at the sketch. The spatter of bold slashes and strokes conveyed the violence of the crime, and his blood turned stone cold in his veins. He focused on the face centered amidst the random images on the page. His heart shot to his throat. He swallowed hard, unable to pull his eyes away from it.

"You're certain?"

"I am certain," she said. "What does it mean?"

Her tone dipped with concern for the boy. Jackson swallowed again. "It means my client is innocent," he said finally. "And a killer walks free."

Chapter 3

Daisy's mood grew as dark as the sky. Thick clouds sailed overhead. The wind blew harder. She tightened her shawl around her, cursing their foolishness for declining Mrs. Rhodes's supper invitation. The mountain trail could be trying in the best of weather conditions, but traveling in the rain would demand more stamina than she could muster after her draining visit with Andy.

She clenched and unclenched her fist to awaken the numbness that still lingered in her hand. Her arm felt like lead.

"We should forgo the logging trail and take the main road down to town," she advised.

Jackson shook his head. "I need to get back to Troy. We'll take the shortcut."

"The rain could make the trail dangerous. And if it rains hard enough—"

"We have plenty of time before the storm hits," he replied, glancing skyward.

"You don't know that. You're not familiar with this territory. These storms—"

"You're not going soft on me now, are you, Mrs. Lansing?"

She huffed, rolling her eyes. "Why is it you lawyers think you know everything?" she asked. "Is arrogance a requirement for your profession?"

"Absolutely." He laughed.

But ten minutes later, he wasn't laughing anymore. Daisy cowered in her seat, holding tight to the bonnet flapping against her ears. Lightning flashed through the trees, and the sound of thunder rumbled closer and closer. Rain blew on a wind so fierce the drops hurt when they hit.

The urge to remind Jackson that she'd told him so clogged in her throat with the fear things might only get worse. Felled branches hindered their pace. Twice already Jackson had had to climb from the wagon to drag the gnarled limbs off the muddy trail.

The horse plodded on, the wagon lunging and bounding behind. The wagon plunged into another deep rut, tipping forward as it lurched to a stop. The horse strained to pull the buried front wheels from the muddy bog, but this time the old rig wouldn't budge.

Jackson hopped out to inspect the situation. "Damn it!"

The two words said it all. Even without looking, she knew it was hopeless. The wagon was mired in mud, and there was no sense wasting time. They needed shelter. Waiting out the storm beneath the bed of the wagon was no option now.

"Cuffy's shanty is just up ahead," Daisy shouted above the wind. "We can make it on foot."

Jackson helped her down from the driver's side, then scrambled to unhitch the nervous horse from the wagon. He stuffed Daisy's case and some other supplies into saddlebags and tossed them over the horse. Daisy trudged behind, cursing Jackson under her breath as he led the mare through the slippery muck.

The foolish man's rush to return to the city had them ankle deep in mud and neck deep in trouble. They trekked to the shanty, where Jackson tied the horse to a nearby tree. Daisy didn't bother to wait before pounding on the door. When no one answered, she pushed open the door and stumbled inside.

Yanking off her soggy bonnet, she shook the rain from her head, stomping the mud from her shoes. She spun to face Jackson. "I told you!"

He barged past her, his gaze darting around the dim room. During a flash of lightning, he reached for a lamp.

"I knew we shouldn't have taken the trail. Why didn't you listen to me?" she said to his back.

He lit the lamp. The small room came alive with light in the darkness of the storm outside. "We'll be fine here," he said. But his voice was filled with more irritation than confidence.

"What about the wagon?" she asked. "How do you propose we get back to town?"

Jackson ignored the question, tossing his hat to a small bench near the fireplace. He bent to start a fire as Daisy paced behind him. "You and your big hurry to get back to Troy," she said. "You—"

"I want to free an innocent man before he dies!" He stood to face her. His brows slanted above cold blue eyes. She blinked hard at his loss of temper. He took a breath, collecting himself. "Randal Morgan is ill. He doesn't have much time. I'm trying to clear his name before he dies behind bars. Thanks to your sketch, I may now be able to do that," he said. "Not to mention aid the authorities in apprehending the man who murdered Andy's father."

She lowered her gaze, shamed by her selfishness. It wasn't as though she'd forgotten about Andy and what he'd witnessed, but she was trying hard not to think about it. Her stomach turned. How she'd hated making the poor boy relive it. While she couldn't regret using her ability in this instance, the wrenching memory of his pained little face spurred her to tears. She blinked them back. Despite everything, her vexation at Jackson lingered.

"It's almost dark now; we'll never make it tonight," she muttered. "This is a nightmare."

"Calm yourself and come sit down," Jackson said. The fire sparked into a nice blaze in no time. Jackson peeled off his coat and hung it over the back of the chair. "Sit."

Daisy sighed. Hiking up her heavy wet skirts, she strode to the chair, then plopped down in front of the fire. "A nightmare," she uttered again, crossing her arms to her chest.

He dragged a small chair from the sawbuck table, then sat next to her. The wobbly thing creaked beneath his weight, and she wondered how Cuffy hadn't yet landed on his rump atop a pile of splinters. "We'll be safe here until morning," Jackson said. "We'll get the wagon at daybreak, then slip back into town as discreetly as we left."

"What if we can't get the wagon out?"

Jackson frowned. "Then we walk back."

She took a deep breath, trying hard to stay calm. "I don't suppose we have much choice," she said. Inside, though, her mind was whirling with worries. Her hard-earned reputation was at stake, and although she had no regrets for her actions today, she couldn't afford trouble.

And no matter how persuasive the arrogant attorney was at downplaying the situation, there was no disputing the fact that spending the night in a cabin in the middle of the woods, alone with Jackson Gallway, definitely qualified as trouble.

* * * *

Daisy couldn't stop shivering. Rain battered the roof. Dripping water splashed into a coffee tin in the corner. Despite the discomfort of sitting in damp skirts, she refused to take off her clothing. Jackson, on the other hand, had no qualms about stripping down. His fine coat and shirt hung, drying by the fire. A small towel covered his bare shoulders as he rummaged around, unabashed by his improper lack of attire.

She shivered again.

"Drink this," he said, handing her a tin cup. "It will warm you up."

The scent of whiskey filled her senses as she raised the cup to her lips. She took a deep sip, felt the heat of the whiskey flow through her veins. Hugging the quilt around her, she began to relax. Her feet were soaked. Jackson tossed a pair of wool socks onto her lap.

"Take off your shoes and put those on," he said. "I'm sure your friend, the giant, won't mind if you borrow them."

Daisy turned away from him to remove her shoes and unroll her stockings. She hung the filthy things over the bench by the fireplace and set her muddy shoes on the hearth alongside Jackson's large boots.

The sight of their footwear, drying side by side in the firelight, seemed so intimate. She stole a glance in his direction. His dark hair was tousled, and there was a wildness about him that she hadn't noticed when he'd been properly dressed. Below the thin towel draped over his shoulders, muscles flexed as he leaned casually with his elbows on his knees. His lack of modesty in her presence was unnerving. And exciting.

For the briefest of moments, she wondered what life might be like with a man like him. A man near to her age, vital and strong.

She guzzled her drink, feeling warmer. Lighter. Rain dripped from his hair, beading on his naked back below the towel. Drops slid slowly down his spine. His skin glistened in the firelight, and she swallowed hard against the impulse to touch him.

Warmth tingled through her core. She straightened in her seat, regaining her senses. The man was bad news. His wanderlust was no secret, as was his commitment to bachelorhood—Tessa had told her as much. Still, Daisy found her mind drifting....

"So," she said, "how long have you been working with the Markelson Law Firm?"

"My position is only temporarily. Markelson offered me this case after my resignation from Kressler and Associates."

"Resignation?"

"Forced resignation," he clarified boldly.

"Oh." She lowered her gaze. What on earth had he done to earn a forced resignation?

"Let's talk about you, Mrs. Lansing."

"What about me?"

"I saw you with Andy," he said. "While you were entranced."

She turned to him, feeling struck. "You were supposed to wait on the porch."

"I've never seen anything like it."

"I'm sorry you were startled, but if you'd waited outside—"

"I wasn't startled."

She eyed him skeptically. "You watched me transfer Andy's thoughts into a sketch, and that didn't startle you?"

"No, Mrs. Lansing, it did not," he said with a slow shake of his head. "It scared the hell out of me." He smiled at the truth in it, and then she smiled too. "It's an extraordinary ability," he said. "How did you learn it?"

"I did not learn it," she said.

"It just came to you naturally?"

There was nothing natural about it. The ability to transfer people's thoughts to paper was borne of something else. She blinked back the memory of blinding smoke and flames.

"I've always been artistically inclined," she said quickly. "The discovery of my *extraordinary* ability came later."

"Are your parents artistic, as well?"

"I never knew my parents." She lifted her chin against the pain of her childhood. "I was raised in the orphan asylum until I was nine. After that I was placed out with several families in Troy." She fiddled with her hands. "When I was a girl, I used to imagine my parents were great artists." On a fortified breath she added, "So, I am certain I inherited the artistic aspect of my talent from them."

"So am I." He smiled.

Her heart skipped a beat, and she smiled too. He was so charming. The compassion in his handsome face—or the whiskey she'd drank—filled her with longing. Heat slithered through her chilly bones. It had been so long since she'd felt such yearnings—since she'd allowed herself to feel them. Lawry had done his best to tame her desires, but unlike Lawry, she knew Jackson could handle them. She stared into his eyes, her gaze trailing to his mouth. His lips looked so soft. So inviting. She'd never see him again.

She barely felt herself leaning toward him, barely felt his light breath on her face as she moved closer and pressed her lips to his. She heard a sharp intake of breath before his mouth softened against hers. She leaned into the gentle pressure of his lips, closing her eyes. He smelled of leather and rain, and everything wonderful.

He eased his mouth from hers, his breath soft and warm as he lingered a mere inch from her lips. "I'm not sure why you did that, Daisy, but I caution you not to do it again." The husky tone of his voice told her why.

The irresistible impulse to kiss him had stunned her as well. Heat blazed in her cheeks as she drew away. "I—"

"You'd better get some sleep." He ran a hand through his hair. "You take the cot. I'll make a bed here on the floor."

She fumbled for her stockings, scrambling around. "We have to be up at first light," she reminded him. She tossed the stockings on the cot. "It's a long walk back to town, if we can't get the wagon out." But tomorrow's tribulations wouldn't surpass her folly tonight, and she found herself rambling. "I'm attending a meeting tomorrow for Misty Lake's Overseers of the Poor."

"Of course you are," he said with a smile.

She smiled too, feeling better. "My involvement is what led me to the idea of a day home. Membership support is crucial for the success of my plan. I suppose I have to prove myself as well, if I want people to trust me with their children."

"You'll be home in plenty of time for your meeting," he assured her.

She crawled onto the cot, wincing at the thought of whatever else might be crawling there with her. She lay on top of the musty blanket, wide awake, listening to the rain battering the roof. She stared across the room at Jackson, mesmerized by the amber glow of firelight licking his bare back, his broad shoulders. The taste of his kiss was still fresh on her lips, and she pressed her fingers to her mouth, wondering how she would ever forget it.

* * * *

Daisy awoke to the sound of a slamming door. She bolted upright. Clutching a blanket to her chest, she searched the dim room for Jackson.

"Whoa, there!" Jackson stood with his arms raised in surrender beneath the towering shadow of Cuffy and his rifle.

She flung her feet to the floor, shoving them into her shoes. "Cuffy! Don't shoot!" Daisy raced to Jackson's side. "It's me, Mrs. Lansing!"

Cuffy narrowed his eyes. "Mrs. Lansing?"

She nodded furiously. "Yes, yes. Please put down that gun."

Cuffy lowered the rifle. "Whatcha doin' in my place, Mrs. Lansing?"

"I'm sorry, Cuffy. We got stranded in the storm." She grabbed Jackson's arm. "This is Mr. Jackson Gallway."

"How do, Mr. Jackson." The small pair of antlers on Cuffy's cap bobbed with his eager handshake.

Jackson exhaled in relief. "I was just heading to get my wagon," he said. "It's stuck a quarter mile or so up the mountain, and I could use some help getting it out."

Cuffy puffed his massive chest. "I'm strong as an ox. I can get yer wagon out for you."

Jackson turned to Daisy. "Get your things."

She complied quickly, then hurried outside to join them.

"You have the sketch?" Jackson called over his shoulder.

"Good heavens," Daisy said as she circled back to get the case, which contained the sketch she'd drawn. She chased after the men, who'd wasted no time as they led the horse up the muddy trail.

The rain had stopped sometime during the night, but the morning sun was no threat to the streams of water trickling down the rutty trail.

When they reached the wagon, Cuffy assessed the situation, then wedged a few strong branches under the mired wheel. With a few deep grunts, he and Jackson pushed the wagon free. Daisy couldn't be more grateful to the gentle giant who stood with mud up to his thighs.

"Thank you so much, Cuffy," she said.

Cuffy wiped his forehead with his flannel sleeve. "It wasn't nothing," he replied. "Not for me," he added with the candor of a child.

Jackson struggled to catch his breath. "We'd appreciate it, Cuffy, if you wouldn't mention to anyone that you helped us today," he said between breaths. He placed some coins in Cuffy's large hand.

Cuffy's eyes widened with gratitude. "No, sir, I won't."

Daisy smiled in relief. "Thank you again, Cuffy," she said as he helped her board the wagon.

The long ride back to town was slow and awkwardly quiet. Jackson stared straight ahead, his concentration fixed on the challenge of driving. Oh, why had she kissed him? Her embarrassment came in second only to her fear she'd not make it home undetected—though it would serve her right after her shameful behavior.

She pushed away thoughts of her folly. "Do you think Andy is safe?" she asked.

"I believe he is. For the time being, anyway. His future safety will depend on the authorities and their willingness to consider my new evidence."

Daisy nodded, hoping Jackson could convince them. "Please let me know if I can do anything else."

"You've done more than enough," he said. "I owe you my thanks."

She accepted his gratitude with a smile, then turned back to the road ahead.

They finally emerged from the woods, and a mix of relief and disappointment greeted her at the end of the trail. The warmth of the sun intensified as they clattered down the main road back to town.

Jackson stopped the wagon when they reached the fork in the road where they'd met yesterday. "I'd drive you home but—"

He turned toward the sound of rambling wheels around the bend.

"This is fine," she said, standing. Her heart pounded. "If anyone stops me, I'll tell them I was out sketching ferns."

He helped her down as the sound of the distant carriage grew louder.

"Have a safe trip to Troy," she said, turning.

He reached for her arm. "Thank you again for your help."

His gentle touch held her in place, as did the gratitude in his eyes. A tentative smile curled his lips, and Heaven help her, she wanted to kiss him again. "Of course," she uttered, wanting so much to say more. "Good-bye." She walked as quickly as she could. He snapped the reins, and the wagon rolled past her, ambling down the road toward the livery. Clumps of mud still trailed in its wake.

A few minutes later, a purple carriage buzzed by. Felice Pettington and her maid, Myrtle, gave haughty waves. Daisy's relief at their timing helped divert her focus from the aching sadness that lingered when she thought about Jackson on his way back to Troy. And how this perfect stranger had affected her more in one single day than her late husband had during six years of marriage.

* * * *

The meeting was about to come to order. The loud chatter waned to a quiet din as the members of Misty Lake's Overseers of the Poor began to take their seats in the stuffy meeting room in the town hall.

Daisy settled in her seat, pleased by the turnout. Attendance was better than she'd expected after last night's storm. Last night's storm… She exhaled a long breath, but the memory of kissing Jackson remained.

She forced her thoughts to the present and the matter at hand. This meeting was important to her future, and she had to focus on securing support. Straightening her shoulders, she recited in her mind the presentation she'd prepared about her plans for the day home.

"I'm looking for Mrs. Lansing."

Daisy spun toward the familiar voice, her pulse pounding.

"I see her. There she is over there!" Cuffy's booming voice echoed through the room as he stooped through the entranceway. Heads turned, all eyes following the giant man as he zigzagged through the rows of chairs, antlered cap and all, looking as proud as Lucifer.

She shot to her feet. From the corner of her eye, she saw Felice Pettington and the equally snide Gertrude Hogle creeping closer. Daisy's heart pounded faster in the room's sudden silence as Cuffy charged toward her. He reached into his tattered coat.

"I found this in my bed after you and Mr. Jackson left this morning." He whipped out Daisy's stocking. The filthy thing dangled from his fist as he flaunted his find like a bagged goose. He leaned close. "And I didn't tell no one I helped ya'll with the wagon."

Daisy stared stunned. The deathly silence of the room lapsed into gasps, which quickly droned into murmurs. The buzz of the crowd intensified, growing louder, but the only words Daisy heard were the ones in her head.

She was ruined.

Chapter 4

Daisy's dream for the day home was as dead as her reputation. No one would entrust her with the care of their children now. Tears welled in her tired eyes, but she brushed them away. She had to fix this.

During the long ride to Troy, she'd convinced herself she could. Her head swam with the memory of the stunned faces of those who'd witnessed Cuffy's surprise appearance at the meeting yesterday—her ears buzzed with their gasps and hushed innuendos. Her stomach lurched. Those not present for the scene were sure to hear all. Felice Pettington would see to the task. Daisy uttered a curse at the loss of all she'd hoped so hard to attain.

The memory of the Palmers, the couple who'd taken her in and then tossed her away, incited her anger. To be rid of her in the wake of that horrible night, they'd shamed her into marrying a man more than twice her age. She'd had little choice in the matter, but she'd paid her penance for the scandal she'd caused by using her entranced drawing so frivolously.

And now here she was, being punished for using it to help a child. It was all so unfair… She glanced out the carriage window, felt the crush of her past all around her. Memories crowded the sidewalks and streets, surrounding her like an angry mob. Every familiar sight and sound was a reminder of the fire and all she strived so hard to forget. The lost lives, the guilt. Her life had been spared, but surviving the tragedy had changed her forever.

The carriage rolled to a stop, and she lifted her chin. The street lamps lining Troy's Washington Square glowed softly in the early evening dusk as Daisy climbed from the carriage and made her way to the impressive brownstone. Inhaling a breath, she trudged up the stairs as though facing the gallows, and then rang the bell.

"Good evening," she said to the elderly housekeeper who'd answered the door. "I wish to see Mr. Gallway."

"I'm sorry, miss…"

"Mrs." Daisy snapped. She forced a smile, reclaiming her manners. "Mrs. Lansing," she said, calmly.

"I'm sorry, Mrs. Lansing, but Mr. Gallway is…" She glanced over her shoulder at the wide parlor doors. "Presently engaged."

"But he's home?"

The woman blinked. "Well, yes, but—"

"I must see him immediately," Daisy said as she brushed past the sputtering woman and into the wide foyer.

"But he has instructed me not to disturb him."

"Then you shan't," Daisy said. She tossed her wrap to a chair by the umbrella stand and marched down the hall.

"Mrs. Lansing…"

Ignoring the harried housekeeper chasing behind her, Daisy pushed open the heavy doors and charged into the room.

Jackson shot to his feet, eyes wide. "Mrs. Lansing." His surprised expression deepened the stark blueness of his eyes. Her heart skipped a beat. She'd almost forgotten how handsome he was. She managed to drag her gaze from him, glancing to his companion. The young woman lounging on the settee straightened, fluffing her skirts. Her pursed lips were painted with red lipstick, and her cheeks were flush from more than rouge.

"I tried to stop her, Mr. Gallway," the housekeeper said, clenching her hands.

"It's all right, Josephine," he assured her before she slipped from the room.

Jackson strode toward Daisy. "I haven't yet had an opportunity to review your late husband's will."

Two glasses of bubbling champagne sat on the table. "Yes, I can see you're a busy man."

He frowned at her sarcasm.

"But that's not why I'm here," she said. "I have an urgent matter to discuss with you."

He stiffened, sobered by her tone. "What's happened? Are you all right?"

The concern on his face almost made her feel sorry for the blow she was about to strike him. The lipstick stain on his cheek chased her sorrow away.

"I'm fine," she said. "But I must speak with you." She glanced past him to the woman on the settee. "Privately."

The woman's frown of displeasure at the interruption deepened.

"I'll see Miss Swootz to her carriage," he said. "Have a seat."

He escorted the flamboyant Miss Swootz to the door, murmuring his apologies as Daisy settled into the seat the woman had vacated. The strong smell of perfume filled Daisy's senses, fueling her ire. Had she really expected Jackson Gallway to be sitting home alone in front of the fire, nose buried in a book?

She huffed at the ridiculous notion of it, glancing toward the two champagne flutes. Despite all common sense, her body stirred at the memory of kissing him. The feel of his warm mouth on hers...the sting of his hasty rejection.

As though standing on the ledge of some dark precipice, she squeezed shut her eyes, praying for the strength she needed to jump—to deliberately plunge into the depths of future regrets.

Jackson returned to the room moments later, closing the doors quietly behind him. "Now, what's the matter?"

She took a deep breath, straightening her spine. "I am ruined," she said.

He blinked. "What are you talking about?"

"The entire town of Misty Lake knows we spent the night together."

"How?"

Her temper flared at the note of skepticism in his tone. Did he think she was lying? "What difference does that make?"

"We were discreet. The situation cannot possibly be as bad as all that."

"It is worse, I assure you," she said. "Cuffy made a surprise visit to my meeting yesterday."

"Cuffy?" He narrowed his eyes. "What happened?"

"He had my stocking. He—"

"Your stocking?"

"I'd forgotten it, and he found it in his bed."

"Christ," Jackson muttered. He sank into a chair across from her, completely deflated.

"He meant no malice of course, but everyone knows," she said, staving back tears.

"That crazy coot." Jackson moved to the settee to console her. "It's all right," he said, clasping her hand.

She relaxed, welcoming the familiar scent of him. Her body melted in the heat of his nearness, the solid grip of his hand. She nodded in relief. "I must admit I was afraid you wouldn't understand."

"Of course I understand."

She placed her hand atop his, feeling so grateful. Hopeful. "Neither of us expected to marry under these conditions, but it's the only recourse—"

"Whoa." Retracting his hand, he shot to his feet. "Who said anything about marriage?"

She stared incredulously. "But you just said—"

"I said nothing of marriage."

She frowned at his back as he turned away. He paced the floor, a caged animal desperate for escape.

"There must be some other way," he said. "Something else we can do."

She bristled at his audacity. While she'd expected his distress, she'd also expected he'd have the decency to try to hide it. "We can do nothing without risking Andy's safety," she said. "Not that disclosing the circumstances would change things. We spent the night together. Alone."

The reiteration forced him to silence for what seemed like forever.

"I just need a minute to think," he said, pacing some more.

"It's all been arranged."

He stopped in his tracks, turning to face her.

"Your brother took care of everything."

Jackson frowned. "Of course he did. I'm sure Dannion was only too happy to help."

That Jackson was now angry at Dannion as well fueled her ire. "He wasn't the least bit happy about anything, I assure you. But he and Tessa will be here tonight. The ceremony will take place in the morning."

"Tomorrow?"

"Yes. Tomorrow. I will not return to Misty Lake as a scandalous widow. I can't. I won't."

"And what about me?" he demanded. "I had plans for my life."

"So did I," she shot back. "And they certainly did not include getting married again. Especially to someone like you."

He blinked at the insult before his face turned to steel. "And yet, here you are."

"And here I will stay until you agree to do the honorable thing."

He snorted. "The honorable thing."

"A foreign concept to you, I'm sure. But you will do what is right." She couldn't help herself. "According to your brother you've been in need of *rightening* for quite some time."

"Is that so?"

"He told me about the circumstances leading to the loss of your position at the law firm."

The taut line of his mouth tightened. "I see."

"We have no choice," she said, veering back to the matter at hand. "We've made this mess and must now clean it up."

"And how tidy things will turn out for you."

She narrowed her eyes. "What is that supposed to mean?"

"The Gallway name carries weight in Misty Lake."

"No thanks to you," she muttered.

He clenched his jaw. "Nevertheless, your plans for a day home stand a better chance with the Gallway name behind you. Not to mention your late husband's funds become available upon your remarriage. You've read the will, surely you know this."

While this was indeed a brighter side to the bleak predicament, she resented the accusation. She took a furious breath. "Now you listen to me, Jackson Gallway, and you listen good." She took an imposing step toward him, pointing her finger. "This is as much your fault as it is mine. My reputation is ruined because I helped you. If you do nothing else in your roguish life, you will marry me. You will do the honorable thing, or so help you—"

"All right. All right." He held up a hand.

"Will you do it, then? Will you marry me?"

His sudden smile took her by surprise. "Are you proposing to me, Mrs. Lansing?"

She frowned, exasperated. He'd resorted to humor to mask his fear, but he was clearly terrified.

"Will you?"

All amusement drained from his face. "Yes." His blue eyes pierced her like daggers. "I will do the *honorable* thing. But let me make something straight."

She swallowed at his somber tone as he stepped closer. She'd never seen him wear a more dire expression.

"There's much you don't know about me," he said. "But what you do know is true. I am a rogue, and I live a roguish life. So as you consider this warning, consider this as well. Are you certain you want to marry *me*?"

* * * *

While Josephine showed Daisy to one of the guest rooms upstairs, Jackson poured himself a brandy, dreading Dannion's arrival. Jackson could almost hear the censure in his brother's booming voice, the smug "I told you so."

Married. Damn Jackson's foolish idea to take Daisy to Barston, and damn the stubborn woman for insisting she go. That she'd conspired with his brother made him angrier. She'd run to Dannion first, enlisting his support to ensure Jackson did the honorable thing. Not that he could blame her for securing reinforcements. She was too smart not to formulate a solid plan of attack.

Even so, their lack of faith in Jackson was like salt in the wound. Would his reputation as a rake always supersede all? He stiffened, clenching the glass in his hand. If so, perhaps his future bride was not as bright as he thought for binding herself to "someone like him."

He knew she'd succeed with her plans for a day home somehow. Then there was the matter of her late husband's estate. He sighed, unconvinced. Money was not the motivation behind their marriage but merely a fortunate benefit. She cared about children. She was protecting the boy by remaining silent, as he was. Jackson shook his head, his thoughts tangling into knots. None of this mattered now; the damage was done.

The whole point of solving the Morgan case was to pave his way to St. Louis. The urge to leave town right now to escape this debacle was hard to resist. A few short weeks ago he wouldn't have thought twice about shirking a case—or a scandal. He dragged around that damn promise he'd made to Morgan like he'd now drag the shackles of a wife.

But it could be worse.

He had to admit, somewhere deep in his anger, thoughts of marriage to Daisy Lansing stirred a certain amount of excitement. Since she'd kissed him that night, soaking wet from the rain, he'd had one hell of a time keeping her out of his mind. His admiration of her remarkable ability was part of the attraction, and the intellect behind her lively eyes appealed to him as much as what lay beneath her skirts. He couldn't remember ever being so affected by a woman. Even Miss Swootz hadn't managed to divert his brain from thoughts of the beautiful widow.

Be careful what you wish for...

The phrase rang in his head almost as loudly as his mother's words. Her constant reminders that he wasn't a marrying man. According to her, he wasn't a working man, either, and Jackson had made sure that most people agreed. He forced away thoughts of his mother and took a long sip of his drink. "To hell with them all," he muttered.

The calming warmth of brandy flowed like blood through his veins, clearing his head. He was wrong to blame Daisy for their predicament. She'd wanted only to help. He'd brought this trouble to her, and she didn't deserve it. It was all his own fault.

For once, he was involved in a scandal that wasn't caused by his lust, and yet he would pay the price for the rest of his life. By this time tomorrow, he'd be a married man.

Proving Randal Morgan's innocence had damn well better be worth it.

Chapter 5

After the grim civil ceremony at Troy City Hall, the wedding breakfast Tessa had arranged on the garden patio behind Jackson's brownstone was a pleasant surprise. Daisy breathed in the scent of the honeysuckle shrubs, welcoming the slight lift to her mood.

Birds chirped in the tall lilac bushes lining the iron-fenced yard; a plush hammock hung from between two pear trees in the corner. Sounds of the city floated on the breeze, distant reminders of the world beyond the serenity of the patio's vine-covered walls.

The wrought iron table was cloaked in lace and set with gleaming stemware and china. In lieu of place cards, small vases containing three daisies each adorned the settings for Daisy and Tessa. The men wore matching flower favors in their lapels. The intimate beauty of the occasion hit Daisy like a slap of reality.

She was married. Again. It all seemed like a dream. An incredible dream that spurred a mix of dread and excitement. All those years living with Lawry, his rules and his ways. His intolerance. He'd been appalled by her entranced drawing. From the day they had married, he'd forbidden her to paint or sketch. Depriving her of her art had been her daily reminder of the mistake she had made, and she'd mourned the loss of her creative passion as she'd never mourned him.

Her new husband was different. Jackson was intrigued and impressed by her strange ability, and from where he'd stood in his life he had little room to condemn anyone's past. While his leniency would be a welcome change, he was a rake, first and foremost. He'd admitted this with no apologies, and she'd do well to shore up her defenses. After Lawry's betrayal, she'd be a fool to trust another man. Especially a man like Jackson Gallway. She had to remember that. Daisy glanced down at the wedding band on her finger, fearing her attraction to Jackson might make her forget.

He'd looked so handsome in his gray frockcoat during the ceremony this morning she'd had to anchor her heels to the floor to keep from being swept away by the fantasy of their marriage. By him.

He'd stood before the officiant, reciting his vows with his usual flippancy, but his trembling hands as he'd slipped the gold band on her finger had given him away. To his credit, he hadn't fled the room as she'd half expected he might. But in each nervous movement, she'd sensed his reluctance to enter into a marriage she was sure he'd regret as much as she would. The kiss on the other hand...

Could two people who craved freedom as much as she and Jackson find some common ground? Could they be happy together? She stiffened against the romantic notion. There was no place in this marriage for futile expectations, but that didn't mean she couldn't anticipate other aspects of their union. The mere thought of tonight—of sharing a bed with this young, vital man—caused her heart to pound wildly.

"Do you like it?"

Daisy spun to face Tessa.

"I thought the garden would suit nicely," Tessa said as she stepped out to join her.

Daisy glanced around at the classical statues and potted rubber tree plants. Painted vases held fan leaf palms. "It's lovely," she offered. "And it looks like the weather will cooperate," she added for lack of anything else to say.

Even in the company of her dearest friend, Daisy felt ashamed of her hasty marriage. For little Andy's sake, she hadn't divulged to anyone the circumstances that led to her spending the night with Jackson. Although she knew she could trust Tessa, she thought it best not to risk it, and Jackson had agreed.

"I just checked with Cook, and breakfast will be served within the hour." Tessa reached to push a stray wisp of hair from Daisy's cheek. "You're a beautiful bride."

Daisy gave a fluff to the skirts of her gown. "It seems so plain," she said, missing the orange blossoms and veil her status as widow denied her.

"You need no embellishments," Tessa said. "You are lovely as you are."

Daisy smiled at Tessa's attempt to lift her mood. "Thank you so much for being here for me. For us."

Before Tessa could reply, Josephine appeared with a silver tray of tall glasses and placed it on the table next to a bottle of chilling champagne.

"Wonderful," Tessa said with a clap of her hands. "I love my children dearly, but sometimes a little freedom feels like such a treat. I can't remember the last time I enjoyed champagne this early in the day."

"You miss them already, don't you?"

Tessa laughed. "Pitiful, isn't it?"

Daisy shook her head. "Not at all. You and Dannion have much to be thankful for." She smiled against a sudden prickle of tears. "Will I never marry a man I love?"

Tessa took Daisy's hand. "Give this marriage a chance, Daisy." Love and concern overflowed in her eyes. "Give Jackson a chance."

Daisy nodded.

"I have hope for my wayward brother-in-law, and I am certain you're just the woman to mold him into shape." She gave a nod toward the sound of the men's voices inside. "God knows his brother needed a little molding."

Daisy smiled at the reminder of Tessa and Dannion's rocky history, feeling better.

"We are true sisters now," Tessa said. "And speaking as your new sister, and from my own experience, there's often more to a man than his reputation."

If this is true, I'm really in trouble. What Daisy knew already of Jackson was almost more than she could handle. The memory of interrupting his tryst with Miss Swootz last night burned in her brain. And then there was the ugly business that had cost him his last job. Most people learned from their mistakes. Jackson took them in stride. But as he'd said, the Gallway name carried weight. Daisy intended to carry it with pride, even if her husband didn't. "While I fear hoping too much from my groom, I'll let you hope for the both of us," Daisy replied.

"Hope for what?" Dannion asked as he and Jackson stepped out to the patio.

"Our husbands," Tessa teased.

Dannion raised his brandy. "I'll drink to that." He took a sip before turning to Jackson. "How are things with Markelson?"

Jackson shrugged as they all took seats at the table. "The man's head is harder than steel. I gave him proof that Randal Morgan is not a murderer, but he refuses to see what's right under his nose."

"You can't blame Markelson for his reluctance, Jax. You haven't exactly earned anyone's trust." Dannion's gaze flew to Daisy, and she felt his regret.

"So you've mentioned," Jackson ground out.

The air between the brothers crackled with the tension. Although Tessa seemed to take the sibling discord in stride, Daisy doubted she'd ever get used to the brothers' strained relationship.

"As you'll soon discover, Daisy, when it comes to my brother citing my faults, no occasion is sacred." Jackson turned back to Dannion. "But for my new bride's sake, I ask you to spare us today."

Dannion gave a nod of surrender, lifting his glass in salute to the truce. His dark eyes softened. "To Daisy and Jax," he said as the others joined in the toast. His booming voice dipped with genuine emotion as he raised his glass higher. "And heartfelt hopes for their happy future."

* * * *

Tessa and Dannion's departure filled the parlor with an awkward silence. Jackson glanced at Daisy, who quickly lowered her gaze to the glass of wine in her hands. Throughout the ceremony, the cake cutting, and other formalities of the small celebration his sister-in-law had arranged, Jackson had managed to tuck his excitement about their wedding night into some nook in the back of his mind. But now...

He could barely cling to his sanity now that they were finally alone and he and Daisy were free to move on to more enjoyable formalities.

Daisy, on the other hand, obviously didn't share his excitement. She'd sipped through a tall glass of wine, and then poured herself another, as though the pending evening—the inevitable consummation of their marriage—was too unpleasant to face sober.

The woman had spent six years in the bed of an old man, so Jackson took her reluctance tonight personally. How could he not? He was more suited to her age, and most women considered him handsome. Daisy had been attracted to him once, but her tentative kiss at the shanty in the woods was offered in ignorance of who he really was. His bride's present aversion was to his lacking character, and it was this insult that bothered him most.

"I don't know what Dannion told you about the affair that led to my resignation, Daisy, but I did not know she was married."

"You didn't?"

He hated the spark of hope in her eyes, the grasping for some justifiable excuse for his behavior. "No," he replied. "But I didn't ask, either."

"Unfortunate."

"To say the least," he mumbled, considering the woman happened to be married to one of the firm's partners.

"How did you land at Markelson's?" Daisy asked.

"I have my brother to thank for that, though it pains me like a sun burn to admit it. Markelson owed him a favor, and Dannion arranged it—cleaned up another of my messes."

Daisy lowered her gaze.

Jackson welcomed the silence. He didn't want to talk anymore. He wanted her to want him again, to look at him as she had at the shanty. He moved to the settee, then sat beside her. The heat of her nearness aroused his every sense. The floral smell of her hair and her skin, the curve of white lace at her perfect breasts. He reached to her hand and gave a gentle squeeze.

She stared down at their hands, his thumb caressing her smooth flesh, spreading her fingers as he entwined them with hers. His pulse spiked in anticipation of what they both knew was coming. She lifted her gaze, and the heady desire inside her blue eyes left him breathless. She wanted him as much as he wanted her. The certainty filled him with pride. The rare appearance of the emotion surprised him.

He leaned slowly toward her and placed a gentle kiss on her lips. With a sigh, she closed her eyes. Her breath smelled of wine, fruity and sweet; her lips were soft as a peach. Her mouth became more pliant, more accommodating, and his heart pounded like a drum in his chest. He kissed her again, slowly trailing his lips to her cheek. Savoring the contact with her satiny skin, he forged a lazy path of light kisses along her jaw to her ear. "Shall we go upstairs?"

She nodded, her eyes still closed.

He pulled her to her feet and led her upstairs. The walk seemed endless as they made their way down the hall. Jackson had ducked into the room earlier to check on the arrangements, and he hoped Daisy would like what awaited her inside. He opened the door.

Josephine had transformed the master bedroom into the perfect bridal suite. Gone were the piles of newspapers and cigar boxes that marked the room of a bachelor. The smell of flowers filled the air. He closed the door quietly behind them, allowing Daisy a moment to peruse their surroundings.

Tall candles burning on the nightstand cast a soft mix of light and shadow on the bed. Golden rays danced across the coverings, which were turned down neatly to the matching linens. A thriving fire crackled in the hearth. The room whispered with an invitation, a prelude to pleasure and the one good thing he could offer her.

He moved toward Daisy, who stood stiffly on the center of the carpet, arms crossed to her chest. She looked more like a frightened virgin than a seasoned widow.

"Are you all right?" he asked.

She gave a slight smile.

"Don't be nervous, Daisy." He took another step toward her. "Not with me."

She swallowed hard. "I'm not nervous." She glanced at the bed, her voice dropping to a murmur. "Not about that, anyway."

He stared in confusion. What the hell else was there? At this moment, he couldn't muster a coherent thought that didn't involve her naked body, and he found thoughts of anything other than kissing her senseless were escaping as the moments passed.

"If not *that*, then what?" He took her hand between his and placed a kiss in her palm. He kissed her wrist, several slow, light kisses against her pulse. The faint tremble in her arm aroused him more than it ought.

She slipped her hand from his, shaking her head. "Jackson, wait," she said, composing herself. "I must tell you something."

He wrapped an arm around her waist, pulling her close. "Are you certain about that?" He nuzzled her neck, breathing the smell of her. Unleashing her passion was so damn hard to resist. "I can think of nothing more pressing than the matter at hand." To his delight, she tilted back her head in total agreement. He smiled against the soft wisps of her hair. "I will please you, Daisy," he murmured in her ear.

"I've no doubt about that," she murmured back. "I only hope you survive."

He pulled back in surprise.

Her eyes flashed wide, as though she hadn't realized she'd spoken aloud. Her freckles faded in the crimson shade of her cheeks. "That's what I wanted to tell you," she said. "It's all very personal, but I thought it fair you should know. "Lawry—"

"What about him?" Jackson asked, irritated by the mention of her late husband on *their* wedding night.

"He…he died…in bed. Right after we…"

Jackson cocked his head as her cryptic words became clear. He'd heard from his associates that Lansing's heart had seized while he slept. He'd obviously heard wrong. Daisy was young and beautiful, and so passionate Jackson was surprised the old man had lasted as long as he had.

"Ah." Jackson considered her dilemma amid his crushing disappointment. "If you need more time—"

"No." She shook her head, and he wanted to jump for joy at her adamant reply. "It's just… I wanted a child, you see. I shouldn't have…"

"Daisy." He took hold of her tense shoulders. The troubled look in her eyes made him ache. "You are not responsible. I'm sure he died more as a result of his age than anything you might have done."

Her face flushed with relief. "You're right, of course," she said. "I just thought you should know."

Comforting her evoked a pleasant warmth in his chest, a swell of contentment that felt foreign and new. "In case you're worried for me, you needn't be. I'm in perfect health."

The start of a smile played on her lips. "That's true."

"And while I appreciate the warning, I am willing to take my chances." He touched his forehead to hers. "There are worse ways to go."

She smiled broadly then, and Jackson had never seen anything prettier. He lowered his head and kissed her hard. She flung her arms around his neck and kissed back. Sliding her tongue against his, she moaned into his mouth, pressing closer. Her open desire aroused him further.

With shaky hands, he undressed her, fighting hard to stay calm. His fingers fumbled at the tiny buttons at her back until her skirts slid with a rustle to the floor. Lifting her from the heap of ruffles and petticoats, he carried her to the bed, sinking alongside her into the plush coverings.

Staring into her face, he felt awed by his want for her. His strong need to please her surprised him. Straining for control, he unwrapped her from inside layers of cursed pantaloons and corsets until she lay naked at his side. His gaze roamed with his hand over the soft curve of her hip. Her nipples peaked like tight buds, her breasts rising and falling with each anxious breath as she awaited his move.

He leaned down and sucked a nipple into his mouth. Her jolt of pleasure beneath his lips made him drunk, and he feared he might burst on the spot. Arching toward him, she raked her hands through his hair, driving him mad.

He sat upright, peeled off his shirt, and then returned to the warmth of her breasts. Circling with the tip of his tongue, he licked and teased her breasts, lost in the sound of her moans, the press of her soft thighs against his, as her legs slowly parted.

A loud knock sounded on the door.

It took several more seconds and several more knocks for his mind to register. "I am sorry, Mr. Gallway, but it's urgent," Josephine called through the door.

With a curse, Jackson pounced bare-chested from the bed and strode to the door. Shielding his upper torso from view, he cracked open the door and reached for the note.

He closed the door, moving toward the candlelight as he unfolded the message. "It's from the jailhouse," he uttered as he read. "Randal Morgan took a turn for the worse. The physician says he won't make it till morning."

Jackson gazed across the room at Daisy. Her knees were drawn beneath the sheet she held loosely to her chest. Her disheveled hair hung to her bare shoulders. The gleam of desire in her eyes faded as she parted her luscious lips. He sensed the one word was as difficult for her to say as it was for him to hear, but she spoke it, anyway.

"Go."

Chapter 6

At the soft click of the bedroom door, Daisy bolted upright beneath the covers. Jackson slipped into the shadowy room, the floorboards creaking beneath his weight as he closed the door quietly behind him. He glanced toward her, the lamplight illuminating his surprised expression.

"Did I wake you?"

She shook her head, straightening her hair into some semblance of order. The mantel clock read half past two, but she felt wide awake. "How's Mr. Morgan?" she asked, swinging her feet to the side of the bed.

Exhaling a weary breath, he stripped from his coat, then tossed it over the footboard, sinking beside her on the mattress. "He died an hour ago."

She scooted closer, placing a hand on his slumped shoulder. "I'm sorry."

He stared down at the floor, shaking his head. "That man didn't deserve to die in a jail cell."

"No, he didn't. But you—"

"I never should have gotten involved. What the hell was I thinking?" He ran a hand through his hair.

"You were defending an innocent man."

The sarcastic snort of laughter didn't suit him. "Markelson assigned me to this case because it was a loser. That's what he called it when he told me to have Morgan plead guilty. Morgan claimed innocence all along but had no money for a proper defense, so Markelson didn't provide one." His face hardened. "He knew I was in over my head."

"But we know Mr. Morgan was innocent."

"We are alone in that belief. Even his children turned against him. He asked me to clear his name for their sake, and I made a promise to do that." The anger in his voice dissolved in sorrow. "A promise I'm not sure I can keep."

The humble admission proved there was hope for him yet. A sudden realization filled her with guilt. In the wake of their sudden marriage, she'd forgotten that it was Jackson's dedication to help Randal Morgan that brought them together in the first place. Why was it so easy to overlook the good in this man? Was it because he was a lawyer? A rogue? Or a combination of both? "You'll clear Mr. Morgan's name, Jackson. You know he's innocent, you just need more proof."

The usual confidence in his sapphire eyes was clouded with doubt.

She lifted her chin. "He entrusted you to clear his name, and you'll honor your promise."

"I've never kept a promise in my life." He shot to his feet, then strode to the table. "Promises are worthless. You said so yourself." He tossed the reminder over his shoulder, reaching for the decanter of brandy. He poured a tall drink. The bottle clanked on the marble tabletop before he snatched up the glass and quickly drained it. The tense lines of his face eased a bit from the brandy's effect. "Let's not talk about it anymore."

The defeat in his voice tugged at her heart. He looked so tired. "All right," she agreed. She watched in silence as he poured another drink. The fear he'd fail Randal Morgan was understandable, but she sensed Jackson feared something more. That he wasn't good enough to see this through. That he'd quit.

Daisy had never struggled with issues of commitment. She'd move heaven and earth to succeed at a cause she believed in, but Jackson had limited ambitions. As Dannion had mentioned, Jackson had the intelligence and education to do anything he set his mind to. Unfortunately, he didn't set his mind to much other than skating through his bachelorhood, no matter how thin the ice, no matter how deep the consequences, until he plunged into trouble. When he was in it up to his ears, his brother was always there to pull him out.

Only this situation was different. This was between Jackson and a dead man. Jackson hadn't saved Randal Morgan in time, but he had to prove the man's innocence to ease his own conscience. Daisy sensed Jackson had something to prove to himself as well, and her heart ached with his burden. She'd been in those shoes.

At the moment, the inappropriate quips Jackson made to lighten bleak situations were sorely missed. Seeing him now, like this, reinforced her suspicion that this case was more than a case to him. The word atonement chimed in her head. Her chest constricted at the thought.

She watched him from across the room, admiring his tall form, his wide shoulders. Beneath narrowed brows, his eyes were heavy with thought. She was consumed with an uncontrollable need to wipe away his turmoil, the painful image of a dying man in a jail cell, and make him forget everything outside this room's walls.

"Jackson." She spoke with tender purpose, her voice gentle but firm. "Come to bed."

His gaze penetrated her flesh like intense rays of sunlight. Heat coursed through her veins. He looked wild and unruly and handsome as sin. He was everything Lawry was not, and she'd never wanted anything more.

No one had ever looked at her this way, as though she were all that mattered in the world. Lawry's disinterest in her as a woman, the Palmers' neglectful treatment of her as a girl, disappeared in Jackson's eyes. He wanted her, and the thought was overpowering.

A surge of excitement shot through her. He set his drink on the table, loosening his collar as he strode toward the bed. After pulling her to her feet, he kissed her hard.

Breath hitched in her lungs; heat flooded her veins. His grip on her shoulders tightened as he opened his mouth, thrusting his tongue between her lips. The taste of brandy, hot and sweet, filled her mouth as he slowed the kiss with long, sweeping glides, the rhythm of his tongue working her body into a frenzy. She clutched his neck and his hair, and he moaned deep in his throat, lifting her closer.

There was nothing rote or meek in his touch, nothing proper in his need. His raw passion was fierce and contagious, and she wanted it all.

Life with Lawry and months as a widow hadn't eased the yearning that had lived like an unwelcome guest inside her. It had been so long since she'd been touched. Even cold hands had been better than none....

Thoughts fled with her zeal to have what she wanted. To take what she needed. Clutching Jackson's shoulders, she drew him closer, the scent of him filling her nose, stoking the sizzle in the pit of her belly.

Reaching to her waist, he slid his hands over the curve of her hips, down the side of her thighs. Clenching fistfuls of fabric, he lifted her night rail. Slowly. His fingers slipped beneath the hem as he lifted it higher. Gazing into his eyes, she raised her arms as the flimsy silk glided upward and over her head.

She shook her head, freeing her hair from the garment. Something sparked in his eyes as he stilled to watch her hair tumble to her shoulders. She touched a finger to his perfect mouth. His lips parted as the simple gesture spurred him back into action.

He caressed her breasts, the taut nipples beneath his thumbs. His palms cupped the weight of her sensitive flesh, igniting a blazing fire through her core.

Burying his face in her hair, he nuzzled her neck, each touch of his lips on her skin sending tingles all the way to her toes. Her knees trembled, her body a mass of sensation and need. She clutched at his shirt, eager to feel him. He leaned to unbutton his shirt. Reaching to assist, she tugged it from the waist of his trousers as he opened it wide. Splaying her hands, she roamed the firm planes of his chest. The soft patch of dark hair tickled her fingertips, then her lips, the virile smell of his skin inciting her further.

In one fluid movement he scooped her off her feet and onto the bed. Tearing off his shirt, he climbed next to her. She squirmed as the tingle between her legs grew stronger. Her heart raced, and her breath came short and hard. She pulled him on top of her, grinding against the thigh he pushed between her legs and the rising sensations. His mouth covered hers, their tongues gliding and swirling. The taste of him in her mouth, the feel of him between her legs, was thrilling and new.

Rolling to his side, he unfastened his trousers. His boots hit the floor with twin thuds. He shimmied his trousers down to his calves, kicking them to the foot of the bed. And then he was naked. Naked and lovely between her legs, his hardness pressing against her thigh, the dampness between her legs. She urged him with her moans, her hands clenching his shoulders.

He kissed her throat, her neck, her ear. She wrapped her legs around his, capturing him so he couldn't escape.

He pushed inside her, filling her with a rush of pleasure she hadn't expected. He was perfect, so thick and so hard. Her head whirled with their movements as she writhed in the wonderful friction, the exquisite feel of him deep inside her. She clung to his back as he moved faster, each thrust driving deeper, winding her tighter and tighter. The knot of sensations between her legs erupted, spreading outward through her body. She cried out in surprise at the overwhelming pleasure. The sound of her release quickly melded with his as he shuddered on top of her.

The room stilled to everything but the sounds of heavy breathing and her heart pounding in her ears. Several moments passed before her pulse began to slow. Her body succumbed to the pleasant ache and the peaceful exhaustion, but her mind couldn't rest. Making love to Jackson had awakened her to a whole new side of marriage.

As she lay in Jackson's strong arms, in the hazy aftermath of their first night together, one joyous thought became vividly clear. She'd fall asleep eventually, and when she did, it would mark the first time as a married woman she'd close her eyes feeling completely and utterly satisfied.

* * * *

Jackson sat in the Chippendale chair by the window, wide awake, despite the ungodly hour. The light of day crept closer, the view of Daisy's form on the bed emerging in the fading darkness. He watched her sleep, the serene expression on her lovely face warming his blood.

He'd watched her sleep the night at Cuffy's cabin, a guilty pleasure he'd enjoyed for only a few moments for fear she'd wake to find him staring down at her for no other reason than he hadn't been able to help himself. That he could now linger on the sight of her for as long as he liked was a bittersweet realization.

She was so beautiful. Waves of blond hair spilled across her pillow. Languid breaths passed through slightly parted lips, the savory taste of which still left him hungry for more.

Sunlight pierced the dim room, a sliver of gold that caressed the skin of her bare shoulder, her partially exposed leg coiled around the tangled sheet. Only two men in this world had the privilege of seeing her like this, and Jackson was one of them. Daisy belonged to him now, and he'd never felt more unworthy of anything.

Pulling his gaze from the enticing sight of her, he walked barefooted to the window. A few short weeks ago his only concern had been choosing a companion for the night and landing a position in St. Louis.

Catching the wrath of an irate husband, then losing his livelihood as a result had been a mere inconvenience compared to his latest dilemmas. Now he had to keep a promise to a dead man and finagle some way to salvage his plans for St. Louis. Plans he couldn't execute with a wife in tow. He wasn't sure which would be more difficult, but he knew what he had to do first. Randal Morgan would be buried this morning, and until Jackson solved this case, someone else's crime would be buried with him.

* * * *

Daisy opened her eyes to see Jackson standing by the open window, gazing thoughtfully to the street below. He turned toward her at the sound of rustling covers as she stirred.

"Good morning," he said. "Did you sleep well?"

She stretched her arms to the rosewood headboard, sinking deep in the pillows. "I expected to toss and turn all night, but I slept very soundly."

"You assumed I would snore?"

She laughed. "No. I've grown used to sleeping alone. I've always had my own bed."

His brows shot upward. "Separate beds?"

"Lawry insisted."

"You snored?"

She laughed. "No. I do not snore."

"I'm happy to hear it," he said with a wicked grin. "Though you could snore as loudly as a saw mill, and I'd still keep you in my bed."

Her cheeks warmed at his words and the sultry thoughts they inspired. Lawry had never spoken to her so boldly—so seductively. Not even in bed.

"My late husband had other concerns," she said. "He believed it was healthier for married couples to sleep separately. We shared a room but not a bed."

Jackson stared at her as though she had two heads.

"He was a very conservative man. I spent a lot of time with children, and he also feared contracting some ailment I might bring home."

Jackson had the good grace to keep any comments to himself. The arrangement of separate beds must seem ridiculous to a man whom she suspected seldom slept alone.

"But you slept well last night?" he asked.

"Very well." She smiled, stretching like a lazy cat onto her side. The bed linen fell just enough to expose her breasts, and she watched his expression turn, her heart pounding, as her nipples hardened in the morning chill of the open window.

"I was about to suggest we return to Misty Lake as soon as possible," he said in a husky voice that quickened her pulse.

"And now?" she asked with a sly smile.

He walked toward the bed. "Now I can't fathom why."

Chapter 7

They traveled from the city in relative silence. While Daisy was curious about Jackson's plans for their future, at the moment, she hadn't the fortitude to hear his answers. Did he expect her to move to his brownstone in Troy? For all she knew, his first order of business when they reached Misty Lake would be to have Kotterman pack up her trunks and ship her and the whole kit-and-caboodle back to the city.

The mere thought of ever living in Troy again clung to her like the perspiration beneath her wool traveling suit. She couldn't do it. She wouldn't. Brief visits were barely tolerable, and up until two days ago, she hadn't been to the city in years.

She had no intention of ever leaving Misty Lake, of ever abandoning her dreams for the day home. Being caught in a scandal with Jackson had veered her off course, but she was back on track now. She'd needed to marry, and she had. She'd deal with any forthcoming problems as they arose.

She turned from the carriage window and the passing scenery to Jackson on the seat across from her. "I think it's important we make a public appearance as soon as possible," she said. "Perhaps we could have supper at the Misty Lake Hotel to announce our nuptials."

"Or we could have Cuffy do it for us." Jackson smiled.

Daisy rolled her eyes. There was nothing funny about the consequence of their indiscretion, but if he needed to make little jokes to deal with those consequences, so be it.

Although she wasn't looking forward to facing people, either, she wanted to get the unpleasant business over as soon as possible. "If the rumor mill that circulated our scandal runs at the same rate, our marriage is already known," Daisy said. "But an appearance at the Misty Lake Hotel will keep the talk focused on our marriage and not what led to it."

"What type of reception are you expecting from the good people of your little community?" he asked.

Leaning back in her seat, she thought of a widowed acquaintance who'd remarried last year. Charlotte had spent three long years in mourning, and still there'd been talk. Daisy had remarried after only ten months. "The mourning periods of some of the town's more stringent families last for years beyond what I deem necessary. I can't control that. I have a new husband now, and people will have to accept our...situation."

What did he expect her to say? That she dreaded facing her friends and neighbors? That she was shrinking with every mile of the narrowing road that took them closer to the country?

She stiffened her spine. The reaction to her second marriage could be no worse than the reaction to her first. Surely she'd be spared the speculation and harsh judgments she'd endured when she'd married Lawry, a wealthy man who was old enough to be her father. Everyone who'd heard about her sordid night with Jackson would know exactly why she'd remarried so suddenly, but at least her motive would be clear.

She glanced at Jackson. He sat comfortably, one leg bent, the other stretched as far as the cab allowed, staring out at the passing landscape as though he hadn't a care in the world—let alone a wife he'd known for barely a week.

The casual pose suited him like a glove. No worries furrowed his brow, and a part of her envied his irritating ability to take everything in stride. Although she and Jackson were close in age, their characters and lives were miles apart. But despite their obvious differences, they shared one thing in common. They both wanted to find the murderer who'd let an innocent man die behind bars.

The haunting memory of that little boy's face after she'd forced him to recall the worst moments of his life wouldn't fade until she knew he was safe. Andy's life was at stake, which made fretting about her own problems seem petty and trite.

"What's being done to find the man who killed Andy's father?" she asked.

"Not much." The frustration in Jackson's curt answer filled her with a sinking feeling that only intensified as he elaborated. "I've reported my findings to the authorities, along with your sketch, but they're as wary of Morgan's innocence as they are of me. They question the credibility of the sketch as well. More so, I'm certain there's a political motive."

"What do you mean?"

"The chief of police is up for re-election. That doesn't work in Morgan's favor. The last thing the city wants is to admit they locked up an innocent man."

"It's all so unfair."

"It's politics. I've considered going to the papers. There should be some warning to the public that there's a murderer at large."

"What's to consider?"

"Any warning to the public is also a warning to the killer, who's been resting easy for months. The boy is safe, so long as the killer believes his crime died with Morgan."

"Yes, of course," she said. "In the meantime, may we pay Andy a visit?"

He pursed his lips as he considered her request. "I'm concerned for the boy too, but strange visitors attract attention."

"Please, Jackson." The use of his name came to her naturally. The tender shift in his features told her he didn't mind. "I'm afraid Mrs. Rhodes has her hands full."

"It can't be easy for the old gal to care for the boy alone," he said. "We'll take a ride to Barston in a day or so. Since there's no telling when the authorities will act, she needs to be warned."

His expression darkened, and Daisy found herself missing his earlier nonchalance. Not even during the most heated moments of verbal sparring with Dannion had Jackson's eyes conveyed such intensity. This case had a rare effect on him—one of the few things in his life that truly seemed to matter to him.

The knot in Daisy's stomach tightened when they reached Misty Lake. When she stepped into the house, she felt better. In addition to taking care of the house, Kotterman was a master in the kitchen, and the aroma of his specialty chicken stew welcomed her home. Following a brief introduction to her new husband, Kotterman bid them an awkward offering for "much happiness and marital bliss," then took their baggage up to Daisy's room. Jackson declined her invitation for a tour of the house, opting instead to disappear into the library with an armful of thick files to review before dinner.

Daisy decided to take a walk down to the lake. She felt herself relaxing as she meandered down the path of stepping stones toward the water. The smell of wet sand and grass filled her senses. Birds sang overhead. Time passed quickly, and she was surprised to see Jackson's tall shadow on the grass next to the bench where she sat. Without a word, he sat next to her.

"It's so good to be home." Daisy took a deep breath. "Speaking of home," she uttered reluctantly, "where are you planning to live?"

"Pardon me, *Mrs.* Gallway?"

She frowned. "I know you've no great fondness for the country, but I intend to remain here in Misty Lake."

He studied her closely, a blank look on his face. "And I have no intention of dragging you, kicking and screaming, to the city." He swatted at a horsefly. "I'll stay in Misty Lake for the summer," he said. "I can work on the Morgan case here and travel to and from Troy as needed, so long as the roads hold out."

Despite her initial relief, a breath of disappointment ached through her. He obviously planned on maintaining separate residences come autumn. She lifted her chin. And that suited her fine.

She stared out at the water, soothed by the calm lull of the waves. "This is my favorite spot in the world." She scanned the view of the lake and distant mountains.

He narrowed his eyes in genuine disbelief. He stood, walked to the water's edge, gazing out at the lake. "I do not understand this fascination with the country," he said with a shake of his head. "It's so quiet. And there's nothing happening. Nothing here."

Something rustled in the weeds near the shore. A tall goose charged from the pussy willows, flapping its wings. Jackson jumped back, then froze like a statue. The enormous bird released a menacing squawk guaranteed to keep him that way. A cockeyed line of goslings emerged moments later, scattering around his feet. Releasing another loud squawk, the mother goose summoned her tiny troops, and they waddled into the water.

"I stand corrected," Jackson murmured, as the geese swam away. "There are geese here."

Daisy laughed. "There's much more than geese here. You'd see that if you took the time to look."

He returned to his seat, his eyes sparkling with mischief in the sunlight. "Oh, I look." He reached to push a strand of hair behind her ear. His fingertips lingered on her earlobe and the dancing pulse at her throat.

She inhaled a deep breath. "And what do you see?"

"I see you. Only you."

The words played soft and smooth on his lips, as though they'd been there before. Staring into his handsome face, she saw the long list of his prior conquests, but she didn't care. Memories of their night together came back in a rush that made her eager for more. "Are you attempting to seduce me?"

Something splashed in the water, startling them both.

"Christ Almighty," Jackson said, looking mildly embarrassed.

"Just a bass," she said with a smile. "The fishing is good."

He frowned. "I don't fish."

"Never?"

"Dannion is the fisherman in the family. I never cared to learn."

"I will teach you."

The offer sparked a full-blown smile. "You want to teach me to fish?"

"I'd be happy to," she said. "You might enjoy living here if you engaged in some of the recreational activities the country offers."

He grinned devilishly. "Oh, I plan to engage in enjoyable activities."

Pretending to ignore his blatant innuendo, she said, "Teaching you to fish would be my pleasure." She dropped her hand to his thigh.

He stared down at her hand, swallowing hard.

It was so easy.

"Fishing, huh?"

She nodded. "Among other things."

He smiled, bending to nuzzle her neck.

She tossed back her head, enjoying his wonderful lips on her skin, his breath in her ear. How perplexing that one night in his bed had made her feel so at ease with him in this way. That she might have her cake and eat it too was a sweet consolation for the bitter confines of marriage.

He kissed her firmly before drawing his mouth away. Lowering his head, he touched his forehead to hers, closing his eyes. He planted a kiss on the top of her head.

The tender gesture sent a chill down her spine. "So, tell me, Jackson. Where is *your* favorite place?"

"It isn't here."

"Be nice," she scolded. "Or you'll be bait for the bass."

He smiled at her playful threat, looking so charming. "I favor so many places, it's difficult to narrow it down to just one."

She didn't doubt it for a second. According to Tessa, Jackson had roamed between Saratoga and Albany before taking up residence in Troy. He was a wanderer, and his wanderlust extended far beyond the borders of geography. She couldn't imagine he'd settle easily in one place. With one woman.

"But I'd have to say that I favor St. Louis," he said. "When I was there several years ago, I sat for hours on the hotel balcony overlooking the Boulevard, the longest I've ever sat alone, through an entire cigar, just watching the action on the street below."

"You bore easily, don't you?"

He laughed. "I've been accused of that, yes. I take after my mother. She always told me we were a lot alike."

"And you agree?"

He shrugged, tossing a blade of grass. "Dannion sure as hell does."

"But it's your opinion in which I am interested."

He looked at her, brows raised, as though this surprised him. His expression turned more thoughtful as he studied her. "I was planning to return to St. Louis—"

"Congratulations, you two!"

They both turned toward the path that led to the house and the couple peering over the picket fence.

"Here we go," Jackson said.

"Brace yourself," Daisy uttered. She waved, forcing a smile. "You're about to meet the town's nosiest neighbors."

"I'm all aquiver."

Suppressing a laugh, Daisy nudged him with her elbow as the fence gate swung open. Tom Wyman strode toward them, his tiny wife practically running to keep up. Daisy took a deep breath. "Jackson Gallway, these are my neighbors, Tom and Nadine Wyman."

"Congratulations are in order, we hear."

To Daisy's surprise, Nadine embraced her with the same unbridled enthusiasm in her voice.

Tom shook Jackson's hand with a grip so forceful Daisy feared he'd yanked Jackson's arm from its socket. Jackson turned to Nadine, flashing one of his signature smiles. Bowing to her petite level, he reached for her gloved fingers and gave them a squeeze. The flirtatious gesture proved his arm was intact, and Daisy scoffed at his honeyed routine and Nadine's schoolgirl reaction to his flattery.

While Tom bombarded Jackson with questions ranging from law practices to road conditions, Nadine leaned toward Daisy. "I've always thought the summer season the best season for scandal. Talk fades quickly when there are other entertaining distractions. The winter months on the other hand…"

The woman's observation wasn't meant as an insult, and Daisy couldn't help nodding at the truth in her words.

Nadine patted Daisy's arm. "Your story is old fodder already. Folks are still chewing on the shocking business with the Shaws. Stories about broken marriages have more meat than stories about new ones."

"The Shaws?"

"How have you not heard?" Nadine's eyes lit with her eagerness to fill Daisy in on the tale. "They ran a nice little farm up the mountain. A while back, Mary Shaw abandoned Marty and their children and ran off to the city. With a peddler they say. Marty put an ad in the all the papers that she left without his consent, and he wasn't responsible for her debts. Then he sold the farm, packed up the children, and moved out west."

"Oh, my."

Nadine nodded. "Barston used to be such a quiet town. And now folks are still reeling from that murder. But at least the scallywag who killed that poor farmer is dead. We heard so this morning. The Good Lord's justice, if you ask me. Imagine being shot down in your own home." She shook her head. "Terrible."

Daisy stiffened. "Yes. Terrible."

"Too many peddlers from the city coming and going," Tom chimed in.

The tight line of Jackson's mouth softened. "With so much peddler traffic, one might wonder if they arrested the right man." He spoke casually, scrutinizing Tom's response behind a mask of indifference. In Jackson's calculating eyes, Daisy glimpsed the lawyer he was. An expert at honing in on reactions. A man trained to seek justice and truth—by any means—and twist accordingly.

"What do you mean?" Nadine's eyes widened in alarm. "Are you saying that Morgan didn't do it?"

"Of course he's not," Tom said. "The man is no fool. You read the papers, Nadine. They all but caught him red-handed."

To Daisy's relief, Tom brought the conversation to a halt.

"We'll let you newlyweds settle in," he said, reaching for his wife's arm.

"That's a good idea." Nadine gave a pat to Tom's hand on her arm, and they started away.

Daisy waited until the couple disappeared into their yard to raise an issue she hadn't considered before now. "Does anyone in Misty Lake know that you were defending Randal Morgan?"

Jackson shook his head. "I haven't made it known, although that may all change."

It may change a lot of things, Daisy thought. Jackson had tested the waters with the Wymans, and those waters ran cold. People would be unhappy, to say the least, about Jackson defending a man they believe was a murderer. Despite her best efforts to put her selfish fears aside, Daisy couldn't help thinking about the impact her husband's cause might have on her plans for the day home.

But if Jackson had the conviction to stand by his decision to honor the promise he'd made to Morgan, then she would too.

Chapter 8

Later that night, Jackson climbed into bed next to Daisy, anticipating their second night together between the sheets.

"I hope the open window won't bother you," she said as she fluffed at her pillow. "It's much warmer upstairs than I'm used to."

He narrowed his eyes. "This isn't your room?"

"Because of Lawry's health restrictions, our room was downstairs. I moved into this room after his death."

Jackson nodded. At least he wouldn't have to share his sleeping accommodations with the ghost of a dead man. He inhaled a deep breath to fend off his irritation. His damn jealousy had spread like a rash all day. That Daisy had made love to another man—that she'd unleashed that fierce passion on someone other than him—stung like hell.

He was jealous of a dead man, and the pathetic fact didn't bode well with him or his pride. What was it about this woman? He shook off any attempt to answer. Daisy was his wife. Husbands were supposed to be protective and possessive of their wives.

Jackson reached to the table next to the bed to turn down the lamp. He paused, his attention fixed on the small object atop the lace table covering.

The framed miniature depicted a portrait of a young woman. He picked it up and looked closer. The image inside the aged frame had faded with time, but it was Daisy. Beneath the crown of daisies she wore, her eyes stared out at him, only something in their blue depths was different. Happier.

"Did you paint this?" he asked, rolling onto his back.

"No." She took the miniature from his hand. "It was painted by a man named James Blackstone," she said, staring down at it. "He was my foster father. And a talented artist. He encouraged my interest in art, and he painted that portrait of me as a gift for my sixteenth birthday."

"Sounds like a good man."

"He was. And his wife, Tildy, was a good woman." She stared at the miniature, her eyes glistening in the lamp light. "They died in a fire that very night."

He winced. "On your birthday?"

She nodded. "I was dragged unconscious, from the house, but the Blackstones died. This piece was the only thing recovered in the rubble. The only thing that survived," she uttered. "Besides me."

Beneath the sorrow in her voice, he heard something more. Her guilt for surviving ripped at his heart. He turned, propping up on his elbow to face her. "I'm sorry, Daisy."

She blinked several times, as though fighting back tears. "Shortly after the fire I discovered my ability to draw while entranced."

He propped higher, intrigued.

"That's when the Palmers took me in. I'd been placed as a maid in a working home next door to them. To amuse the household staff, I would play games using my new ability. A subject would concentrate on a series of numbers or letters and I'd scribble it down while entranced. They found it entertaining, and I found myself popular." She shrugged. "Eventually, I learned to transfer images from their minds."

"You became more practiced," he said.

"Yes. The Palmers heard about my ability and invited me to stay with them as their daughter's companion. Grace was of marrying age, and the Palmers were determined to marry her well. They brought me to entertain some friends at a party one night. It wasn't long before the Palmers began receiving invitations to parties and dinners at the homes of the best families in Troy."

Jackson didn't like where this was going.

"On the night of the Taylor's party, the Palmers stressed how important it was I not only entertain the guests, but leave them enthralled."

"Why?"

"One of the guests included a young man they hoped to match with Grace."

"Ah."

"Yes. Well, anyway, everything was progressing wonderfully. From Mrs. Hasting's thoughts, I produced a sketch of her cherished rose garden, in perfect detail. Much to Mr. Glasser's awe, I sketched an image of his prized mare. Everyone applauded my little show, but I sensed the Palmers wanted something more impressive." She lowered her gaze. "So I delved deeper into the thoughts of my next subject."

"Mrs. Taylor," Jackson said. There was no use pretending he didn't know that much. The Taylor's divorce was infamous in Troy.

Daisy nodded. "I went deeper into her thoughts than I'd ever gone before. Since I have no idea what I'm sketching while entranced, I cannot censor what I draw. By the time I'd opened my eyes, it was too late."

"What had you drawn from her thoughts?"

She lifted her chin. "A picture of a man lounging on a bed. Naked."

Jackson blinked.

"The man I drew was the best friend and business partner of Mrs. Taylor's husband, who was present, as well."

"Holy Hell," he muttered.

"Mr. Taylor went crazy. The sketch confirmed his suspicions of an affair. Pandemonium ensued, and the Palmers and I were promptly ushered from the premises. That began their exile from the upper echelon of society— not to mention ending any chance of Grace marrying into wealth as the Palmer's had hoped."

"And they blamed you," he said.

"They were selfish, greedy people, but they had every right to blame me." She stared up at the ceiling. "The ability I'd used to get people to like me made them despise me instead." She smiled sadly. "Of course, no one would hire me as a maid after that. The Palmers reminded me of this fact every day."

"They kept you on in their home?"

"Not for long," she said. "A prominent gentleman, who'd heard of their misfortune, offered to help them. He set them up in a fine house in Newport, complete with his assurance Grace would be well received. That man was Lawry. And all he wanted in return was me."

Jackson gaped, stunned by the sacrifice she'd made for these people.

"I had to do it. I'd ruined so many lives. And I owed the Palmers that much. They'd taken me in."

"They used you," Jackson snapped.

"Yes," she said. "But I was as guilty as they for abusing my ability." She shook her head as though clearing her thoughts. "Anyway, I married Lawry, moved to Misty Lake, and here I am." She smiled.

Despite the lump in his throat, Jackson couldn't help smiling back at her. She'd lived through so much, and she'd survived it all. The orphanage and the fire. The Palmers. She'd served six years for sins not her own, sentenced to a life in the godforsaken country and into the bed of a stingy old geezer, and still she could smile. She was beautiful—inside and out—and he'd never been drawn to anyone more. "Yes, indeed, here you are."

He eased the miniature from her hand, then put it aside. He settled closer, into the scent of her hair and her skin. He kissed her with one, two, three, soft presses to her warm lips. Lowering her to the bed, he kissed his way to her ear. "And you are finally free."

* * * *

Jackson's warm breath filled her ear, and she sighed, sinking into the ecstasy as though into a steamy bath. Deluged by pleasure, she felt boneless. Nerves and muscles unfurled beneath each lingering kiss to her neck.

His mouth traced her jaw, slowly, exquisitely, to her throat before meeting her lips in a sultry kiss that left her trembling and weak. He drew away, his gaze melding to hers.

"You're so beautiful," he whispered.

The intense regard in his eyes stilled her heart. Her breath. Her world.

He touched her face, staring into her eyes, to her soul, to the woman she was deep inside. She felt naked, and exposed, and closer to him than she'd ever felt to anyone.

She pulled him toward her, drowning in it all. Spreading her legs, she clung to him in the need to feel him between her thighs. To have him deep inside her.

He kissed her neck, taking his time. The pace of his languid torment countered the race of her pulse and the urgency flooding her veins. She calmed, drifting on the pleasure as his lips skimmed her shoulder. Her flesh tingled, and she writhed slowly, pressing her breasts to his chest. The pleasure was heavenly and cruel, and she moaned against the building intensity of both.

His hot mouth covered her nipple, and she arched on the bed. She ground against his thigh, silently pleading, but he refused to be rushed.

Dismissing her flurry, he reached with one arm to hold her in place. He smiled against her breast. "Patience. I promise I'll make it worth it."

She sighed in protest and then surrendered beneath his flickering tongue. He moved down the length of her body, kissing every inch of her. He nipped and teased at her stomach and hips, and she reveled in the pleasure. The rock-hard shaft that brushed her leg proved he enjoyed pleasing her too.

Stretching her arms above her head, she drank in the sensations, feeling precious and priceless, and drunk from it all. She writhed beneath his hands and mouth. A promise for her patience. "*…I'll make it worth it…*"

He dipped his head between her thighs, and she all but screamed out loud. Raking her fingers through his hair, she ceded to his words, and the sheer bliss, as he honored them.

* * * *

Daisy nestled into her pillow with the sound of Jackson's peaceful breathing behind her. Tonight he'd made love to her with such tenderness, such rapt devotion, she feared she might cry. The ills of her past had ceased hurting with each touch and caress, each sweet, whispered word.

Guilt faded in pleasure, and she felt whole again. Jackson's want for her filled more than her body, more than her womanly desires, sating places in her soul that had been empty for years. Their second night together had proved she'd been starved for affection. She realized now, she'd been starved for it her entire life.

While unveiling her past to Jackson, she'd heard in her words, felt in her shame how she'd used her ability in a hapless attempt to form a connection to someone—anyone. She'd sold her soul for the recognition of total strangers. People who cared nothing for her. The Blackstones' kindness had magnified the neglect of the rest. Her time with them had been the happiest she'd ever known, the closest she'd ever felt to being loved, and that's why she treasured the miniature so dearly.

She winced against a spasm of guilt. Always the guilt. The possibility she might have caused the fire that killed the Blackstones clogged her throat, left her struggling for air. She'd suffered with the blame for so long, the pain was a part of her now, a chronic ailment that gnawed at her from the inside out, eating her alive.

But in bed—entangled with Jackson and blinded by bliss—all the pain disappeared. *"You are finally free."*

And yet she wasn't alone. She could reach out and touch him right now. The revelation struck her soundly, and echoed in her ears. Even in Lawry's presence, she'd been lonely. A caged bird displayed in the corner, she'd lived on mere crumbs, always hungering for more. The promise of children had fed her through the years, as had Lawry's lies.

She shrugged off the pain of her past. Love was not won or earned; it was given. And she'd ceased trying to buy something that was offered for free to countless others every day—even those more undeserving than she.

Rooted firmly in the reminder, she brushed off any whimsical fantasies about the man lying next to her. While she would revel in the pleasant diversion of their bed, she had her own plans. Independence was a sound substitute for love, and the pursuit of self-reliance was necessary and worthwhile.

Love, on the other hand, was neither.

Chapter 9

The Misty Lake Hotel bustled with guests. While most of the town's summer residents returned year after year, there were always some new faces among the familiar ones, and this season was no exception. Several locals were in attendance as well, including Dannion and Tessa, whom Jackson had arranged to join them for supper.

Daisy was relieved to share their first public appearance as a married couple with her closest friend, and having his brother at his side might make assimilating to a new community easier for Jackson as well. Although he'd met a handful of people over the years during sporadic visits to his brother's home and, no doubt, the taverns in town, most of tonight's patrons were strangers to him.

Not that he seemed at all worried about people's opinions of their sudden marriage. He drank and laughed without a care in the world, and as the evening progressed, she found herself fretting less too.

After only two weeks, the reaction to their marriage was better than she could have imagined. Of course she knew there'd been talk, but since arriving tonight, an endless parade of people had stopped by their table to extend congratulations.

"Good evening."

Daisy smiled up at Landen Elmsworth and his very pregnant wife, Gianna. Jackson stood, relinquishing his seat to Gianna before greeting Landen with a hardy handshake that conveyed they'd met before.

"Last I'd heard, you'd set your sights on St. Louis," Landen said. "I am happy to find they landed elsewhere," he added with a smile aimed at Daisy.

The men conversed behind them as the ladies chatted at the table. Gianna beamed with all the radiance of an expectant mother. Despite Daisy's happiness for the couple, she felt herself sinking into the void of her own disappointment. She'd tried so hard to conceive a child with Lawry. Too hard, it turned out...

Gianna prattled on, extending her best wishes for Daisy's marriage to Jackson, before she took Daisy's hand between hers. "I've been so eager to tell you how much I admired the portrait you painted of Felice Pettington," she said.

"Thank you." Daisy smiled, flushing with the compliment. "It was the first piece I'd painted in years."

"Well, it was remarkable," Gianna said. "In fact, my husband and I were thinking of giving our Aunt Clara a portrait of herself as a gift."

"I've met Clara." Jackson smiled. "And I'm certain she'd enjoy being immortalized on canvas immensely."

"Anyone who knows my aunt would have to agree," Landen said.

Everyone laughed in good humor at the old woman's notorious vanity.

"So what do you think, Daisy?" Gianna asked. "Would you paint the portrait for us?"

"I'd be happy to," Daisy replied honestly. She'd always enjoyed her brief meetings with the Elmsworth family and had often wished for the opportunity to get to know them better.

"We would like it to be a surprise, though. Felice mentioned you painted her portrait from memory."

"My wife has an exceptional memory," Jackson said.

Daisy basked in the pride in his eyes.

"Wonderful," Gianna said. "And in case your memory of your subject needs refreshing, Aunt Clara will be attending the Westcott Ball with us next month. My sister-in-law, Alice, will be there too. Perhaps you might make it this year, as well?"

All these years in Misty Lake, and Daisy and Lawry had never once attended the annual event. "Yes, perhaps," Daisy said, amid a spark of excitement.

The Elmsworths bid them good night, then made their way to their table.

"The Westcott Ball is the highlight of the season," Tessa informed Jackson.

"Is that so?" He glanced to Daisy for her opinion.

She shrugged. "I've never been, but I've heard it is so."

"I enjoy the ball almost as much as the Pederson's harvest festival," Tessa said. "They host a lively party each fall in their pumpkin patch."

"Pumpkin patch?"

Disregarding Jackson's incredulous expression, Tessa reached for his hand. "It will be such fun to have you here in Misty Lake, Jax." Genuine emotion gleamed in her eyes. "The four of us will be as thick as thieves."

Jackson laughed, his gaze fixing on Dannion. "Did you hear that, Brother? Thick as thieves."

Dannion pursed his lips.

Tessa peered toward the door. "The Wymans are here," she said. "Have you met them yet?" she asked Jackson.

"Tom and Nadine," he replied with a nod. "They practically hurdled the fence in their haste to welcome us home."

Everyone laughed as Jackson refilled their glasses from yet another carafe of wine. George and Dorthea Thompson stopped at the table to invite Daisy and Jackson to one of their infamous bridge parties. To his credit, Jackson managed to listen politely as George broke into a lengthy oration on their weekly bridge competitions, followed by an interrogation on Jackson's familiarity with the game.

A few minutes later, Dannion rescued Jackson with the excuse of wanting to introduce him to some of his friends. Daisy and Tessa remained at the table, drinking wine and catching up. It had been so long since Daisy had socialized like this. Lawry's frequent malaise had restricted them to daytime engagements, and she was enjoying the evening immensely.

As she watched Jackson across the room, laughing and drinking with his brother and the rambunctious group of men he'd met during dinner, she realized her concern for his assimilation was for naught.

Although Dannion's standing in town likely warmed the waters of Jackson's reception, she had to admire how easily Jackson swam the social currents. The man could charm a snake. She wasn't surprised that, in a matter of hours, he'd befriended so many.

Of course, his newfound friends were sure to scatter once they got wind of his involvement with Randal Morgan. But until then, Daisy couldn't help being impressed by how easily Jackson had gained their acceptance.

He looked so handsome in his black coat. Every glance at him made her feel like a bride. The wonderful things she was discovering in the marital bed were exciting and new. She enjoyed their late-night suppers and leisurely breakfasts on the patio. As uncertain as she was about tomorrow, she knew one thing tonight. Jackson affected her like no man ever had. In and out of their bed. He was easygoing, required little upkeep, and he laughed a lot. Daisy was having the time of her life.

Pleasantly surprised by the admission, she craned her neck for a better view of him across the room, just as Hannah Pederson, the eldest and prettiest of the six Pederson girls, insinuated herself inside the circle of men. Hannah drifted to Jackson's side, laughing at something he said.

Daisy stretched her neck farther. Hannah placed her hand on Jackson's arm. The familiar gesture prompted the possibility the two had met before. Daisy's stomach clenched. Although Jackson's visits to the Gallway mansion had been rare, it was more than plausible their paths had crossed there.

Jackson tipped his head toward Hannah's dark curls as she whispered something in his ear. He glanced across the room at Daisy, and she quickly averted her eyes. When she glanced back, he was gone.

So was Hannah.

Swallowing down the remaining wine in her glass, Daisy scanned the dining room for any sign of them. The heat from the wine she'd consumed mingled with her angry disbelief at Jackson's shady disappearance. She could barely contain her simmering temper.

She'd be damned if she'd allow her new husband to make a fool of her during their very first public appearance. What the devil did he think he was doing? She shot from her chair, excused herself to Tessa and the other woman at the table, then made her way to the edge of the room.

She nodded curtly to acquaintances she passed on her mission to seek out Jackson and Hannah, wherever they hid, her anger growing more intense with every step she took. A pair of wide doors was propped open to cool the crowded room.

Clasping her hands into fists, she headed toward the doors and prepared for the worst. She swallowed against the sick feeling in her stomach as she slipped outside onto the shadowy veranda overlooking the lake. The damp air felt good on her face but did little to cool the heat flooding her veins. Two men stood to her right, smoking cigars. She passed them as she strolled alongside the railing toward the stairs, which led to the patio below.

Through the distant sounds spilling from inside the hotel, she could hear Jackson's voice. She walked slowly, peering around. She craned her neck over the railing and saw the shadows of two partially exposed figures on the patio beneath her. Their voices carried on the silence around them.

Jackson and Dannion. Her chest swelled with relief. Jackson had merely stepped out for a smoke. She hadn't noticed Dannion's absence in her haste to believe Jackson was up to no good, and she felt guilty for her hasty assumption.

With a calming breath, she turned to duck away before they spotted her, but Jackson's icy words froze her in place.

"I can't do it," he said. "Nosy neighbors, bridge parties, rabid geese." He shook his head. "It's too much."

"You're in the country, Jax. It comes with the territory," Dannion said. "Misty Lake is a close-knit community. You're married now and—"

"Damn it, Dannion, I made a mistake."

Daisy's heart pounded through the sudden silence.

"This marriage was a mistake," Jackson said. "I can't do it. I don't want to do it." He tossed his cigar, and sparks burst on the lawn. "I had plans to be in St. Louis come autumn, not cavorting in some pumpkin patch. Marriage ruined everything."

"Where have I heard that before?"

"Don't." Jackson's anger was clear. "Our mother has nothing to do with this."

"She has everything to do with this, and you know it."

Jackson didn't reply.

"You have a wife now, Jax. Forget about St. Louis and make the best of it."

Daisy backed toward the doorway and slipped inside undetected. Her stomach turned. She knew nothing about Jackson's mother, and at the moment, she didn't care. Her infatuation with Jackson, with the man he was in their bed, had fooled her into hoping he could change. That he might want to change. A tingle of tears stirred in her eyes. Jackson's regret stung more than it ought, more than she'd thought possible given her past.

Years of rejection hadn't inured her from the wrenching disappointment consuming her now. She should have known better. She had caged Jackson, just as she had been caged. His blunt admission that their marriage was a mistake ached through her core as the reason for her reaction became painfully clear.

He was right.

* * * *

Daisy was unusually quiet the next morning at breakfast. Jackson watched as she stared down at her plate, mindlessly poking and pushing at the eggs with her fork.

"Too much wine last night?"

She glanced up as though suddenly realizing he was there. "I'm fine. A bit tired is all."

He wasn't surprised. By the time they'd returned home from the Misty Lake Hotel, it was well past midnight. He'd kept her awake for hours after that, not that she'd complained. In fact, she'd seemed more eager than ever. As much as he prided himself on his skill in that department, he'd had to credit her amplified enthusiasm to her fondness for wine.

She'd amazed him with her fervor, even more so than usual. She'd indulged her passion like a woman devouring her last meal, and the mere memories of it now were making him hard.

Unable to sleep, he'd tossed and turned, Dannion's words ringing in his ears. As angry as he'd been when he'd heard it, the advice his brother had crammed down his throat had become easier to swallow. The appealing sight of Daisy sleeping at his side, the sweet scent of her, had diverted any search for alternatives.

Making the best of their marriage was his only choice, though he'd wrestled against the truth of it for hours. By the time darkness had succumbed to the morning sun, he'd surrendered too. After the Morgan case was solved, perhaps he and Daisy could visit St. Louis. She might enjoy such an adventure. Her ability would prove interesting at the card table, and he smiled at the thought of the mischief they could cause.

Daisy gave a final poke at her eggs, then dropped her fork to her plate. "Since I now have a husband to manage my inheritance, am I correct to assume I can access my funds?"

He shrugged. "It's your money, Daisy. You can have it whenever you want."

She nodded, looking relieved.

"You're going forward with the day home?"

"Eventually," she said. She narrowed her eyes. "No objections, I hope?"

He eased back in his chair, studying her closely. "None." The skepticism in her eyes took him aback. Did she want his assurance in writing? He supposed he couldn't blame her lack of trust. After the demeaning limitations Lansing had placed on her inheritance, and the underhanded maneuvers his attorneys had made to enforce them, she had a right to be skeptical about finally having access to what was legally hers and the freedom to move ahead with her plans. "You made it clear from the start how determined you are on the project." He smiled. "I know better than to get in the way when you set your mind to something."

She withheld the smile he expected as she sipped her coffee. "Good." She set down her cup, her weary eyes fixing on his. "Over the past few days, I've been thinking about some things."

"No doubt," he said with a teasing grin.

"While I appreciate the sacrifices you've made by marrying me, I can't help thinking about the reaction your defense of Randal Morgan will garner from people here in Misty Lake."

The serious conversation was deflating his mood. "You're not suggesting I quit?"

"No, of course not." She took a deep breath. "But community support for the day home is crucial, and any resistance to your cause may hinder mine."

"That's possible."

"I've decided to postpone my endeavor until you've cleared Morgan's name. After which, I'll proceed with my original plans, and you can do the same."

"What do you mean?"

"I have access to my money now, Jackson. You did the honorable thing by marrying me, but surely, you had some plans of your own before—"

"Have you been talking to Dannion?"

"What has Dannion to do with this?"

"Nothing," he said, closing his mouth.

"As I was saying, we did what was necessary at the time, but since returning home, I've realized that I don't want a husband any more than you want a wife."

He summoned his voice through the clench in his chest. "Is that so?"

"Yes." She fidgeted in her seat. "But I have devised a solution that will make this marriage tolerable for us both."

He sat speechless as he absorbed her words.

"Before we were interrupted by the Wymans at the lake, you mentioned going back to St. Louis."

"And?"

"And here's my solution." She fluffed at her skirts. "If you agree to stay here in Misty Lake, as my husband, for the entire summer, you can pursue your plans in St. Louis come autumn."

"Daisy, what the hell—"

"I'm not finished." Her blue eyes flashed with the same warning they'd held back in Troy, when she'd demanded he marry her. He'd underestimated the desperate young widow that night—but there was no underestimating the determined woman sitting before him now.

Daisy straightened her spine. "I'll remain here in Misty Lake, and we'll remain married, in name only. You will have total freedom, in *every* sense of the word, if you agree to one condition." She lifted her chin. "You must give me a child."

Chapter 10

Jackson gaped. "A child?"

"I want a child, Jackson. More than I've ever wanted anything."

He couldn't believe what he was hearing. "So what you're saying is that if I give you a child—"

"You can have your life back."

He sat, awed, absorbing her words. Just last night, he'd wanted nothing more. And here she was, offering escape on a silver platter. Still, he couldn't help feeling deluded. A spike of anger flared through him. Daisy Gallway was a cunning woman.

"Our marriage continues to serve you well."

"Pardon me?"

"You'll have everything you want. Your reputation, your money, your day home, and a child."

Her affronted expression actually looked genuine, but she wasn't fooling him again.

"Things couldn't have worked out any neater had you planned them that way," he said.

"Are you suggesting I planned this marriage?"

"You may not have planned it, but you've maneuvered your way around it remarkably well." He leaned forward, facing her challenge head-on. "You saw another opportunity to get what you wanted, and you took it."

She shot to her feet. "I took nothing!" Her eyes were blue fire. "And I certainly didn't want this!" She waved her hands between them.

"Then why—"

"I heard you last night, Jackson!"

He stared, speechless.

"I heard what you told Dannion. I was there." Her chest heaved, but the anger in her shaky voice didn't cover the pain in her eyes. She took a deep breath, collecting herself as she dropped to her seat. "I was upstairs on the veranda, and I heard every word."

It all made sense to him now. Her abrupt desire to end their marriage—to be rid of him. His gut clenched with thoughts of what she'd overheard. He'd ranted to Dannion in frustration and anger, but he'd never intended to hurt Daisy. "I didn't mean it."

"Yes, you did."

He couldn't lie to her. He was shameless to the core, and as absurd as it seemed, while he was certainly capable of getting her pregnant, then abandoning her, he could not lie to her. "All right, I did mean it. But I'm willing to try. I can adapt to—"

"I don't want you to adapt to being with me. I've lived my entire life with people who did not want me." She lifted her chin. "I refuse to do it any longer."

Her expression filled with the shadows of her past—years of abandonment and neglect, paying for the sins of others. She'd endured too much to be hurt again. His throat tightened amid his faltering argument. "You might have considered all this before the wedding."

"Before the wedding, I had hope."

The words stabbed through him like a knife, but it was the sorrow in her voice that cut his insides to shreds.

She took another deep breath. "You can't tell me this doesn't come as a relief. Think about it sensibly. You have no urge to settle down, especially in the country, and I have no intention of leaving Misty Lake. There's no reason we can't both have what we want. Is there?"

The apprehension in her question confused him. Was he expected to argue or agree? At the moment, he could do neither. A part of him did feel relieved. But a part of him… "And the child?"

"You can visit." She shrugged. "Since neither of us wishes to be married, it makes sense we stay married to each other."

"There's some logic in that, I suppose."

She nodded. "When the time comes, you can go to St. Louis on an extended trip that eventually becomes permanent. I'll make the excuses for your absence here. I'll explain to Dannion that the separation was my idea. That I wanted you to leave."

He listened in silence. She had it all figured out.

"Once you clear Mr. Morgan's name, you'll be free to move on."

Free to move on. The words should elate him. *Protect and cherish your freedom, no matter the cost.* He'd lived by his mother's mantra; he'd been raised by it. He'd aspired to nothing else.

Daisy had grown up an orphan, devalued. And he with a doting mother who'd favored him with a false sense of worth. Bitter disappointment consumed him. Marrying Daisy had been the only selfless thing he'd ever done. But in her solid reasoning, it was clear she understood what he'd known all along. He could never make her happy. Eventually, he'd do something to hurt her; hell, he already had. The admission reignited his anger, and he clenched his jaw to bridle it back. "You're right."

She lowered her gaze. "I know."

"We'll live as man and wife until the end of the summer or until you conceive, and then I'll be on my way. I will handle any necessary explanations to my brother before I go." He stood. "In the meantime, this arrangement we've made stays private." He pointed a finger. "We tell no one."

"Of course not."

He pushed in his chair. "I'm going to Barston this morning to check on Andy and Mrs. Rhodes."

"Am I welcome to join you?" The faint tremor in her voice tugged at something beneath his anger. The sudden vulnerability in her eyes almost made him forget just how fiercely strong she really was. Independence was as close to freedom as a woman could get, and Daisy had claimed hers today.

"Jackson?"

His thoughts shifted to the matter at hand. Daisy's concern for Andy could not be denied, and Jackson needed her help. The sooner this case was resolved, the sooner he could recover his life.

"Make yourself ready."

* * * *

Daisy closed the door behind her, wiping the tears that had formed on her way to their room. She'd done the right thing by releasing Jackson from their marriage. She knew it in her heart. Still, she could have sworn that she'd hurt him, somehow. The thought was ridiculous. She'd heard his true feelings last night, and only because she'd confronted him had he tried to recant.

She hadn't planned on telling him what she'd overheard, but he'd been so adamant in his accusations that she'd connived him into marriage that he'd left her no choice. Did he really think she was capable of such a dirty deed as to snare a second husband to gain access to her former husband's money?

As desperate as she was at the time, she was surprised she hadn't resorted to it. Jackson was a lawyer, though, and she supposed it was only natural for a lawyer's mind to suspect such schemes.

She hadn't realized until last night on the veranda how deeply she'd hoped Jackson might come around to their situation. That over time he might grow to care for her. Many men sowed wild oats, then settled down with women they cared for. That was the difference between those men and Jackson. Jackson cared for no one but himself.

At least neither of them was sailing under false colors now. They both knew where they stood. She dressed quickly, confident in the arrangement they'd struck. She would go with Jackson to Barston today, and she'd help him prove Mr. Morgan's innocence in any way she could.

They would live together as a married couple for the summer, but there would be no surprises come autumn. And no expectations in the meantime, no pointless hope things might change with the season.

With any luck, Jackson's parting gift to her would be a child of her own. Her desire for a child may have cost her first husband his life, but Jackson Gallway would be luckier. He'd have his life and the freedom to live it the way he wanted—with miles between him and the chains that would bind him.

And Daisy's heart would remain intact.

Chapter 11

"We'll take the main road to Barston," Jackson said as he helped Daisy board the wagon. Her eyes met his, and he stepped back in time to the fateful trip that had prompted their marriage. "I want to get a feel for the layout of the village and the route Morgan traveled the day of the murder," he said to prod through the awkward moment.

He hopped up to join her, then situated himself on the bench. As always, the scent of her nearness filled his senses to overflowing. Desire, lust, denial—a maelstrom of conflicting emotions that frustrated the hell out him. The only constant in her presence was his total state of confusion and arousal.

Oblivious to his dilemma, Daisy focused on her bonnet, adjusting the wide brim against the sun. "Do you know what stops Mr. Morgan made during his travels that afternoon?"

"Yes. I made him retrace his every step, and I recorded each stop, including everyone he saw or spoke to along the way." He shrugged. "He peddled his wares in Barston only twice before, so he wasn't that familiar with the village or the people."

"That certainly doesn't help matters," Daisy said. "Have you any idea how many other salesmen passed through town that day?"

"Not yet. I'm guessing one at least." He turned to face her. "You brought your sketch pad?"

She nodded.

"Do you think you could sketch another likeness of the man Andy saw?"

"Yes, of course." The sparkle of pride in her eyes was well deserved. He'd seen for himself the scope of her talent.

She reached under the seat for her case of sketching supplies and started drawing. Even the bounce of the wagon didn't hamper her determination as she worked. She bit her lower lip, her face set in concentration. Wisps of blond hair blew beneath her bonnet, fluttering against her slender neck. He admired her profile, struck by her simple beauty as though regarding some masterpiece displayed in a museum.

Shaking his head, he returned his focus to driving. He blamed his escalating attraction to Daisy on her decision to hand him the mitten. Rejection engendered strange responses. It was human nature to crave something denied. Or in this case, something soon to be denied. Jackson had always relished the challenge of the hunt, and his limited time with Daisy spurred a need to get all that he could. And why not? She'd given him license, free and clear, for the next three months, anyway. He may as well enjoy it.

"Finished," she said, snapping him back to attention. She held out the sketch. Jackson was amazed at how accurately she'd replicated the original he'd given to the chief of police. She did, indeed, have an exceptional memory. Right down to the finest details.

"How do you do it?" he asked. "Few artists can capture the likeness of a subject without the aid of an actual subject."

She shrugged. "I can't explain how it comes to me so easily. The picture in my mind just flows from my brain to my hands, and then onto the page."

"As it does while entranced?"

"I suppose so, yes."

"Have you ever considered using your talent to help the authorities solve crimes?"

She tilted her head, eyeing him warily.

"I'm serious," he said. "Your skills are unique." He warmed at the blush in her cheeks. The sprinkle of freckles on the bridge of her nose accentuated her fresh-faced allure. "But then again, so are you."

Her pensive smile became broader, and then she burst out laughing. "You honestly can't help it, can you, Jackson?"

"Can't help what?" he asked with his most innocent expression.

"Flirting," she said, laughing some more. "Using flattery to seduce."

He smiled. "Is it working?"

She shook her head at his hopelessness. She saw clearly through his shallow composition, but unlike most women, Daisy ensured that he knew it. The fact was as unnerving as it was liberating. In this temporary arrangement he could be himself—whatever that meant—and the result wouldn't matter. The outcome of their relationship was already set.

"Nevertheless, I meant every word that I said."

"Let's see how I do with helping you with this case before you hire me out to the Troy City Police Department."

"Fair enough," he said, enjoying her smile and the effortless ease it brought to his soul. He didn't know what he expected from this woman, but come autumn, when all was said and done, he knew he couldn't bear for her to hate him.

"Can we stop at the general store in the village?" Daisy asked. "I'd like to get some licorice sticks for Andy."

Jackson nodded. "I can show your sketch around the store, see if anyone recognizes the man. Someone must have seen him at some point."

Daisy frowned. "It vexes me to no end that this man thinks he got away with murder."

"But we know better, don't we?"

"We just have to prove it," she said.

"And we have to be careful. You let me do the talking when I question people about the sketch. Witnesses tend to be skittish about getting involved."

"What's the plan?"

She considered them partners, and surprisingly, he didn't mind. "We'll start at the store. Then we'll go door to door if necessary, until we find someone who remembers seeing the man. Someone had to have seen him somewhere between the Wendell farm and Troy."

"You think he headed to Troy?"

"It makes sense. This man is a bad egg. He could have killed Wendell, stashed the items he stole from the house in Morgan's cart, returned to Troy, leaving Morgan as the patsy. He may have known Morgan, who knows."

"Jackson, look." Daisy pointed to the sky in the distance. A thick haze hung in the air, a gray cloud hovering above the treetops.

Hair prickled on the back of Jackson's neck. "It's smoke."

Daisy gazed toward the mountains, squinting beneath the brim of her hat. "Smoke?"

The alarm in her voice was justified. Jackson felt a twinge of the same in the pit of his stomach. "Probably smoke from a fire at one of the logging camps. We're almost to the village," he said, slapping the reins. The wagon picked up speed. They drove along at a steady pace past acres of rolling fields dotted with cows and neat rows of newly planted corn.

When they reached the edge of town, a wagon was stopped on the road in front of a small farmhouse. The passengers in the wagon were talking with a couple on the side of the road.

"Something's going on," Jackson mumbled. He pulled back on the reins, slowing the horse as they neared. An assembly of faces turned toward them, all wearing the same troubled expression.

With a sweeping wave, an elderly man dressed in baggy denim overalls and a straw hat directed Jackson to pull the wagon up behind the other. The plump woman at the farmer's side hurried toward them. The strain of her pace and suppressing the forthcoming news left her cheeks so flushed Jackson feared she might burst.

"There was a fire on the mountain," she announced. "A bad one."

The old man hobbled over as fast as his weary bones allowed. "The house was burned to the ground."

"What house?" Jackson asked.

"The Rhodes house."

"Oh my God," Daisy gasped.

Jackson's hand on her knee kept her from jumping from the bench. "Is everyone all right?" he asked amid the rising panic swelling in his chest.

"Mrs. Rhodes took it bad in the lungs," the farmer said.

"What about Andy?" Daisy croaked.

Jackson eased her back in the seat, trying hard to stay calm. "What of the boy?" he demanded.

The woman lowered her head.

"No word on the boy yet," the farmer said. "They took Edna over to the Carney place where the doctor's working on her."

"She's a tough one," the woman added. "She'll pull through. I don't care what they're saying."

Jackson gave a nod, then snapped the reins hard. "Hang on," he told Daisy as they sped around the other wagon and down the dusty road.

Daisy was clenching her skirts so hard her knuckles were white. Jackson hadn't the words to soothe her fears, so he just reached for her hand and gave it a squeeze. Her fingers gripped his, and she held tight as they raced through town. Passing people abuzz with the excitement of the early morning fire, they maneuvered through the traffic at the intersection and headed up the mountain.

The smell of smoke permeated the air; the haze became thicker and thicker. He identified the Carney house even before he saw the name painted in white letters on the huge boulder at the bottom of the crowded drive. On the porch, a solemn group gathered in vigil for Mrs. Rhodes.

Jackson snapped the reins harder, a futile attempt to spare Daisy from the sight of the house and the dismal imaginings of what was happening inside.

They reached the charred remains of Mrs. Rhodes's house, and Jackson's stomach turned in revolt. The house where he'd sat drinking cider that day was completely destroyed. The devastation was so vast, so ugly. A lifetime of comfort and memories drifted off in the billowing smoke. Jackson steeled his emotions as he helped Daisy from the wagon. They hurried toward one of the volunteer firemen surrounding the smoking skeleton of the house.

"What happened?" Jackson asked.

"It went up fast. From what we got from Edna, she must have left on a lamp when she went to bed, and one of those damn cats knocked it over. The lamp was on the table by the window so the curtains went up and that was that."

"What about Andy?" Daisy asked, frantically.

"We're looking. He may have gotten out. We have men searching the fields," he said. "Got men ready to search the rubble, too, but we can't get near it yet."

Daisy's legs buckled beneath her, and Jackson caught her around the waist. The man stepped toward them. "Better get her out of here, mister. This ain't no place for a woman."

"I'm fine." Daisy regained her footing quickly, but her voice trembled. "I want to help look for him. He may have gotten out of the house. He may have run away."

"We're hoping so too, ma'am. If he's out there, we'll find him. I promise."

Jackson led Daisy away, turning her from the sight of the house. He held her face between his hands. "They'll find him safe and sound." The anguish in her eyes mixed with tears. She didn't cry, but he could tell she wanted to. She'd lost her foster family in a fire; she'd lived this nightmare before. He drew her into his arms and held her tight, struggling against his own fear for the fortitude to calm hers. "We should go see Mrs. Rhodes and find out how she's doing."

Daisy nodded against his chest. She eased from his embrace, then stiffened, clenching his arms. She gaped over his shoulder. "Andy!"

Jackson spun around to see two men charging from the field. The taller man carried a boy. Jackson smiled as the other searchers and spectators erupted into cheers.

Daisy broke free of Jackson's grip and raced toward the field. Recognizing her immediately, Andy squirmed from the man's arms, then jumped down, running through the tall grass toward Daisy as fast as his little legs could carry him. Daisy dropped to her knees, and he flung himself into her arms.

Relief coiled through Jackson, and he swallowed against the tight knot of emotion in his throat. The boy wrapped his arms around Daisy's neck. Hanging on for dear life, he buried his face into the safety of her golden hair.

Jackson cleared his throat, blinking hard as he watched. Daisy's bonnet hung behind her as she shielded Andy from the horror of the charred ruins just a few yards away. The scene reminded Jackson of everything that was good in this world, all the things that truly mattered. Things like love and faith and charity—things he'd touched on the surface, but never quite felt.

The spectators and volunteers circled the two men who'd found Andy, eager for the story. "I found him up at the Shaw place," the man who'd carried Andy explained. He pointed to the bearded man beside him. "This is Jacob Squires. He bought the Shaw place. Andy was sleeping on his porch."

Jacob shrugged his burly shoulders. "Didn't even know the boy was out there," he said, "until I heard the ruckus." He adjusted his spectacles. "Me and the misses just moved in last week. She's a dainty creature, and the trip from Pennsylvania about did her in."

The crowd gathered around Jacob, bombarding him with questions and welcoming him to town. Jackson walked to Daisy and Andy. He tousled Andy's hair, and the boy gave him a crooked smile.

Jackson's relief that the boy was safe was shadowed by suspicion. The possibility the fire was arson could not be ruled out. An eerie premonition crept up his spine. The celebratory mood in the air only heightened his fear. Andy might be in true danger. Until the man in Daisy's sketch was apprehended, no one was safe.

Chapter 12

No one who'd witnessed Andy's tender reunion with Daisy could object to her suggestion she and Jackson take the boy to see Mrs. Rhodes. Andy sat in the wagon between them with a tabby cat, the sole survivor of the seven strays that had shared the house with him and Mrs. Rhodes. They drove most of the short distance to the Carney house in welcome silence. After the chaos of the fire, Daisy found solace in the rhythm of the moving wagon and the simple presence of their company.

Her relief that Andy was safe mixed with her sympathy for his terrible misfortune. First the murder of his father and the loss of his home, and now the loss of his foster home. But he had survived. As she had. She wiped at her tears in a futile attempt to contain her emotions.

Jackson, on the other hand, was all business. His inquisitive manner befit a lawyer's when he asked, "Did you notice any strangers around the house lately, Andy?"

Andy stroked the cat on his lap, his small hand tensing suddenly on its coat of striped fur. "No," he uttered, lowering his gaze.

"Are you sure, Andy?" Daisy asked.

He shrugged. "I thought I saw a man in the window, but Mrs. Rhodes said it was only shadows from the tree branches, and that I have a strong 'magination. Then she tucked me in, and I went to sleep. Tabs woke me up. He kept meowing till I opened my eyes. They were hurting from the smoke. I called for Mrs. Rhodes, but she didn't answer. Tabs jumped out the window. I was scared, so I followed him into the field."

"That's a smart boy," Daisy said, wrapping her arm around him. "Tabs saved your life."

Andy nodded.

Daisy glanced at Jackson. She knew from his grim expression that he wasn't at all convinced that Andy had imagined a man in the window. For the boy's sake, and to Jackson's credit, he held any frightening suspicions to himself.

When they reached the Carney house, they were greeted by jubilant cheers and applause. Apparently, someone from the fire site had raced ahead with the news Andy was safe. They climbed from the wagon and then walked to the crowded porch.

"I'll wait out here," Jackson said.

Daisy gave him a nod before ushering Andy through the door. If possible, there were more people crammed inside the small front room of the house than there were out on the porch. A heavyset woman hurried toward them. "I'm Mrs. Carney," she told Daisy. Planting her hands on her ample hips, she pinned Andy with a stern frown. "You gave us quite a scare, young man. Whatever possessed you to run away like that?"

Andy lowered his head.

Daisy reined back the urge to lambast the woman. How dare she scold the boy for surviving, regardless of how he'd managed to do it? "How is Mrs. Rhodes?" Daisy asked instead.

"She's doing better. The doctor says she'll be right as rain in a few days."

Daisy exhaled a breath of relief. "Oh, thank goodness. May we see her?"

"Of course. This way."

They followed the woman to the back of the house to the last room at the end of the narrow hall. "Edna, look who's here," Mrs. Carney announced.

Mrs. Rhodes glanced up from the bed. Her disheveled gray hair seemed grayer around her pale face, and she looked as though she'd aged ten years since the last time Daisy had seen her. After the ordeal of the fire, Daisy wasn't surprised. The old woman's life had been spared, but her place in the world had been reduced to a smoking pile of rubble.

Mrs. Rhodes struggled upright on the pillows, holding out her arms. Her groggy eyes welled with tears. "Oh, thank you, Lord." She croaked out the words, the pain audible as they rose from the smoke-raw hollow of her throat.

Andy hurried toward her, then hugged her tight.

"Oh, what will become of you now?" she cried, hugging him tighter. "I'll have to go live with my sister in Albany," she said to Daisy as she released the boy. "This poor child will have to go to the orphan asylum for sure."

Daisy's heart sank to her feet. "Is there no one else who can care for him?"

Mrs. Rhodes shook her head, sinking back to the pillows.

"Folks are busy running their farms," Mrs. Carney said. "This tyke is too small yet to be of much help."

"Don't fret, Mrs. Rhodes," Andy said in a frightened little voice. "I'll be all right." He spoke the courageous words through trembling lips as he consoled the old woman who had taken him in when no one would.

Daisy despaired, contemplating his plight. Memories of her years at the orphanage came back in a rush. A faceless child among dozens of faceless children. The stark longing for love. With another glance at *this* child, Andy Wendell, her melting attempt to stay strong became a puddle of mush. He'd been through so much already. "Of course you'll be fine, Andy. You will come to stay with me and Mr. Gallway in Misty Lake."

The boy's face lit up. "Tabs too?"

"Tabs too," Daisy assured him.

"Oh, how kind of you," Mrs. Rhodes exclaimed. "He'll be no trouble at all, will you, Andy?"

Andy shook his head.

Daisy smiled. She supposed she should have consulted Jackson before extending the invitation. He was her husband, and they shared a home; he had a right to consider who lived in it. But his role as her husband was short-term. After a lifetime of seeking permission from people who'd dictated her decisions, she relished the freedom to do as she pleased. Especially in this instance. Strangely, she felt confident Jackson trusted her judgment. The reassurance that Andy would be safe under their watchful eyes cemented her decision. "You stay here and visit with Mrs. Rhodes for a bit. I'll go give the happy news to Mr. Gallway."

* * * *

Jackson milled around a bit, making small talk with the group of people outside. Three men sat side by side on the porch railing, the sleeves of their flannel shirts bulging with muscles. Sawmill workers, he presumed, or lumberjacks. Jackson was reminded suddenly of Cuffy, and how they certainly grew them large on the mountain. Daisy's tap to his shoulder jolted him from his thoughts.

"May I speak with you for a moment?" she asked.

"How is she?"

"She'll recover. But she'll be moving to her sister's home as soon as she's able."

"And Andy?"

Daisy shook her head. "There's no room for him there. I've offered to take him home with us." A shadow of apprehension crossed her face. "It's either that or the orphan asylum, Jax, and I can't let that happen."

He needed only to look into her eyes to understand her reasons. Andy was an orphan like she was, and she wanted to give him a home, if only temporarily. Humbled by her benevolence, he managed a smile. "No, of course you can't."

She smiled too. "How is it going out here? She scanned the assembly of people, which was beginning to wane. "Have you shown them the sketch?"

"I was just about to."

Daisy followed as he meandered to one of the large men perched on the railing. "Curtis, is it?" Jackson asked.

"That's right."

"My name is Jackson Gallway." Reaching inside his pocket, he pulled out the sketch, unfolded it, and held it out. "Do you recognize this man?"

"Can't say as I do. Who is he?"

"He's a suspect in a case I'm working on. I believe he was around these parts a few months ago."

"What's he done?"

Jackson glanced to the women nearby. "I'd rather not say in mixed company," he said. "But it's imperative that I find him."

"You a lawman?"

"I'm a lawyer."

"Lawyer?" The man winced.

Ignoring the insult, Jackson moved on to the next two men in the line. "Do you recognize the man in this sketch?"

The men glanced at Curtis, who was the obvious leader of the trio. "No, sir."

"No, sir."

"How about you?" Jackson asked a young woman who'd inched closer during his canvas of the men.

She craned her neck toward the sketch, and her eyes widened. "I—"

"My sister ain't seen him, either." Curtis's fierce glare at the girl tamped out the spark of recognition Jackson had seen on her face. "You go on home, Corine," Curtis said. "Mama's waiting on you."

Corine scurried off with no argument, not that Jackson blamed her. Curtis's tone alone was menacing. That he could back it up with two hundred and fifty pounds of oak-hard muscle was almost enough to send Jackson slinking behind her.

Instead he held up the sketch. "Anyone?" He moved in a circle, rotating the sketch for all to see. "Has anyone seen this man around the Rhodes's house?"

"The Rhodes's house?" Curtis hopped from the railing. "What exactly are you saying, mister? That this man set the place on fire?"

"I'm saying there's a possibility—"

"Mrs. Rhodes is an old woman who lived with a houseful of crazy cats. The fire was an accident." He narrowed his eyes. "Who exactly are you working for?"

Jackson sighed. His agenda would come out sooner or later. "I'm trying to find the man who murdered your neighbor, Ray Wendell."

Amid an eruption of protests, Curtis yelled, "They caught that bastard, and he's good and dead!"

Jackson shook his head. "I don't believe Randal Morgan killed Mr. Wendell."

"And you're trying to peddle this nonsense? Here?" Curtis's eyes were wide; a vein bulged in his neck.

"I'm trying to find the truth."

"Trying to frighten the women more like it. And maybe scare up a name for yourself in the process. That's what men like you do. Men who defend murderers for a living."

"That's not true!" Daisy took a step forward. "There's evidence to support Mr. Gallway's suspicion, and if he's correct, there's a killer at large here in your backyard."

"It's all right, Daisy," Jackson said. While he appreciated her loyalty, she was an outsider like he was—and they were sorely outnumbered. Drawing her back, he conveyed this with his eyes before addressing the crowd. "It's been a long day for everyone. Sorry for the trouble, folks." He turned to Daisy. "Go get Andy."

"Hold up," Curtis demanded. "You're the folks taking the boy in?"

"We are," Jackson said.

"I ain't no educated lawyer, but I know Edna Rhodes. And she ain't about to send the boy off with you or anyone else in cahoots with the city trash who murdered his father."

"We'll see what Mrs. Rhodes has to say about that," Jackson said.

Curtis took a step closer. "No, sir, we won't."

"Are you refusing to allow us—"

"You're damn right I am." Curtis took another imposing step toward Jackson, blocking his access to the house. His two pals flanked him like trees. "We know what's best for the boy, and it's best the two of you be on your way."

Daisy shook her head furiously. "I'm not leaving without Andy."

"We take care of our own," Curtis said. "The boy stays with me."

Jackson's blood pounded in his ears. "Now, wait just a—"

"Git!" Curtis shoved up his sleeves, posed in a stance that warned he meant business.

Jackson stared down the challenge, clenching his fists. While he'd earned his fair share of bruises in the past, he knew this man would crush him to pulp. The image of Daisy's distraught face gazing down at his broken body flashed in his mind, spurring him to reason. He pointed his finger. "You take good care of that boy," he said. "I'll be back to make sure that you do." He inhaled a deep breath. "In the meantime, I suggest you take a few minutes, or an hour, or however long it takes for that pea brain of yours to consider what a horse's ass you've been here today." He tossed a glance at the women huddled nearby. "I apologize, ladies, for this unpleasantness."

"But, Jax—"

"Go say good-bye to the boy," he said as he urged Daisy toward the door. "Tell him we'll be back to check on him soon."

With a sigh, she did as instructed. Feeling like a trapped rabbit amid a pack of wolves, he waited, relieved by Daisy's sense to withhold the protest that might cause them to pounce.

When she returned, he wrapped his arm around her waist and led her away.

"That went well," he mumbled as they boarded the wagon. "How was the boy?"

"He likes Curtis's dog," she said. "He says he'll be fine."

Jackson patted her arm. "We'll return to check on him in a day or two. Let things settle down."

They drove down the mountain in silence. The scene with Curtis had Jackson's blood boiling, but he'd done the right thing by walking away. A bruised ego was preferable to a bruised body, but he couldn't help dwelling on the fact the man had publically shamed him that way.

"Is that Corine?" Daisy pointed to the roadside up ahead. "Curtis's sister?"

"Yes," he said. "And I'd like to speak with her." He pulled back on the reins.

Daisy called down to Corine as the wagon rolled to a stop. "My name is Daisy Gallway, and this is my husband. May we offer you a ride home?"

Corine glanced to the long road up ahead. "Thank you," she said with a smile.

Jackson's rush of optimism was premature, but he sensed Corine knew something about the man in the sketch.

Daisy placed a hand on Jackson's forearm. "Don't drive until I tell you to," she murmured.

With a nod, Jackson hopped down to assist Corine. A moment later the woman was sitting beside Daisy in the wagon. Jackson returned to his seat. Even as he pondered Daisy's motives, his brain couldn't deflect from the pleasing smell of her hair.

"Your brother has offered to take in little Andy," Daisy said.

"He has?" Corine furrowed her brow. "Mama will sure be surprised," she muttered.

"You and your family will take good care of him, won't you?"

"Yes, ma'am, we will. I know Curtis seems a gruff sort, but he's a good man. He'll do anything to protect his neighbors."

"We're counting on that," Jackson said. "Keep a close eye on the boy. Until the man I'm searching for is apprehended, you're all in danger."

Corine wrung her hands on her lap. "That fella you're looking for. I've seen him. A while back."

Jackson leaned forward to face her. "Where?"

"You can't tell my brother. He don't want me involved."

"Where?"

"I can't recall." She shook her head. "For the life of me, I can't recall. But I know I've seen him before."

"Think." Jackson didn't mean to sound harsh, but he needed her to remember. He handed her the sketch of the man. "Look at it again."

Corine stared down at it, shaking her head. "I'm sorry."

Daisy reached for her sketch pad at her feet. "Corine, would you indulge me for a moment?" she asked.

Jackson sat at attention, and let Daisy take over.

"When I'm trying to remember something, it helps to close my eyes. Can you do that for me now?"

Corine eyed Daisy warily. "I suppose."

Daisy smiled. Positioning the pad on her lap, she prepared for business. "Now just relax," she said. "Close your eyes and try to concentrate on the man you saw. Try to picture the surroundings, any details you can."

Corine followed Daisy's instructions. Dipping her head forward, she closed her eyes.

Jackson shifted in his seat, bracing himself to witness Daisy's talent up close.

"Can you see him?" Daisy asked softly.

Corine nodded.

Daisy closed her eyes too.

A moment later, her hand twitched on the pad. Jackson sat riveted, watching as her trembling fingers gripped the pencil. Her head lulled to the side. Her vacant eyes opened a crack, but she seemed fast asleep as she moved. The pencil glided across the paper, short strokes and long. Manic, incoherent scribblings poured onto the page, faster and faster. Among the jumbled drawings, an image appeared, taking shape, stroke by stroke before his eyes.

Daisy flinched, blinking hard.

Jackson's pulse raced as she awoke from the trance. He touched her trembling shoulder, and she patted his hand, assuring him she was fine. As awed as he was by her curious ability, it still unnerved him to the bone to see her in that ghostly state.

"He was on horseback," Corine said. "I remember." She looked down at the sketch on Daisy's lap. Her eyes flashed wide. "On that horse," she uttered, clearly amazed. She leaned away from Daisy. "How did you do that?"

Daisy shrugged. "I can't explain it," she said simply. "It's just something I can do."

Corine furrowed her brow in disbelief or confusion or both. "You can't let Curtis know about this," she said. "He wouldn't like it."

Jackson was inclined to agree.

Corine stared down at the sketch of the black horse with distinct white stockings. "I remember those white hooves," she said. "The man you're looking for was on that horse. I saw him when I was coming out of the post office 'bout two months ago."

Jackson stilled. "Do you remember which direction he was going?" he asked.

"Up the mountain."

"Thank you, Corine," Jackson said. "You've been very helpful." The wink he flashed earned him a smile before he snapped the reins and they headed down the mountain.

Jackson's heart raced in a surge of excitement. This mystery man was real, and Jackson would find him. With Daisy working her magic in his corner, he couldn't lose. In this moment, he felt capable of anything, and his gratitude for Daisy's help overwhelmed him. It was all he could do not to stop the wagon and kiss her, right there in front of Corine.

"Nice job," he said with a smile.

She smiled back, and he was struck, once again, by the impulse to kiss her.

When they were finally alone, he said, "It's all starting to fit now. Randal Morgan insisted that someone stashed the items stolen from the Wendell place in his cart." Jackson held up the sketch. "This man."

Daisy's face filled with fear. "I'm so worried for Andy."

Jackson couldn't help feeling guilty. The incident with Curtis had cost her the boy. Had Andy been with them now, she'd be resting easier. "We'll see him soon."

"Not if Curtis has his way."

"He won't," Jackson said. "Next time I'll be prepared."

She arched her brow. "Engaging in fisticuffs with him?" she asked. "I imagine he packs quite a punch."

Jackson gave a firm nod. "I imagine he does. But I'll be packing a gun."

Chapter 13

Over the next week, Daisy noticed an obvious change in Jackson's mood. Despite the sunny weather, today's breakfast on the bluestone patio was a dismal affair. The furrow of his brow deepened by the moment, and any attempt at conversation was locked tightly behind his nonexistent smile.

A pang of guilt ached through her, and she couldn't help feeling sorry for his sullen transformation. His carefree days as a city bachelor appeared miles behind him. Now he trudged between Misty Lake and Troy, lugging the burden that had landed so heavily on his slumping shoulders. Responsibility. And more of it than he'd likely ever carried before. He stared out at the lake, his long legs stretched from where he sat at the wrought iron table, looking lost in thought and so displaced.

Sunlight reflected off the water, forcing glimmers of light into his forlorn eyes. Like a waning candle, the flame inside him was dimming, suffocating in his current circumstances and the doldrums of his surroundings. She missed his easy smile, his light-hearted humor.

To pile on the agony, he'd been shown up in public by Curtis and practically chased down the mountain by an irate mob. Daisy admired Jackson's diplomacy in handling the ugly confrontation, but men were men, and their egos were more fragile than eggs.

Daisy felt melancholy too. Although Jackson and she were in agreement that Curtis would keep Andy safe, she couldn't shake her disappointment at losing the chance to care for the boy. For a moment, in the sheer bliss of her excitement about taking Andy home, she'd felt a sense of completion, a hope fulfilled by the promise of a child beneath her roof. Someone to love. Someone to love her in return.

She had until the end of the summer to do what she could to secure that hope. If Jackson lasted the summer in Misty Lake. At this moment she wasn't so sure he'd last another hour. But tonight... At night he came back to life.

While they made love, nothing else seemed to matter. In the haven of their bed, they followed their bodies into the pleasure, far away from the ills of the world. They were using each other, plain and simple. But she cared for him too. Very much.

Since living under one roof, she'd come to enjoy the little things about him, the way his hair looked in the morning, all wild and mussed. The way he walked across a room with those purposeful strides, so full of confidence. But most of all, she enjoyed the way he listened when she spoke. The interest he took in what she had to say was more alluring than his sapphire eyes.

These endearing feelings were acceptable, she supposed. They were husband and wife, and whether in name only or not, married couples should, at the very least, like each other. Since she planned on becoming the mother of Jackson's child, this reasoning seemed especially just. A civil union would ensure a civil separation, which would be for the best.

A man like Jackson couldn't bear the lifelong responsibility of fatherhood. Some men couldn't. Her own father, whoever he was, had abandoned the duty.

She swallowed back her guilt for leaving Andy, and tried to push her gloomy thoughts from her mind. Flipping casually through the pages of the Misty Lake Sun, she realized she could use a boost to her mood as well. And then she saw it. With a glance at Jackson, she folded the papers quickly, certain she'd found the perfect diversion for them both.

"Are you free this afternoon?" she asked, tossing the papers aside.

"I have some notes to go over this morning, but after that my day is clear. Why?"

"Are you up for some recreation?"

His eyes widened in a mock expression of horror. "Me? Surely you jest." He flashed his first genuine smile in days, and she basked in the familiar warmth it induced.

"Wonderful. Heaven knows I could use a bit of fun."

"Is that so?" Arching a brow, he eyed her, looking so handsome. "I can't decide whether to be inspired or offended."

Daisy considered this during the split-second before he broke out laughing. The welcome sound wrapped around her like a reassuring embrace. She smiled, relieved that his old self was resurging.

He turned toward the sound of squawking geese in the distance. Mama and goslings swam toward the shore. Reaching for the uneaten toasted bread on his plate, Jackson said, "If you'll excuse me, I have company."

"Friends of yours now?" she asked as he stood.

"We came to a truce over a handful of bread."

The geese proceeded up the lawn for their breakfast.

"Come help feed our guests," Jackson said as the geese scrambled around his feet.

Daisy grabbed some more bread and joined him in his task. They laughed at the antics of the tiny family that raced and pecked for the bread. Jackson tossed mama goose a piece, and she snatched it mid-air.

"They've grown since I last saw them," Daisy said.

Jackson pointed. "Especially that one," he said. "He's a bit of a bully."

Daisy smiled. "So how often do these visits occur?"

He shrugged. "Every day. I come out here to clear my mind. The mornings are quiet." He smiled. "Until this crew arrives."

Jackson swiped the remaining crumbs from his hands, cueing the geese his supply had run dry. Mama goose headed toward the lake, the goslings chirping behind her as they waddled away.

Surprised by the sudden lift to her mood, she said, "Now that your guests have been fed, I'll have Kotterman ready the carriage. We shall depart at noon."

"Depart for...?" His dubious expression bordered on dread.

No doubt he imagined a tedious Saturday spent attending the weekly church social or some such event he'd safely avoided until now. On a mischievous whim, she withheld any assurance to the contrary. She shook her head, suppressing a smile. "While I'll not divulge our exact destination, I guarantee a fun-filled afternoon."

"Your idea of fun may differ from mine." He smiled in that wicked way she'd come to know so well, and the suggestive wit in his eyes filled her with longing.

"Don't be so sure," she said with a wicked grin of her own. She'd abandoned all reticence in speaking her mind, but why bother being shy? The pretense of modesty was ridiculous in the wake of their passionate nights. Hours spent naked, repressing nothing. This man brought out everything, the deepest aspirations of the stagnant woman who'd been bottled inside her body for years. And now her truest self poured freely. In bed and out.

Unlike Lawry, to whom she'd always tried to be the proper wife, she now lived to please herself. The consequences of each move she made no longer mattered. She had nothing to prove to Jackson, and she expected nothing more from him save the intoxicating delight of his company. And if he left her with a child, all the better.

"We can enjoy public recreation as well as private," she said in a sultry voice she barely recognized. "I'll prove it to you today."

"But you won't tell me what you have planned?"

She shook her head.

"It's not fern picking in the woods, is it? A butterfly hunt through the fields?"

She laughed, rising from her chair. "Just promise to keep an open mind."

"Now I truly am worried."

"I know." She kissed his cheek in reward for the good sport that he was. The spicy scent of him filled her nose, igniting her senses. "I'm having fun already."

* * * *

An hour later, they were on their way to Logan's Field for what Jackson suspected was a picnic. Croquet, potato salad, and lemonade. Good, wholesome fun. Suppressing a chuckle, he glanced at Daisy, his mood much improved as Kotterman drove the carriage through the Saturday traffic in town. The bustle of activity outside the carriage window roused his energy and the roguish side of his nature that had been dormant since his arrival in Misty Lake.

Aside from dinner at the Misty Lake Hotel and a few brief visits to the local taverns, he'd devoted the remainder of his time to the Morgan case. The focus on business was a clear departure from his usual summer slate. If not for Daisy, he was certain he would go mad in his bumbling efforts to solve this case and honor a promise he was unqualified to keep.

Randal Morgan deserved better. He'd trusted Jackson to protect his children by clearing his name, which only proved how truly desperate the man must have been.

Fending off his biting insecurities, Jackson returned his focus to Daisy. Although he didn't expect much from whatever recreational event she had planned today, he'd keep an open mind. He appreciated her attempt to provide some much-needed fun, and he wouldn't disappoint her by not enjoying the day.

Besides, just being in her company lifted his spirits. She stimulated his mind as well as his body, diverting his attention to more pleasant matters than the fear he'd fail Randal Morgan. Jackson was homesick for the city, and if anyone could aid in the remedy for everything he was missing in Troy, it was Daisy.

She sat on the seat across from him, gazing out the open window and wearing a green dress he'd never seen but was fast becoming his favorite. The matching ribbon on her straw bonnet wafted in the breeze; tendrils of blond hair danced around her face. The sight stirred him physically, her soulful blue eyes, so full of warmth and intelligence, her ruby lips, so eager to smile and so sweet to kiss.

His gaze traced her profile across the line of her jaw, down her throat, to her lace-trimmed bodice, and then lower. Her breasts rose and fell with each breath, each jolt of the carriage, and he all but moaned out loud his appreciation—his yearning—for what was heaven-on-earth beneath the green silk.

From head to toe she was perfect. Like the modest flower for which she'd been named, her soft-spoken beauty flourished naturally and required little care. Resilient and firmly rooted, no matter how brutal the sun or how fierce the storm, the sturdy bloom survived. Just like her.

Perusing her attributes stirred his blood and the growing hardness between his legs. The uncontrollable and inconvenient effect she had on him came as no surprise. He'd accepted his arresting attraction to Daisy long ago. What he could not understand, though, was why her? He'd seduced dozens of beautiful women out of their skirts, but Daisy seduced him out of his mind, and this reversal, of sorts, was a first.

Daisy's eyes met his, and he took a deep breath, his brain grappling for something to say. "You truly enjoy living in the country, don't you?" he asked.

"I truly do."

Jackson withheld the reflex to ask why. "You never miss the buzz of the city?" he asked instead.

"I prefer the buzz of the bees. My life in the city left me lost to myself. I wanted a home. When Lawry brought me to Misty Lake, I knew I'd found my place."

Jackson nodded, wondering if and when he'd ever find his. Was there one place on this earth he belonged? He thought about the wanderlust he'd inherited from his mother, his plans for St. Louis, and all the cities he'd roamed.

"What about you, Jackson? How did you land in Troy?"

He smiled at her apt choice of words. "I attended school there. Actually, I attended two other schools before that, but was expelled from both for abandoning my studies to sneak off to the city."

She chided his antics with a tsk-tsk and a grin. "What was your childhood like?"

He shrugged. "It was…fun."

Daisy laughed, and he realized how fond he'd become of the familiar sound. "I raised all sorts of trouble, but my parents indulged me."

"Dannion too?"

"Dannion and I were complete opposites growing up." He smiled. "We still are, in case you haven't noticed. He was the first born, and my mother was hard on him. Their relationship was strained for as long as I can remember."

"But you got on well with her?"

"I was her favorite. An honor she never let me forget." He shrugged. "She never let Dannion forget, either. I suppose that explains a lot about my brother."

"And you, as well."

The simple observation opened a chasm of complex issues into which he'd rather not delve. His mother's bitter warnings against marriage echoed through his head. He shook off the past by changing the subject. He pointed toward the sparkling lake. "Look at all the boats."

Daisy admired the array of vessels and their colorful sails. "It's a lovely day for boating," she said. "The locals, and summer guests alike, take full advantage of the many lakes in the area."

"I'm not one for boating. Haven't partaken in years."

"What a shame," she said. "You don't know what you're missing."

"Yes I do. Drowning."

She rolled her eyes. "A ride in a boat doesn't guarantee drowning."

"No. But it sure as hell increases the odds."

She smiled. "I suppose I must give you that." She straightened in her seat, adjusting the brim of her bonnet. "Speaking of odds, I'd wager you're curious to know where we're going."

"And you'd win that bet."

Leaning toward the window, she pointed at the approaching intersection and a large wooden arrow pointing left. The placement of the arrow-shaped sign at the side of the road was surely recent. Jackson had traveled this route several times and would have noticed the colorful advertisement that was now impossible to miss. He turned to Daisy, smiling with gratitude for the trip she'd arranged.

She leaned back in her seat, beaming in satisfaction. He fought the urge to pull her onto his lap and kiss her senseless for knowing him so well. Excitement coursed through his blood as he anticipated a day spent enjoying one of his favorite pastimes.

"While it's not Saratoga," she said, "I'm hoping it will do."

He turned back to the sign, his smile growing broader as he recited the display of bold words. "Welcome to Logan's Field and Opening Day of the Race Track."

Chapter 14

By the time traffic allowed Kotterman to drop them at the gated entrance to the field, the day's event was well under way. The lively sound of strumming banjoes poured from the gazebo Daisy and Jackson passed as they hurried through the crowd. People stood in clusters at the wooden fence surrounding the crude track. The rows of long benches that served as the grandstand were crammed to capacity. Jackson led Daisy to a shady spot beneath a patch of elm trees, where they were lucky enough to find an empty bench among those occupied in the picnic area.

The smell of roasting beef and popped corn floated on the light breeze, and the air all but crackled with the anticipation of the first race of the season. For years, Daisy had wanted to attend the summer racing event, but Lawry had always refused her. Despite the numerous women in attendance, according to Lawry, it was unseemly for proper ladies to partake in such activities, and so he'd attended without her.

The memory of Lawry's antiquated ideas magnified the reality of their marriage. The age difference, his dominance, her docility. From her current viewpoint, she could see clearly the relationship that was more like father and daughter than husband and wife, distorting the illusion she'd fostered in her mind for so long—because she'd had no other choice. Like a set of eyes peering out from a portrait, the vivid truth of that union stared back at her now, a truth that had left her bankrupt, mentally, physically, and financially.

Even from the grave, he'd tried to control her.

She glanced at Jackson, and words like partnership and equality filled her with warmth. The ache of neglect melted away. She'd never felt so accepted for who she truly was. Even her entranced drawing hadn't made him look at her differently. Jackson didn't make her feel ashamed of her ability. Quite the opposite. He encouraged her to use it—and for something that mattered. To help solve crimes.

The renewed swell to her spirit was a sweet misery. Her marriage to Jackson had given her the chance to be herself, hope for all she wanted and deserved, and the confidence to accept no less. Whether he gave her a child or not, when all was said and done between them, she'd always be grateful for that.

Shaking away the grim mood that threatened to befall her, she took a deep breath, turning to the man at her side. He looked well within his element, relaxed and comfortable. That she had helped lighten his mood, lightened hers too. He perused the racing program he'd been handed at the gate. Humming softly to the lively music in the distance, he studied the various races and the riders, composed of local hobbyists, assigned to each horse.

His dark hair fell forward as he read, and she suppressed the urge to push it from his forehead and kiss every inch of his handsome face.

"Gallway."

Daisy glanced up to the middle-aged man peering down at them. He wore his fine suit with a distinguished air and a smile. Despite the jaunty greeting, his gray eyes betrayed a maliciousness that made Daisy uneasy.

Instead of rising to greet the man, Jackson dropped the program to his lap and leaned back on the bench. "Buchanan," he murmured in a tone that increased Daisy's unease.

Jackson's rebuff seemed to please Buchanan, whose smile widened beneath his drooping mustache. "I can't say I'm surprised by your presence," he said. "You're not one to pass by a good time." He glanced at Daisy. "Or a pretty lady."

"This is my wife." The chill in Jackson's voice grew stronger. "Surely you've heard."

Buchanan's knowing smile said he'd heard it all. Every scandalous detail leading up to their marriage and then some. "You've been busy." His face hardened. "In other aspects as well. Since you've never been much of a lawyer, earning a favorable reference must prove difficult, indeed. But grasping at straws with this Morgan case? Why you refuse to let the matter drop is beyond my understanding."

Jackson blinked against the force of the insult but maintained his usual apathy. "And why you harbor the notion that I give a damn what you think is beyond mine." He leaned forward. "Like it or not, I am a lawyer—"

"You're a blemish on the profession."

"That may very well be," Jackson said. A muscle clenched in his jaw. "But this is *my* case. *My* business. And I will do what is right."

This garnered a chuckle. "Like you did right with Easterly's wife? You lack the morals to do what is right."

Daisy's heart lurched in her throat. Fearing the worst, she stole a glance at Jackson. His profile was hard and set like steel. But to her surprise, he remained unflappable. He merely crossed his arms on his chest, as though he'd been expecting the reminder of a topic he'd grown bored with long ago.

Buchanan seethed with frustration. The bear he poked refused to be riled, and his hostile glare deepened. "You're no more than a joke. So is this mission to proclaim Morgan's innocence. Give it up before you're laughed out of town." He glanced to Daisy. "Best of luck to you, Mrs. Gallway. You'll need it." He turned on his heel and strode away.

"Buchanan was one of the partners at the firm from which I resigned," Jackson said before she could ask. "Mr. Easterly is a more forgiving husband than most."

Certainly more forgiving than Mr. Taylor had been after Daisy had exposed his wife's affair so publically.

"I see." She fiddled with her hands, wondering what to say next. Jackson's past was shadier than a forest, but somehow she'd forgotten just how unscrupulously he had behaved. The more time she'd spent with him, the easier it had become to overlook the way he'd lived his life.

But Buchanan had insulted her husband in her presence, which insulted her as well. Daisy was nothing if not loyal, and the instinct to defend Jackson came naturally. Unfortunately, the words didn't. "That man has horrible manners," she uttered.

Releasing a snort of agreement, Jackson returned his focus to the racing program in his hand. Daisy frowned. That was it? No explanation? No apology?

Surely, he had to be embarrassed she'd witnessed the ugly encounter. Ashamed, even. And yet, here he sat, his body slack, his face serene, as though he'd already erased from his mind the entire incident and any emotions it stirred—though there appeared to be none.

"Which horses do you like?" he asked, pointing toward the makeshift paddock.

She took a deep breath and tried to refocus as he awaited her answer. The regard in his eyes did the trick. She smiled, pleased by his request for her input on selecting a horse on which to place a bet. Her opinions mattered to him, and the remarkable fact was a boon to her pride. She watched in excitement as the horses were led in a line toward the track.

"They're so tall," she uttered. "I enjoy watching them run, but I can't help fearing for the riders."

"Saddle racing can be dangerous," he agreed. "Not that sulkies are safer."

"There's just something about being mounted high on a running horse. I can barely manage to stay seated at a trot."

He tilted his head. "I thought you country girls were at home in the saddle?"

She smiled at his teasing tone. "I was raised in Troy, remember? I never had the opportunity to ride growing up. By the time I'd moved to the country, my lack of confidence in the saddle had developed into full-fledged fear."

A gunshot rang out, signaling the start of the first race. The crowd broke into cheers. Daisy's heart pounded in the thrill of it. She jumped to her feet, joining Jackson as they craned their necks to better their view. In the midst of the excitement, though, came obtrusive reminders. Like whiffs of manure on the shifting breeze, Buchanan's odious words lingered, sporadic assaults she did her best to fend off as she watched the horses race around the track.

The day brought other offenses, as well. Several residents of Misty Lake were in attendance. Most made a point to confront them with their opinions that Randal Morgan was, indeed, a murderer.

Apparently, the news that Jackson was attempting to prove otherwise had trickled down the mountain with Curtis, the man who had taken in Andy. Several of Curtis's cronies were also in attendance.

It seemed everyone was of the same opinion, and Daisy felt the brunt of their scorn like a physical blow. If Jackson felt the same, he didn't convey it. Or he simply didn't care.

Disappointment prickled inside her. As his wife, she'd pay the price for his sins, but shouldn't he ante up too? After the debacle at the Taylor party, society had treated her harshly, so she could relate to the stigma Jackson bore. But she'd done everything in her power to improve her reputation and atone for her mistakes. She'd strived to be a proper wife to Lawry, forfeiting parts of herself in the process. Her charity work was appreciated, and eventually, people in Misty Lake had accepted her, though she'd made very few friends.

She released a long sigh, remembering that Jackson had warned her of his reputation before the wedding. He'd offered no promise to change, yet she'd married him, anyway. Her spirits plunged lower. Jackson proceeded through the day as usual, ignoring the rude looks and whispers that buzzed around them like flies.

Despite the possibility of another ugly scene, Daisy insisted she and Jax seek out Curtis to inquire about Andy. There was no telling when they'd get an opportunity to visit the boy in Barston, and Daisy was concerned for his welfare.

She held Jackson's arm tightly as they approached the burly man, who was easy to spot in the crowd. He stood with Mrs. Rhodes's neighbor, Jacob Squires, the man who had discovered Andy after the fire, and three other fellows. All five held mugs of beer, the effects of which Daisy feared might escalate matters if the meeting became heated.

"Curtis," Jackson called.

The man squinted, his eyes widening in surprise as he recognized them. "If it isn't the lawyer and his artist wife." He tipped his hat at Daisy, his lips pursed tight.

"Good afternoon," Daisy said.

Jacob and the other men greeted her in kind before she turned back to Curtis. "How is Andy?"

He studied her intently, as though weighing his answer. "The boy is fine. Safe and sound. I meant it when I said we take care of our own."

"I'm glad to hear it," she replied.

Curtis turned to Jackson. "This boogeyman you and your wife conjured up to frighten folks into believing your tale doesn't exist. I'm seeing to it that everyone knows it's all hogwash."

Jackson nodded. "From what I hear, you've done a fine job."

Curtis frowned at the smart-aleck response. His eyes narrowed into slits. "Wendell was my friend, Gallway. You're courting trouble by defending his killer."

"I'm no stranger to trouble," Jackson replied. "Ask anyone." He took Daisy's arm and led her away. "Christ, I hate these small towns."

"They're not exactly singing your praises in Troy," she reminded him.

He winced at the barb, pursing his lips.

She lowered her gaze, regretting her words, but her vexation grew. Jackson had no one to blame but himself. If not for his disreputable past, people would be more apt to trust his judgment in this matter. Everyone made mistakes, but had he learned nothing from his?

"True enough. But unlike the country, where distractions are fewer, everyone in the city is not privy to the color of my socks."

"Among other things," she uttered, unable to stop herself.

He eyed her warily. "Among other things, yes."

"Hence your fondness for St. Louis?" she asked.

"The larger the city, the better." His answer conveyed it all. His wanderlust carried on his voice, shone in his eyes. His refusal to be caged by the rules and censure of society—even marriage—spurred his quest for escape. For something better. And so, he would do as he always had. He'd spread his wings and fly toward the open skies a new city offered.

His desire to leave offended her personally. How could it not? After a lifetime of loneliness, she'd grown used to his company. His looming departure punched a hole in her heart, but she plugged it with anger. Anger at herself for wishing he could be more. Anger at him for not caring enough about himself, or anyone else, to try.

"Come on, there's still one race to go." Jackson pulled her along. She shuffled to keep up as they made their way back to the picnic area. After Daisy was settled on the bench, Jackson said, "I'm going for a beer. Would you like one?"

She'd never been offered a beer. Lawry had forbid her from drinking it, and she felt somewhat devilish for her rebellious desire to enjoy one in public. "I would."

Jackson strode toward the vendor tables on the far side of the track. He moved with a virile grace and confidence Daisy couldn't help admiring. Maneuvering through the crowd, he hastened his steps in his goal to make it back for the next race and his need for a drink.

"Pardon me, Mrs. Gallway."

Daisy turned to find Jacob Squires approaching from a copse of trees behind her. She stiffened in surprise. The woolly man's shy smile quickly put her at ease.

"Sorry for the intrusion, but I wanted to talk to your husband." He shifted from boot to mud-stained boot. "About the man I saw by the Rhodes's place the day before the fire."

Daisy straightened to attention. "Yes. Yes, of course. My husband went for refreshments, but he'll be back soon. Please have a seat."

Jacob scanned his surroundings. Behind his thick spectacles, his nervous glances told her he didn't want to be seen. He shook his head. "I don't want Curtis and the other boys to know about this." He shrugged. "I'm new in town, and I don't want any trouble. Curtis wouldn't like it if he knew I was helping Mr. Gallway."

"I understand." Trying her best to restrain her eagerness for answers, she spoke calmly. The man's reluctance might overpower his decision to help if she pressed too hard. "You had a good look at this man?"

"Yes, ma'am, I did."

Her heart pounded.

"But he didn't much resemble the man in your sketch."

She exhaled her disappointment. "My husband will still want to speak with you. Perhaps we can pay you a visit—"

"No." He lowered his voice, glancing around. "Someone might see you."

She nodded. "Can you come to our home in Misty Lake?" When he didn't answer right away, she said, "This information might be important. I could draw a sketch of the man you describe."

"All right," he agreed. "I have a lot of work to do at my farm, but maybe tomorrow. Or the day after?"

"That would be wonderful, Mr. Squires. We're on Lakeshore Lane. Thank you so much for coming forward."

Glancing around to be sure no one was watching, he tipped his weathered hat, then slipped into the trees like a thief in the night.

Daisy took a deep breath. Finally, someone willing to help. Even if the man Jacob described was no match to the sketch, the lead was still worth pursuing.

She couldn't wait to tell Jackson, and she filled him in on the development the moment he returned.

"And he saw this man the day before the fire?" he asked.

Jackson's enthusiasm was contagious. "Yes," she replied with an encouraging nod.

"But no resemblance to the man in the sketch?"

"That's what he said. But, Jackson, I can help him remember other details, like I did with Andy and Corine. And then we'll be sure."

Jackson considered this for a moment, then raised his mug of beer. "This day just got even better."

She took a sip of the frothy beer he'd delivered. "Yes, indeed."

Laughing, he reached to her lip, scooped off the foam, and then sucked it from his finger. She stared at his perfect mouth, a slow heat flushing through her veins. Vivid memories of those lips on hers hitched her breath, and she shifted in her seat to quell her arousal.

"There's still one race to go," he reminded her. "I'll bet you that my pick wins.

"What shall we wager?" she asked, intrigued by the bet.

His thoughtful expression melted, his mouth twitching with humor. "If my horse wins, you must take a ride with me. On horseback."

She grimaced at the challenge. "You're a wicked man."

He winked, and she couldn't resist being charmed. He excited her beyond reason, and in so many ways. "Since I've no intention of losing this wager, I accept." She smiled as the perfect reprisal sprung to her mind. "But if my horse wins, you must take a ride with me." She straightened her spine and lifted her chin. "On a boat."

His brows shot up in surprise as he stared, aghast and impressed by her dare. "Touché, Mrs. Gallway." Amusement danced in his eyes. "Touché."

Chapter 15

The heat of the day lingered after sunset, which made for a stuffy carriage ride home. Jackson was looking forward to a cool drink on the patio when they arrived back at the house just after nine.

"I'll go change my clothes for the boat ride," Daisy said. "I suggest you do the same."

He stopped in his tracks. She couldn't be serious. "Boat ride? Now?"

"Yes, now." She planted her hands on her hips. "You're not trying to wiggle out of paying your debt, are you?"

"It's almost dark out there."

"There's a full moon tonight," she said, moving closer. "There will be plenty of light." She nudged him toward the staircase.

He hung his head, exaggerating his displeasure, though not by much. The last thing he felt up to was a boat ride, but he owed Daisy, and for more than winning their bet.

Today he realized how severely she was suffering the effects of being his wife. Because of him, she'd been forced to postpone her plans for the children's day home. People she'd known for years were treating her cruelly or snubbing her altogether. Her involvement in aiding with the Morgan case would only make matters worse. And to think she'd married him to save her reputation….

Jackson turned his focus to the upcoming boat ride as he changed into a pair of light trousers and a linen shirt. A few minutes later, Daisy joined him at the bottom of the stairs, a blanket and picnic basket in hand.

"In case the exertion of rowing depletes your stamina," she said.

The suggestive gleam in her eyes sparked an awareness. She had more in mind than a moonlit cruise. Suddenly, he was eager to sail off in the cursed boat and proceed with her plan.

He took the items from her, then followed her outside. Daisy's prediction about the full moon was correct, and the path to the lake was well lit. When they reached the shore, Daisy climbed into the boat unassisted, so Jackson unmoored the thing from the dock. To his dismay, the small craft seemed even smaller once he was seated on the bench inside. He took hold of the wooden oars, and after using one to shove off from the dock, he began to row.

The oars squeaked softly in their hinges in a peaceful rhythm as the boat drifted with ease on each stroke through the calm water. Stars twinkled in the sky. The humidity in the air seemed less prevalent on the water, but the breeze was gentle and warm.

Jackson's nerves tightened as their distance from shore increased. He took a deep breath, reassuring himself that the craft was solid and free of leaks that could sink them. The fear he might be forced to test his feeble swimming ability lessened as he relaxed in the unexpected beauty of his surroundings.

Moonlight forged a path that rippled across the lake to the small island up ahead. Fireflies blinked above croaking frogs on the darkened shore. The hoot of an owl echoed from the trees. Nature awoke like a napping child, animated and full of life.

All at once, Jackson felt so alive. Attuned and restless. Aroused. Daisy leaned back, her arms braced on each side of the boat as the breeze blew through her hair. Humidity had transformed her wavy tresses into wild curls that cascaded to her shoulders. Her wholesome beauty took his breath away. She'd donned a simple white garden robe, but it was the most fetching thing she'd ever worn. Or perhaps it was the lack of undergarments beneath that earned this distinction.

If he were an artist, he'd paint her like this. The miniature depiction of her as a girl had nothing on the picture he saw now. And then he noticed it. The one thing he'd seen in her eyes in the miniature, but hadn't seen until now.

Happiness.

He swallowed hard. She was happy. Sitting before him, on a bench in a boat, in the middle of Lake Nowhere, she beamed. And he was struck with the need to pretend he was the reason why. Not money or independence, or the prospect of a child. Just him.

"Keep rowing toward the island," Daisy said. "I'm confident you can manage from here."

"Planning on going somewhere?" he asked with a grin.

She reached to the ties of her robe, and all humor escaped him. She held his stare as she slowly untied each tiny bow. With her shrug, the robe fell away. She sat across from him, stark naked. His breath caught in his lungs. She was flawless. Like a vision from a dream, light and shadow cast reflections from the water on her golden hair, her perfect breasts.

He sat mesmerized, the oars dead weight in his grip. She leaned toward him, sliding her hands from his trembling knees to his thighs. Parting her lips, she raised them to his. He inhaled the sweet scent of her, the warmth of her breath. The heat in his blood ignited like fire as she slipped her tongue through his lips with a sultriness that caught him off guard.

Opening her eyes, she eased her mouth from his, a small smile curving her lips. The next moment she was on her bare feet, the boat rocking precariously beneath her jarring movements.

"Daisy, what are you—"

She flashed him a smile, then dove overboard. The sound of a splash echoed as she disappeared beneath the water. He clutched the oars tightly, drops of water dripping from his nose. He craned his neck for the sight of her. His pulse pounded.

She emerged a few feet away, swimming in the moonlight. He sighed in relief. Tension eased from his neck and shoulders as he began to row after her. She sailed through the water like a nymph in the night. Her feet kicked behind her, the strong strokes of her arms propelling her toward the nearby island.

The sound of her laughter aroused him further. Flipping to her back, she watched him with a smile as she swam backward. He kept rowing, spurred by the fleeting glimpse of her breasts in the moonlight.

Daisy reached the island first. She waded from the water, her shimmering body beckoning to him with the sway of her hips, her perfectly rounded bottom. Turning toward him, she stood shameless in the moonlight, arching her back as she wrung water from her hair.

He rowed faster.

"Don't forget the blanket," she called as the boat bottomed out on the sandy beach.

He hopped from the boat, then dragged it ashore. Opening the blanket, he said, "And you call me reckless." He draped the blanket around her shoulders, capturing her inside as he pulled her against him. Her wet breasts felt cool against his chest. She smelled like summer mist, so fresh, so clean.

"I've acquired a sudden fondness for recklessness."

"So I've noticed," he said.

"Perhaps you're rubbing off on me."

She pressed closer, and he could take no more. He lowered his mouth to hers and kissed her hard. With a moan, she threw her arms around his neck, opening her mouth to his tongue with a ferocity of her own.

The blanket fell to the ground. They followed suit, sparing barely a moment to spread the blanket on the sand before he pushed her to her back and covered her body with his. She groped at his clothing between frantic kisses that spurred him out of control.

Her damp skin greeted his naked body as she wrapped her legs around his waist. The primitive setting had freed his savage desire for her, his insatiable lust, and he'd never wanted anyone more. He thrust inside her.

His thoughts spiraled amid the pleasure of his body. The divine feeling of being inside her was consuming. She clutched at him. The way she wanted him, needed him, jarred a part of him that had never been touched. A base protectiveness for someone besides himself. His relevance in the world.

He buried his face in her fragrant hair, drinking her in. He moved faster, and she followed as he got closer and closer. She cried out his name, luring him, urging him, until he was there.

Afterward, they dressed together in the moonlight, then returned to their flannel bed on the shore. Daisy emptied the contents of the wicker basket to the blanket: a bottle of wine, a wedge of cheese, a hunk of bread, and some grapes. He watched as she arranged the items on a napkin, then uncorked the wine.

She'd thought of everything to ensure the perfect moonlit picnic. The trip to the race track had been arranged for him, and now this. She overwhelmed him. She was generous and compassionate and alluring as hell. A treasure he'd discovered tucked away in the boondocks. Did no else realize how special she was?

He brushed off his maddening infatuation and replaced it with reason. He'd never spent so much time with one woman—never bothered to get to know his prior conquests. His affection for Daisy was a natural result of living together under one roof. Yes, he was sure that must be it. Had he not come to know Daisy so well, he'd not be mooning over her like a schoolboy.

And it would be easier to let her go.

He exhaled against the clench in his chest. "Daisy, I've been thinking."

"Uh-huh," she uttered as she handed him the wine.

He took a deep swallow. The fine vintage helped loosen the tight knot in his gut. "Perhaps it would be better if I stayed in Troy for a while."

She set down the bread she'd been tearing, then looked up to face him. "Better for whom?"

Frowning at the accusatory look in her eyes, he said, "Believe it or not, I am thinking of you."

"So am I," she snapped. "We made a deal. You can't very well get me with child from your bed in Troy."

And there it was. The reason he was here with her. The reason she'd made love to him under the stars. The reason she was standing by him, when no one else would. Daisy wanted a child and was doing what was necessary to get one.

"No, I can't," he said. "But until things settle down, I think we should consider putting some distance between us. Misty Lake is your home. When I'm in St. Louis, you'll still be here. Why subject yourself to—"

"I don't care."

"Well, damn it, I do!"

She stared at him, her blue eyes glistening with tears. "Please, Jax."

With an exasperated sigh, he reclined in resignation on the blanket, his mind whirling. She lounged next to him, engaged in thoughts of her own. They stared up at the stars in tense silence.

"Buchanan was right about me, Daisy."

"What do you mean?" Rolling to her side, she propped up on her elbow, regarding him with her utmost attention.

"I've done much I'm not proud of. But worse than that, I never cared who was affected."

She showed no sign of surprise, merely stared down at the blanket between them. "What did Buchanan mean when he mentioned earning a reference?"

"A reference from Markelson for a job in St. Louis. That was my original reason for taking the Morgan case."

"I see." The disappointment in her sinking tone filled him with shame.

"But something has changed. Morgan trusted me to help him, to clear his name for the sake of his children. I know he was desperate, but he was counting on me. And now, because of my past..."

"Everyone makes mistakes."

"That's just it. I've never regretted mine. Not really. But today, when Buchanan said those things in your presence, when I saw how badly people were treating you, I *was* sorry."

Her eyes brimmed with compassion. She touched his face, tracing a finger along his jaw. "Every saint has a past, Jackson. Every sinner has a future." She rolled to her back. "You'll prove Morgan's innocence, and then Markelson will give you a glowing reference for St. Louis." She took a long breath, staring up at the sky. "And with any luck, you will give me child," she murmured, more as a prayer.

And you will be rid of me. He closed his eyes against the pang of sorrow in his chest. Aside from Morgan, no one had ever put such faith in him. Despite any protest, it pained him to admit how deeply he'd grown to care for a woman he didn't deserve. A woman who wanted nothing from him, save a child. A woman with only one expectation. That he would stay true to his immoral form and leave her and their child without looking back.

When they finished their picnic, they rowed back toward the dock at an easy pace. The trip was a quiet one. When they did speak, their conversation consisted of trivial matters, which suited him fine.

All this melodrama was enough to make one's head ache. He missed the carefree days he'd enjoyed before stepping foot in Misty Lake. He needed a miracle to solve this case, and he needed it fast. The longer he stayed with Daisy, the more deeply he sank in the mire of his conflicting emotions about leaving her.

But he would leave her. He would pull himself from the insanity of his growing feelings for her, and he would go to St. Louis. When all of this strife was miles behind him, he would come to forget.

But Daisy had given him a night to remember. He knew with all certainty that no night shared with any woman in any fancy hotel could match the passion he'd experienced with his wife on a blanket in the sand.

They reached shore, and Jackson secured the boat to the dock. He assisted Daisy from the boat but didn't release her. Blinking in wonder, she gazed up at him as his grip on her elbow held her firmly in place.

"Thank you for today," he said. "And for tonight." He smiled. "I've a newfound understanding of your fondness for nature."

She smiled too. "It was my pleasure," she said in a husky voice that made him want her again.

He kissed her. Softly. The night was still young, and they would soon be in bed. He reached for the picnic basket at his feet. The sound of a gunshot exploded in the silence.

Grasping for Daisy, he shielded her body as they slammed to the dock. But it was too late. She clutched his arm, gaping in horror at the patch of blood seeping through her robe.

Terror trapped in his chest. He cradled her tightly, his heart pounding as he tried to stay calm. Her trembling grip on him weakened. Panic surged in his throat. Her gaze flew to his in helpless surrender before her eyes fluttered closed, and she collapsed in his arms.

Chapter 16

Daisy opened her eyes to a roomful of worried faces. She lay in her bed, beneath a heavy quilt, her arm swaddled in a sling across her chest. Blinking hard, she groaned against the throbbing pain in her shoulder and a roiling wave of dizziness. She tried to sit up, which made both ailments worse.

"Easy." Jackson helped her to a sitting position, arranging the pillows behind her. "Welcome back." A smile of relief softened his handsome face.

"I told you she'd be right as rain," Doctor Gregory mumbled between puffs as he lit his pipe. His gruff reminder suggested Jackson had given him a difficult time of it.

"How do you feel?" Jackson asked.

Daisy's stomach turned at the overpowering smell of tobacco smoke wafting toward her. She swallowed hard to combat her nausea, then summoned her voice. "It hurts."

Dr. Gregory stepped forward, emerging from a halo of smoke. "You're a lucky little lady," he said. "That bullet went through cleaner than a preacher's sermon." He fished his watch from his vest pocket, checked the time, and then snapped it shut. "Looks like I'll make it home in time for breakfast after all." He smiled and gave Daisy a pat on the hand. "I'll be by tomorrow to change that dressing." He collected his coat and bag from a chair by the door, then turned to Jackson. "Continue with the laudanum," he said before he left the room.

"Bullet?" Daisy asked.

Jackson sat on the edge of the bed. The sagging motion of the mattress beneath his weight caused a new wave of dizziness. She closed her eyes tightly until it subsided.

"Are you all right?" Jackson's weary eyes were full of concern.

"A bit dizzy is all."

With tentative fingers, he brushed back the errant curls from her face. "You were shot." His words were barely audible. Or perhaps the buzz in her ears made it seem that way. She felt disoriented and confused.

Behind Jackson, she saw Tessa and Dannion huddled together by the window. From the sunlight pouring through the lace curtains and Doctor Gregory's mention of breakfast, Daisy deduced it was morning.

The last thing her foggy brain recalled was standing on the dock with Jackson. She'd no idea what had transpired while she'd slept, but she could see in the distressed faces around her that it had been a taxing ordeal for them all.

Vague recollections of sporadic moments of consciousness flickered inside her head. Little snippets like memories from a wild dream. Doctor Gregory tending to her shoulder, the excruciating pain, Jackson's soothing voice whispering in her ear.

On and off throughout the night, she'd awakened to find Jackson pressing a cool compress gently to her face. He'd spoon fed her liquid heaven that had eased the pain and numbed her fear.

"Who shot me?"

"I don't know." Jackson's face tensed in his failure to hold his emotions in check. He fixed his gaze on his brother. "But I will damn well find out."

Dannion stepped forward. His version of a whisper came out in a loud hiss that could be heard clear across the room. "Be sensible, Jax. The sheriff is on his way. Let him do his job."

"The hell with the sheriff." Jackson stood, his voice rising with his temper. "I'll take care of this myself."

"How?" Dannion challenged. "What are you planning to do?"

"I'm going to kill the son-of-a-bitch who shot my wife, that's what I'm going to do." He ground out the words between clenched teeth. "Tell me you wouldn't do the same."

Daisy wasn't surprised when Dannion did not deny it. "Let's just think on things calmly for a while. Is there anyone who would want to hurt Daisy?" he asked, as though she weren't in the room and merely three feet away.

"You know as well as I do that whoever fired that shot was aiming for me." Dannion did not deny this, either. "One man is responsible for this," Jackson said. "He killed Ray Wendell, and he almost killed Daisy."

Sheriff Coons waddled through the open door behind him. "You don't know that," the man bellowed in a tone as obtrusive as his sudden presence. "Hell, there are dozens of men with axes to grind against you." The snarl of disgust on his pudgy face made evident his opinion of Jackson even before he voiced it. Tension filled the already crowded room "This incident has nothing to do with the Wendell murder."

"The shooter could be someone angry at Jackson for pursuing that case," Dannion said.

"The whole damn town is angry as a wet hen about that," the sheriff replied. "You gonna accuse 'em all of shooting her? Of killing Wendell?" He fixed his scolding eyes on Jackson. "And starting that fire on the mountain?"

Daisy blinked hard several times, dizzied from the drugs and vivid memories of blazing flames. Getting shot.

"Daisy should rest," Tessa said. "Perhaps you gentlemen could continue this conversation downstairs?"

The sheriff blinked in surprise at the jarring interruption. His irritated expression dissolved as he glanced to Daisy, lying helpless in bed. "I'm happy you're recovering, Mrs. Gallway," he said as Tessa shooed him from the room. "We'll get to the bottom of this."

Jackson turned to Daisy. "I'll be back soon," he assured her. Something about him seemed different. True, he was angry, but there was a commanding tone in his voice, a decisive focus in his weary eyes. As if overnight he'd aged with a strength of purpose she'd never seen in him before.

Tessa closed the door softly behind the men. Daisy welcomed the silence as Tessa walked toward her, then took Jackson's spot on the edge of the bed.

"You're going to be fine." Tessa smiled down at Daisy, tears glistening on her lashes. Her eyes were puffy and red. Daisy's heart ached for the worry she'd caused her friend.

Nodding, Daisy reached for Tessa's hand and gave it a squeeze. "What about Jackson?"

"I thought he'd go mad with worry," she said. "I'd never seen him in such a state. But he's much better now that you're awake." She grinned. "He wore Doctor Gregory's patience to a thread."

Daisy smiled in the knowledge of Jackson's concern for her. There was such goodness in him. Such tenderness. His possession of these noble attributes was lost on people who hadn't the inclination or the privilege to know him as Daisy had come to know him.

Tears rolled down Tessa's cheek as she rested her head on Daisy's chest. Daisy stiffened against the pain in her shoulder but voiced no complaint. Instead, she moved to console Tessa, planting a kiss on the top of her head. How grateful Daisy was for the friendship of this wonderful woman. Her one true friend in this world.

"Go home to your children," Daisy said, blinking back her own tears. The laudanum was making her weepy as well as drowsy, and she needed to sleep.

Tessa sat up, wiping her cheeks. "Yes, enough of my theatrics. I shall let you get some rest." Tessa blew Daisy a kiss, then started for the door.

"Tessa?"

"Yes?"

"Keep an eye on Jackson for me." Her voice cracked with emotion and fear he might do something foolish.

Tessa nodded. "Dannion and I will watch him like a hawk."

Daisy relaxed at the reassurance and the effects of the laudanum. For the first time in her life, she felt the comfort of being part of a family. With a contented sigh, she smiled, nestling into her pillows. Tiredness overcame her. "Like a hawk," she said as she closed her eyes and drifted to sleep.

* * * *

Jackson paced the carpet in the parlor, his mind racing. His relief that Daisy would recover rushed like a drug through his veins, sedating the anger twitching under his skin.

"What were you and your wife doing down at the dock so late?"

Jackson turned to face the sheriff, who'd made himself at home on the sofa. "We'd been boating."

The sheriff narrowed his eyes. "In the dark?"

"The moon was full," Jackson said. "But none of that's relevant right now. I have a sketch of the man the Wendell boy saw kill his father."

The sheriff sighed, exasperated by Jackson's reference to the Morgan case. "A sketch composed by your wife? That's more convenient than persuasive, if you ask me," he said. "She could have swayed the boy's description to suit your agenda. Especially since the boy never said nothing about anything until you and your wife got to him."

"I have another witness who saw this man in town around the same time as the killing. And another came forward just yesterday to say he'd seen a suspicious man by the Rhodes's house the day before the fire."

The sheriff considered this. "The same man in the sketch?"

Jackson averted his eyes. "I'm not certain. That information is forthcoming. But you could question them yourself—"

"I'll take a look outside," the sheriff said. With a grunt of exertion, he heaved his hefty body from the sofa. He wobbled for a moment, Humpty-Dumpty in a badge, before regaining his footing. "Then I'll question the neighbors." He pinned his gaze on Jackson. "Unless you got to 'em first?"

"I've spoken to no one since Daisy was shot," Jackson snapped. "Do your damn job, or I'll do it for you."

The sheriff's face blazed like a furnace. "I have a whole county to tend to. In the meantime, you may want to concentrate on tending to your wife. Whatever trouble you're in got the poor woman shot. Don't stir any more."

"I am trying to find out the truth," Jackson ground out.

"The truth is a woman was shot, and I take that seriously. Randal Morgan was guilty. The man is dead, and your case is too. And while folks aren't taking kindly to your crusade for the man who murdered one of their own, they are decent, hardworking people. So it's more likely this trouble followed you from the city."

Jackson absorbed the sheriff's version of the truth, his anger fizzling in his hopelessness. His lack of credibility would cause him to fail Randal Morgan. Worse, fail Daisy.

Satisfied he'd hit his mark, the sheriff pushed on his hat. Jackson watched in silence as the sheriff trudged outside to inspect the property by the lakeshore, leaving Jackson alone with his brother.

"I take it you and the sheriff are acquainted," Dannion said.

"He's as stubborn as an ass," Jackson said as he continued to pace the carpet.

The sheriff blamed Jackson for what had happened to Daisy, and he was right. Jackson had brought this trouble to her, no matter how he looked at it. Each breath Jackson took inflated the guilt that was swelling inside him.

"Have a drink with me, Jax." Dannion fixed them both a whiskey, then handed one to Jackson. Jackson drank it down in one swallow, then motioned for another.

"I've never seen you like this," Dannion said as he poured.

Jackson frowned. "My wife was shot. I believe I'm entitled to more than one drink. Besides, I'm seldom without a drink in your presence; surely you've noticed."

As usual, Jackson's sarcasm did not deter Dannion from speaking his mind. He handed Jackson the refilled glass. "That's not what I meant."

Jackson struggled for patience. "Spit it out," he demanded.

"I've never seen you this invested," Dannion said. "This riled...afraid."

Jackson stiffened. The observation was dead-on, and it irritated the hell out of him. "My wife was shot. I—"

"You love her."

Jackson blinked. He stared at his brother, who regarded him with the same arrogance he always displayed when he knew he was right—which was far more often than Jackson cared to admit. "I do not—"

"You do, Jax. Face it. You've fallen in love with your wife." Dannion lifted his glass. "Trust me, Brother, it happens."

Jackson said nothing.

Dannion's grin widened. "Denying it won't change it. And admitting it won't end your life. Accept it and be happy."

"Like our parents were happy?"

Dannion's grin perished in a frown. His eyes darkened dangerously at the subject of comparison. Dannion's reaction to any mention of their parents was always the same. But Jackson hadn't the energy for it today. Despite his regret for goading Dannion with the question about their parents, he readied his defenses as best he could.

"Our mother could never be happy," Dannion said. "No matter what she had."

"Do not speak of her—"

"She spent her life pining for something else. Something better. And she filled your head with her rancid disappointments. She was incapable of happiness. With any man. She punished our father for her misery and—"

"I'm warning you, Dannion."

"She punished me, as well!" Dannion's face was wrought with fury. Pain. He pursed his lips, as though he'd disclosed some secret he hadn't intended to share. He turned away.

The thunder of Jackson's heart eased to a rumble as he stared at Dannion's back. "What are you talking about? Why would she punish you?"

Dannion's shoulders slumped. He turned to face Jackson, looking incredulous. "Have you never wondered why she hated me so much?"

Jackson lowered his gaze to his drink. All his life he'd struggled with the guilt of being his mother's favorite. To the point he could barely stand to look his brother in the eye to face the sadness that lingered there. The envy and contempt. The unfairness of it all.

Dannion had worked hard for everything he had, including his family, and suffered much strife along the way. In business and family, his success was hard earned. Jackson, on the other hand, had always had it easy. He'd simply coasted down a path that, somehow, always led to trouble, leaving one mess after another in his wake for Dannion to clean up.

"Our mother hated me because I knew what she was," Dannion said. "What she was doing beneath our father's nose. In our father's bed."

"That's a lie."

"Grow up, Jackson, goddamn it!" Dannion tapped at his ear. "I am deaf in this ear because I caught her. Because her lover was infuriated by the interruption of her ten-year-old son!"

Jackson's empty stomach lurched. He couldn't believe it, didn't want to believe it. But he could see in Dannion's distraught face that the story was true. Thinking back, Jackson could see it in his memories as well. No one had ever spoken of his brother's injury. As a boy, Jackson had once asked why Dannion's ear didn't work. His mother had flown into a rage, a rare response from the woman who'd never so much as raised her voice to her youngest son. An hour later she'd showered him with treats.

A heavy blackness invaded Jackson's chest and settled there like a weary traveler. Had Jackson been so self-involved growing up he'd not noticed his mother's deceptions? Or had her lies simply been too sweet to resist?

She'd fooled Jackson by spoiling him so completely he'd never turn against her. She'd openly favored one child above the other, and for no other reason than to punish Dannion for serving as a living, breathing reminder of her sins.

"I didn't know," Jackson uttered lamely.

"You had the luxury of ignorance," Dannion replied. "I grew up a thorn in her flesh, while you were the light of her life. But she jaded us both, don't you see? She taught me that no woman could be trusted. She taught you that no woman could be enough."

Jackson guzzled his drink. The truth in the words was as bitter as the whiskey burning in his throat. All his life he'd known their mother was different. Troubled, even. But an adulterer? Somehow, thinking back on it now, it all made sense.

For as long as he could remember, she'd warned him against imprisoning himself in marriage. His mother and he were kindred spirits, she'd told him, special people who were meant to be free. She'd recruited Jackson into believing that no one else mattered. His mother's justifications for such selfishness were all lies, and she'd fed them to him like crumbs to a damn goose.

Jackson had felt privileged by the favoritism his mother had displayed, and he'd taken full advantage of it. In her eyes, he could do no wrong, so he'd done whatever he'd pleased. She'd indulged and coddled him. And he'd grown up accountable to no one.

"I'm sorry, Dannion."

"It wasn't your fault, Jax. Stop blaming yourself for being her favorite." His mouth twitched with a smile. "As I have."

Jackson swallowed hard. Dannion didn't despise him. The weight of a burden Jackson had carried for years fell away. He'd never felt closer to his brother than he did in this moment.

They both turned to the sound of footsteps in the hall. Tessa entered the room, failing miserably in her attempt to appear chipper. "May I join you for a brandy?" she asked.

Dannion poured her a drink, and she thanked him with a tender kiss. "She's sound asleep," Tessa said.

Jackson worried Daisy was sleeping too much. She needed laudanum, he knew, but he feared the effect of the drug just the same. Tessa must have sensed his concern.

"Doctor Gregory said she needs to rest. She's been through a terrible trauma, but she will mend."

Jackson nodded. "Thank you for coming, Tessa," he said. He turned to Dannion. "You, as well."

Dannion lifted his drink. "That's what families are for."

Jackson smiled. So this is what it took for him to finally realize how much his brother cared? Years of Dannion's nagging for him to grow up suddenly seemed quite justified.

"Tessa and I will postpone our trip to Saratoga. I'll do whatever I can to help with this mess," Dannion said. "Just name it."

Jackson shook his head. "Thank you, Brother, but no. This is one mess I will clean up on my own. I owe it to Daisy."

Tessa smiled, and then kissed Jackson's cheek. "You're taking wonderful care of her, Jax. And you're proving to be one jewel of a husband."

He returned her smile in spite of the sick feeling in the pit of his gut. The compliment had the opposite effect and brought him no comfort. Jackson could never be good enough for Daisy. This incident proved it. Tessa would sing a different tune when she discovered his intentions for St. Louis. And then there'd be Dannion's reaction.

Jackson took another swallow of whiskey to drown out thoughts of anything other than Daisy's recovery and finding the son-of-a-bitch who'd shot her.

Chapter 17

Daisy watched Jackson as he studied the checkerboard between them, contemplating his next move. Despite being confined to her bed, the four days since the shooting had breezed by. Each morning Jackson brought their breakfast upstairs, and they'd eaten supper together too.

The laudanum made her drowsy, and she'd often drifted to sleep as he read aloud from books and newspapers. They played checkers and dominoes and even poker.

Having the use of only one arm restricted Daisy from performing the simplest tasks. Jackson cut her meat at meals, brushed her hair, and even helped her bathe.

In fact, Jackson barely left her side. He sat in the chair next to her bed, keeping her company and tending to her shoulder. Doctor Gregory had shown him how to change the dressing on the wound, which was healing so well it was no longer necessary for the doctor to make daily visits.

Daisy had never been the object of such devotion. Usually, it was she who cared for others. Lawry had suffered from a variety of maladies, and this change in circumstance was pleasant, indeed. Not that she'd enjoyed being shot, but she had to admit, she was enjoying certain aspects of her recovery. Spending so much time alone with Jackson was almost worth the ordeal of having a bullet ripped through her flesh.

Her thoughts drifted back to last night and the bath. He'd treated her with kid gloves as he'd helped her slip into the warm, rose-scented water. With great care, he'd ensured the bandaged wound on her shoulder remained dry while he sponged her body with lingering caresses, cleansing and soothing every inch of her. Then he'd toweled her off in front of the fire.

With no expectation of making love, he'd patted the towel to her wet skin, her breasts and stomach. Turning her around, he'd dried her bottom, her thighs, and between her legs. Even with the acute pain in her shoulder, it was the most erotic, intimate encounter she'd ever shared.

The memory was a pleasant diversion from her current worries. While she knew Jackson blamed himself for her injury, she knew he cared for her as well. Caring paled in comparison to her affection for him, though. Perhaps it was the temporary status of their union that drove her burgeoning feelings, but she could not seem to stop them.

Her chest tightened with sorrow. She'd lived her entire life without passion, and she'd accepted that. Until Jackson had introduced her to everything she'd been missing. Now that she'd experienced these wonderful feelings, she didn't want to live without them. Without him.

She loved him. She supposed she'd known this for some time, she just wouldn't allow herself to believe it. She couldn't. She loved a man who was incapable of committing to marriage, and the admission was difficult to bear.

Jackson needed more than the tedium her world would provide. A one-woman-man he was not. Variety was the spice of his life, and it wouldn't be long before he found Daisy bland.

She stiffened against the thought of his prior conquests, but it was the thought of his future in St. Louis that wrenched through her soul. That he would touch other women as he had touched her.

Shaking off the sting of jealousy, she lifted her chin. She could never let Jackson know how she felt about him. She'd suffered the pain of betrayal before, the despair of being unwanted. But the agony of Jackson's rejection would crush her to pieces. She had to save herself, preserve what remained of the independent woman she'd strived so hard to become.

She'd enjoy the time she and Jackson had left, and then she would set him free. She only prayed for his safety until then. Whoever had shot her had been aiming for Jackson; she didn't doubt it for a moment.

"It's your move," Jackson said.

"Hmm." Daisy studied the board. Jackson had set up his checkers quite nicely, and it appeared he would win again. "Someone taught you well."

"My father enjoyed the challenge of teaching me." He smiled. "Until the first time I bested him."

Daisy smiled too.

"My mother, on the other hand, always let me win." His smile faded as his weary eyes filled with distant memories of the past.

"When did she die?" Daisy asked.

"Several years ago. My father died soon after."

"A broken heart?"

"His heart broke long before that," he mumbled.

She stared, puzzled by the comment.

"My parents had an unhappy marriage," he said.

"I'm sorry, Jackson." She lowered her gaze. Several moments passed before she spoke again. "I like to imagine my parents were madly in love." She smiled. "I know it's silly, but one acquires an active imagination when one grows up in ignorance of who they are and where they came from." She shrugged. "It's the one small perk of knowing nothing about them. I can pretend they were perfect."

"Some people would envy you that." He smiled. "But it's strange."

"What is?"

"I was raised by my parents. Yet during those years beneath their roof, I never knew them for who they were."

"But still you loved them," she said. "And they loved you."

"Yes."

She smiled a sad smile. Perhaps it was the effect of the laudanum, but she felt so blue—so pitifully melancholy. "I never stop wondering why my parents didn't want me." By rote she held back her tears, staring down at the checkerboard. "What I did to make them not want me."

Jackson reached for her hand. "You did nothing, Daise. And I'm certain they wanted you. Sometimes circumstances force people to do things they don't want to do."

Like you were forced to marry me. The thought barged into her head, an unwelcome intrusion she could not deter.

Releasing her hand, he leaned back in the chair. "Perhaps they wanted better for you than they could provide."

She smiled, despite the solemn look in his eyes. "Thank you for that." She added his kind words about her parents to the growing list of things she'd remember always. Sweet memories of their night on the beach, the first time he'd touched her.

Jackson's efforts at consolation seldom failed. Her thoughts returned to the horrible day of the fire at the Rhodes's house, when Andy was missing. Jackson had taken Daisy in his arms, and like glue, his words of reassurance had held her together.

"All a child truly needs is love."

He nodded. "Hence your hope for one of your own."

"Yes," she said. "Lawry promised me children from the day we met, but had little interest in partaking in the activity required to get them."

He shook his head. "Unfathomable."

Her heart melted in his meaning and the blue of his eyes. "Lawry promised me the day home as well."

"He did?"

"He did." She sighed, and the anger of betrayal was tempered by sorrow. "A few years after we married, it became apparent we might never have children. I approached him with my idea for a children's day home in Misty Lake. He refused to allow me to pursue the project, but promised to earmark funds for the future. He needed a wife to take care of him until he was gone, and then the money would be mine."

"He lied," Jackson said.

"For years he led me to believe I'd have my day home someday. He'd often remind me of it to keep me content, I suppose." She shrugged. "But who knows. I never knew what he was thinking." She grinned. "I was often tempted to use my entranced drawing on him while he slept, just for some clue."

He smiled. "Have you ever been tempted to draw my thoughts?"

"There's no need," she teased. "I always know what you're thinking."

"Are you suggesting I'm shallow?"

"Of course not," she said with a smile. "You're just not very deep."

He laughed, and she laughed too.

"So then you know what I'm thinking about right now?" He leaned back, crossing his arms as he gazed at her.

"I believe that I do," she said.

He wiggled his fingers, urging her on. "By all means, tell me."

Humor gleamed in his eyes, softening his handsome face. The appealing pose surmised him perfectly. The slackened shoulders, the strong arms beneath his rolled sleeves, the long legs stretched casually in front of him. A tug of longing stirred inside her, drawing her toward him. She leaned forward.

"I'd much prefer to show you," she uttered in a voice she barely recognized.

His lips parted as he sucked in a breath, and she reveled in that look in his eyes. His throat moved as he swallowed. "If you weren't injured, I would let you." He blew out a long breath, sitting upright. "It's your move," he reminded her with a nod at the checkerboard.

Releasing a breath of her own, she took her turn on the board.

"Will you still proceed with the day home?" he asked. "If things go according to plan?"

She knew what he meant, though he didn't say it outright. But as much as she hated to think about her life without Jackson, she was hopeful she wouldn't be left totally alone. She'd have his child, and that would have to be enough.

"Absolutely," she said. "Once things settle down."

His gaze dropped to the board between them. He blamed himself for her being shot, and his distress broke her heart. She lived with guilt every day. Carried the ghosts of her past on her shoulders, felt the stress of it in her bones. She did not want that kind of torment for him.

"This wasn't your fault," she said. "You did not fire that shot."

He glanced up in surrender. "I guess I'm not very deep."

She smiled against the sorrow in his eyes. "Please don't blame yourself. I couldn't bear being the cause of that." She fidgeted with her hands. "Guilt will eat you alive."

He tilted his head. "Nothing in your past was your fault," he said. You did nothing wrong. The Taylor's marriage was destroyed long before they met you. And you've more than made it up to the Palmers."

While she appreciated his reassurance, she didn't deserve it.

"But not for what I did to the Blackstones."

He narrowed his eyes. "What do you mean?"

The ache inside her spread outward as she voiced the fear she'd never spoken aloud. "I may have caused the fire."

Blinking hard, he leaned back in his seat.

Daisy cleared the lump from her throat. "Mr. Blackstone and I were painting that morning. I'd spilled turpentine on the rug. The fumes were so strong, and it's a flammable substance. A spark from the stove could have—"

"Stop." He shook his head. "You can't know if that had anything to do with the cause of the fire. And you can't torture yourself for what you don't know. For things that weren't your doing."

She nodded, and his fingers tightened around hers. "You are not guilty for surviving what they didn't."

Oh, how she wanted to believe that. How she wanted to unchain herself from the pain of the past and set herself free.

"You deserve to be happy." He gave a firm nod. "Just let it all go."

She stared into his face, lost for words. The persuasive regard in his eyes shifted something inside her. The dark clouds that had shaded her for so long seemed to part as she opened her mind to his simple advice. Hope flourished inside her, sprouting up through the bramble of weeds toward the sun, that there might be a chance the broken pieces inside her could fall back into place.

Chapter 18

Jackson and Daisy ate breakfast in their room as usual, but everything seemed different. She was different.

Falling in love was the one obstacle she'd never considered. She'd sidestepped a ruined reputation, financial woes, the destruction of her dream for a day home, but she could not maneuver her way past her love for her husband. After he left, she'd have everything she ever wanted—even more so, if he left her with a child.

But she would not have him.

She lifted her chin against how much she would miss him. How much she wished things could be different. But Jackson was a free spirit. A wanderer. *Just let it all go.* Until summer's end, she'd enjoy her time with him for the man he was—not the man she'd hoped he could be. Jackson was born to have fun. He'd been raised on it. Unpredictable, to the point of recklessness, he drank in the pleasures of life and apologized to no one for his insatiable thirst. She envied him that. And she was drawn to him, seduced by the liberation she felt in his presence.

He was spontaneous and wild, like an invigorating breeze to be savored before it sailed on to touch someone else. The very traits she loved about him were the ones that would hurt her most.

She brushed off her self-pity. She had to remember the reason he'd come to Misty Lake. To clear Morgan's name and uncover a killer. Andy was an orphan and could be in danger, and Daisy had become so engrossed in her feelings for Jackson she had almost forgotten her promise to Andy—the boy who'd brought her and Jackson together. Perhaps, after Jackson was gone, Curtis would allow her to take the boy in. To raise him and love him.

"Are you going to Troy today?" she asked. The sooner the case was solved, the sooner she could move on with the plans she'd set for herself. Jackson was getting closer to solving this case, and she'd do everything she could to help him.

"Not today," he uttered, glancing up from the papers.

During the week since the shooting, he'd refrained from discussing the case, but still she could see his distraction. He carried on as usual as he nursed her, but the weight of all that had happened was etched in the dark shadows beneath his tired eyes.

"But what about the case?"

The knock on the door interrupted his answer.

"Come in, Kotterman," Jackson said.

Kotterman entered the room with another delivery of visiting cards. "These arrived this morning," he said.

"Did you send our regrets for the Westcott Ball?" Daisy asked Kotterman as he placed the tray of cards on the table.

"Yes, ma'am."

"Thank you, Kotterman," she said as he left. She sank back into the pillows, disappointed she'd miss the ball once again.

"You will attend next time," Jackson said as though reading her thoughts.

Brushing off the sting of his lack of the word "*we,*" she straightened against the pillows. Reaching for the cards, she said, "I haven't had this many visitors since I first arrived in Misty Lake." She shuffled through the cards. "Tom and Nadine Wyman, the Elmsworths, even Felice Pettington."

"Cuffy stopped by as well," Jackson added. "Although he was fresh out of cards."

She smiled at his quip about the simple lumberman. "Suddenly it seems I've become quite popular."

"Too popular. Kotterman has been turning away visitors for days."

After the cool treatment she and Jackson had received at the race track, this news was a nice surprise. She warmed in a glow of pleasure but kept her illusions in check. "I suppose being shot has summoned some curiosity, but I'd prefer to believe people are concerned for my welfare."

"They should spare some of that concern for themselves. There's a lunatic with a gun out there, but they're too pigheaded to see they might be in danger."

"I agree. But they're—"

"They're a bunch of busybodies," Jackson snapped. "You need to rest, not provide fodder for their gossip." He closed the papers. "Everyone's heard about your enhanced drawing."

She wasn't truly surprised. The ability she'd denied all these years had returned from her past and had the town buzzing. "Corine?" she asked.

He shrugged. "She told someone. And someone told Curtis."

"People were bound to find out eventually, I suppose. It's a small town."

"I'm surprised your name hasn't already made the papers," he muttered, before tossing them aside. "I won't have you bombarded by curious visitors."

She sensed he was feeling the pressure of it all almost as painfully as she was. His regard for her welfare was touching, but his worries were getting the best of him.

"I appreciate your concern. But I'm not an invalid. I am quite able to receive a visitor or two."

"In a few days, perhaps."

His guilt for what had happened played some part in his overprotectiveness, but he couldn't shield her from the world forever.

Not wanting to make matters worse, she'd relent to his temporary ban on company. A few more days of rest would do her good. Her need for laudanum was waning, and she preferred to be clearheaded when she faced the curiosity of visitors.

There was one person she was eager to see, though, regardless of her condition. "With the exception of Jacob Squires, of course," she said. "You'll be sure to let me know when he calls?"

"Forget about Jacob Squires."

Daisy narrowed her eyes. "But the man he saw—"

"Was not the man in your sketch. Remember?"

"We still need to get a description."

"I don't want you involved anymore," Jackson said.

"Pardon me?"

"You heard me, Daisy. That's the end of it."

She stared incredulously. *That's the end of it.* She'd heard these vexing assertions all her life. That she was now hearing them from Jackson, the one person from whom she'd never expected to hear them, vexed her even more. She leaned forward. "That's the end of it?"

"I don't want you involved."

"I've been shot, Jackson. I'm already involved."

The reminder was like fuel on a fire. She all but felt the heat of his anger before he replied.

"Exactly. You took a bullet meant for me. That was my fault. I know it. You know it." He flailed an arm toward the window. "Everyone in town knows it. I'm not risking your safety again. I don't need that on my head."

She sighed, staring in silence. Forever thinking of himself. Despite her fruitless hopes, he regarded her as nothing more than a responsibility, a duty. He'd spent a lifetime shirking cumbersome demands, and he considered Daisy one of them.

"No, I suppose you don't," she said. "Rest assured, I've no intention of adding to your burdens by getting myself killed. But, I am a grown woman, and you have no right to tell me what I can and cannot do."

"I am your husband!"

"For the time being!" Her chest heaved. How dare he toss his status as husband in her face? She'd spent her entire life under the control of other people. She had no intention of letting this man control her too. Come autumn he'd be long gone. And he expected her to bow to his will because he was playing husband now? "I will do anything I can to find the man who orphaned Andy Wendell. Anything."

His face turned to steel; his voice was like ice. "I don't doubt your determination. Or your commitment to your plans."

He was no longer speaking of Andy or the Morgan case. True, she wanted a child. She'd made no bones about that. But she'd made love to Jackson because she wanted him more. The admission caused a pinch in her chest. It wasn't the dangling carrot of a child that had led her to make love to him every chance that she got. It was her love for him.

And she was no more than a burden.

She felt like a fool. "Then we're two of a kind, aren't we? We both have designs. I want a child, and you want to carouse in St. Louis."

He narrowed his eyes as he pushed from the chair. "You've spelled it out nicely," he said as he stood. She lifted her chin against his hard tone as he moved toward the door. "Our ambitions are clear. And we're using each other to attain them."

Chapter 19

Jackson spent the next several hours downstairs, keeping company with a bottle of whiskey. Two glasses into it, he still couldn't drown out Daisy's words, but he was giving it his best shot.

You want to carouse in St. Louis. He'd been faithful to Daisy. Hell, since they'd married, he'd never considered taking a mistress or even partaking in a brief affair with another woman. His monkish behavior surprised even him. How could he expect Daisy to believe it?

But the truth was he wanted no one but Daisy. Pity his wife-for-the-time-being didn't want him. She took advantage of every opportunity to remind him of their deal and his impending departure for St. Louis.

She'd have his bags packed and waiting for him by the door as soon as she conceived. Then she'd casually send him down the road as though he were a studhorse.

Why she wanted his child was beyond his comprehension. He was a wastrel, a rake, a wanderer. He supposed she'd found those very traits would serve her well. With her errant husband living miles away, she'd maintain the independence that was so important to her. Yes, Daisy was a clever woman.

But not so clever as to see he was merely trying to protect her. Her involvement almost got her killed. The woman was too damn stubborn for her own good. Had been from the day she'd first learned about the tragic story of how Andy was orphaned. Jackson had sought Daisy out for her help, for his own selfish reasons, but even after he'd tried to dissuade her involvement, she'd insisted on going to Barston with him to help the boy. And what had she gotten for her trouble?

Jackson had seen the blame in the faces of the sheriff and the people who'd stopped to wish Daisy a speedy recovery. He knew what they were thinking. He'd thought it himself. He'd brought nothing but grief to her quiet life in Misty Lake.

Everyone was concerned for her, and with good reason. Her husband had nearly gotten her killed. Jackson tensed. Even Lansing, an old man, had been a better husband than Jackson turned out to be. His jealousy of a dead man incited his anger. Daisy was safe and sound when Jackson had met her, and he would make sure that he left her that way.

Jackson had given Kotterman explicit directions to allow Daisy no visitors. For all Jackson knew, the man who shot Daisy could be one of her neighbors. Tom Wyman or Curtis, even Cuffy.

Jackson shook his head again. His mind was working double time. He was being irrational, and he was dead tired. Resisting the urge for another drink, he returned to the cursed file he'd been studying for weeks. He mulled over endless pages of notes he'd taken, starting from the day he first visited Randal Morgan in jail. He had to be missing something.

He flipped through the pages to his notes on Morgan's movements and the route he'd traveled that morning. Perhaps Morgan had passed the killer on the road to Barston that day. It was possible. And it would explain how the stolen items landed in Morgan's wagon.

Corine had seen the man in the sketch on a horse. A black horse with white socks. Despite the distinguishable description, tracking down the animal would be damn near impossible. Feeling defeated, Jackson tossed the file aside, then ran a hand through his hair.

He didn't know what to think anymore. But he knew the sheriff was wrong. No one from Jackson's past had fired that shot. Easterly hated him, but he'd taken his wife and moved overseas.

Perhaps the man who shot Daisy was merely someone angry at him for pursuing the case and not the man who killed Wendell. Leaning back, he rubbed his burning eyes. For the briefest of moments, he was tempted to accept, like everyone else had, the fact that Randal Morgan was a murderer. It sure as hell would be easier than pursuing the alternative.

As long as he continued this losing battle to prove Morgan's innocence, he was putting Daisy in danger.

He recalled with disturbing clarity the night she was shot, all the blood, her terrified face. When she'd collapsed in his arms on the dock, he'd thought she was dead. He swallowed hard as his stomach turned at the sickening memory of it.

Shaking his head to clear the images from his mind, he closed his eyes in his need for sleep. Nothing seemed worth putting Daisy at risk—what she'd already been through.

Not even honoring his deathbed promise to Randal Morgan.

* * * *

The next morning Jackson awoke with an ache in his head and his heart. Yesterday, after his discussion with Dannion, he'd actually tried to convince himself he could stay in Misty Lake. Was it possible, as his brother had said, that Jackson loved Daisy?

The question had haunted him throughout his dreams that night and greeted him when he woke in the overstuffed chair in the library. He still had no answer, and the fact made him surlier than ever.

He knew nothing of love, but he knew Daisy was special. She was beautiful, yes, but she was so much more. Her heart overflowed with compassion for others. So much so, she blamed herself for things she'd had no control over, and she'd had little control over much in her life. No wonder she refused to heed his demands. Even her quest for independence was admirable, though it hurt like hell to be a casualty of it.

When breakfast was ready, he brought it up to her, as usual. He entered the room and set the tray on the small table next to the bed. Daisy stood, gazing out the window. Her color had improved, and she looked better today. She also looked angry. She spared him barely a glance, then turned back to the window.

"Jacob Squires is downstairs," he announced.

Her eyes flashed wide.

"You'll eat first," he said. "Then I'll bring him up."

She straightened her spine but didn't protest. He'd relented to the visit; how could she argue? The defiance in her eyes faded as she accepted the truce. "All right." She sat at the table, and he joined her.

She poked at her eggs, the tense silence between them like an invisible curtain. "I will be fine, Jackson. It's not as if I'll be performing circus tricks. I'll merely be sketching."

She was right, of course, but he felt no reassurance. He didn't want her involved in the case anymore, but he needed her help. His desperation had driven him down a path he hadn't wanted to go. Or perhaps it was Daisy's determination to help, her unwavering support, no matter her motives, that had urged him to do what was necessary to succeed.

He was treading in unknown territory on this quest to finish what he'd started. He'd never felt an inclination to prove anything to anyone, and he feared the attempt to prove something now would be his undoing. He nodded, pointing his finger to the breakfast tray in front of her. "Eat."

* * * *

Jacob stood in the doorway behind the large bouquet of wildflowers in his hand.

Daisy returned the timid smile on his bushy face and straightened in the chair. "Come in, Jacob," she said.

Jackson loomed behind Jacob as he entered the room, then handed her the flowers. "I heard what happened to you, Mrs. Gallway. I'm happy to see you're all right."

"Thank you, Jacob," she said. "I am recovering nicely."

He took a seat in the chair across from Daisy while she inhaled the aroma of the flowers. "Mmm, these smell wonderful. I shall have them placed downstairs so they'll scent the whole house."

"I've already spoken to Jacob on the time and place of the sighting," Jackson said as he placed her sketch pad and pencils in front of her.

Daisy arranged the pad on the table, then turned to Jacob. "So are you ready to give me a description of the man you saw the day before the fire?"

Jacob nodded. Jackson strolled to the window and gazed out. His mood was still grim, but she was relieved he'd come to his senses by allowing her to sketch the man Jacob had seen. She only hoped it would help.

She situated herself to begin. Once Jacob started talking, she could barely keep up as he recited with great detail the facial features of the man he'd seen near the Rhodes's house.

She sketched and listened and sketched some more. To her surprise, she didn't need to coax the memory from him at all, and the details poured freely from Jacob's mouth to Daisy's pad. "You have a good memory, Jacob," she said. "Most people are unable to recall so easily a face they'd seen for so brief a time."

"I never forget a face," he said proudly.

Daisy had always considered this an attribute of her own. Even as she drew, she had a distinct feeling of familiarity with Jacob. A closeness with this stranger she barely knew. The fondness for the man stemmed, of course, from the jubilation she'd felt upon meeting him for the first time.

Jacob was responsible for finding little Andy after the fire. The desperate search for the boy and her overwhelming fear he had perished in the fire had ended because of Jacob. Daisy's gratitude for his returning Andy safe and sound had etched Jacob's wooly face on her list of things she'd remember always.

When she finished the drawing, she held up the sketch pad. "It's definitely not the man in the other sketch," she uttered to Jackson.

"I'm sorry if it doesn't help." Jacob scratched his bushy head. "But that's the man I saw."

Daisy stared down at the face on the pad. A thin man with a receding hairline, pointy nose, and jutting chin stared back at her.

"I still want to know his identity. A lead is a lead," Jackson said. "We are not ruling out anything at this point."

Jacob nodded. "I should get back to the missus. I don't like to leave her alone for too long."

"Her health suffers?"

"For years now. I moved her here from Pennsylvania hoping the fresh air in the mountains would help her condition, but she hasn't improved much."

He lowered his gaze behind his thick spectacles, and Daisy was touched by his loving care of the ailing woman. Had Daisy loved Lawry the way she loved Jackson, perhaps she'd have minded less about the endless sacrifices she'd made on his behalf.

"I'm so sorry, Jacob," she said. "Please send our regards. I look forward to meeting her one day," she added with a heartfelt smile.

Jacob smiled too. "I best be on my way."

"Thank you for coming, Jacob," Jackson said, patting the man on the back.

Jacob tipped his hat to Daisy before Jackson led him from the room. A few minutes later, Jackson returned.

"I hope Jacob doesn't land in hot water for trying to help us," Daisy said.

"He's new in town, and this won't make him any friends if Curtis finds out."

"The poor man. Running a farm can't be easy while taking care of an ailing wife."

"The man has his hands full, that's for sure."

"When all of this is over, I will pay him and his wife a visit."

Jackson nodded, straightening a stack of notes on the table before stuffing them into a file.

"May I?" Daisy asked.

He handed her the hefty file. "That's everything I have on the case."

She shuffled through the pages on top, skimming the material with a critical eye. "Who is Patty?" she asked.

Jackson shrugged. "I never found out who she was."

Daisy continued to read. "So, Mr. Morgan told you that only you and Patty believe in his innocence?"

"He mumbled that on the night he died. I never got to question him further on it. He was drugged and not making much sense. I assumed at first that Patty was his wife, but found out later that his wife's name was Margaret, not Patty or Patricia. And Margaret died ten years ago."

"What about his children? Have they any idea who she could be?"

"He'd been estranged from them for some time. They weren't too eager to answer my questions, but they told me they hadn't a clue who Patty is or why their father had mentioned her on his deathbed."

"A lover?"

"I asked a few of Morgan's fellow salesmen in Troy if Morgan had a woman, but if he did, they weren't privy to who she was." His brows narrowed in thought. "Unless… What if…"

Daisy tilted her head. "What if…"

Jackson leaned forward. "What if Patty is a man?"

Daisy blinked. "Paddy?"

"It's possible. And it would explain why I've been unable to find out anything about a mystery woman." He leaned back in his seat. "I've always had the feeling that the killer was someone Morgan knew. A salesman, like Morgan, or even a friend." He stood, stuffing the papers into the file. "I'll have to go to Troy soon to do some more digging. But first, I'll go to Barston to retrace Morgan's route the day Ray Wendell was killed."

"Be careful, Jax. There's someone out there who wants to stop you from solving this crime, please remember that."

He glanced at Daisy's sling. "I'm unlikely to forget." He tucked the file under his arm. "I'll be back tonight. I'll send for Dannion and Tessa. They can stay with you until then."

"That's not necessary."

"Daisy—"

"Go, Jackson. Kotterman will take fine care of me. I won't leave this room."

Jackson eyed her skeptically.

"I promise."

Jackson nodded. "There's a gun in the desk drawer in the parlor. I've already told Kotterman where it is, and now I'm telling you. Kotterman is not to answer the door for anyone." He pointed his finger. "Not the nosy Wymans or any other neighbors bearing get well wishes, do you understand?"

"I understand," she assured him. "Now go."

Chapter 20

Jackson rode to Barston on horseback. If he found himself in a position to escape danger, he felt safer mounted on a horse that could run at breakneck speed. The gun in his coat pocket reassured him he'd be prepared for trouble. Jackson was a fine shot, the one skill he possessed that he could truly be proud of. He wouldn't hesitate for a moment to plug a bullet in the man who'd shot Daisy.

Once he reached the main road into Barston, he took a left at the intersection to follow the route Morgan had traveled the day of Ray Wendell's murder.

Morgan had several regular customers in town and a few farther up the mountain. Most people were eager for news from the city, so the length of Morgan's visits varied, depending on the level of interest for said news and the customer's current workload.

Jackson stopped the horse in front of Curtis's large clapboard house and stared at the bright red door. Morgan had stopped here with his wagon before stopping at Ray Wendell's neighboring farm.

If only Jackson knew what had transpired during that meeting. Curtis might be able to provide some insight as to Morgan's mood that morning. Perhaps Morgan had said something about another peddler he'd passed, someone named Paddy, anything that might aid Jackson in piecing together the events that followed after Morgan had left.

"Oh to hell with it," Jackson mumbled as he dismounted. He strode to the red door, and then gave it two solid knocks.

Curtis flung open the door, wearing a scowl.

"I need your help, Curtis."

"Are you out of—"

"Someone shot my wife," Jackson said. "Please."

Curtis sighed. "I heard about that, and I'm real sorry. But I can't help you. Morgan killed Ray Wendell. Just let it be."

"I can't." Jackson took a deep breath. "I spoke to Randal Morgan before he died. He'd claimed his innocence all along, and he claimed it with his final breaths."

Curtis averted his eyes.

"For Christ's sake, I got my wife shot pursuing this case. The whole damn town hates me. Do you think I'd continue to jeopardize my wife's safety if I didn't truly believe there'd been an injustice?" Jackson asked. "Damn it, Curtis, Ray was your friend. Do you want his killer to get away with it?"

Curtis considered this for a moment. His face softened as he opened the door and waved Jackson inside. "Corine took Mama and the boy over to the Leland's for a visit," he said as Jackson followed him to the parlor. Curtis plopped into a worn sofa. "What do you want from me?"

Jackson didn't know where to begin. He'd never expected to get this far with the man, and now that he had Curtis's cooperation, he was unsure how to proceed. He sat in the chair across from Curtis, then took a deep breath. "How often did peddlers from Troy stop by your place?"

Curtis shrugged. "Every week or so. Though lately they've been coming more and more." He frowned. "Corine can barely get her chores done without the interruptions. These fellows come around here charming the women with their wares and stories of their travels, and they ain't nothing but trouble."

Jackson knew Curtis and his friends weren't too keen on strangers intruding on their quiet mountain, but something in the man's tone told him there was more to his dislike for peddlers than the disruption to his sister's chores.

"How long was Randal Morgan here before he left for the Wendell farm that day?"

"About a half hour, I guess. I was out back, splitting wood with my cousin, Billy. I came in for a drink, and Morgan had Corine's ear about some new cooking pot. It was washing day, and Corine had work to do, so I shooed him away so she could finish my shirts. Then I went back to work. Thinking on it, I'm lucky Morgan didn't cut me down too."

"Why do you think that is? That he chose to kill Ray instead?"

"How the hell do I know?"

"Did Ray keep large sums of cash in the house?"

"Ray didn't have no large sums of cash. He was a farmer. But who knows why killers kill. Especially when they're all riled up."

"What makes you think that Morgan was riled up?"

Curtis ran a hand through his beard, a guilty look on his face. "Like I said, when I came in for a drink and saw him making nice with Corine, I shooed him out."

"And?"

"And I gave him my opinion of him and his friends. I warned him to stay away from my sister and my house, and I told him I'd shoot him dead if he ever came back." Curtis swore under his breath. "Morgan was mad as hell when he left, and he took it out on Ray."

Morgan hadn't mentioned to Jackson that Curtis had tossed him out that morning. Then again, in Morgan's line of business, the man was probably used to having doors slammed in his face and may not have thought the detail pertinent.

Salesmen did what they had to do to make sales, and that included making genuine pests of themselves.

"Did Ray have any enemies?" Jackson asked.

"He had friends. Lots of them."

"And the last time you saw Ray? Did he say or do anything out of the ordinary?"

"No." Curtis leaned back in his seat. "Ray was an ordinary man. He'd been hitting the bottle pretty good since the Shaws left town. But he tended to do that when something was bothering him."

"The Shaws?" Jackson asked.

"They owned the farm up from the Rhodes's place. Ray was real torn up about their breakup, but that's only natural. Marty Shaw was Ray's best pal. Ray couldn't believe Marty had left town after all these years without so much as a good-bye." He shrugged. "Hell, I couldn't believe it either, until the news hit about Mary running off like that. When word spread 'round that she might have run off with a peddler, I figured Marty was too humiliated to face us all." He looked thoughtful. "Never would have figured that of Mary," he said. "Guess you never do know."

"Mary didn't seem the type of woman who would step out on her husband?"

"She was one fine-looking woman. The proof is in the pudding." He frowned.

"And Jacob Squires purchased the farm?"

Curtis nodded. "Marty up and sold everything."

"I appreciate your taking the time to talk with me, Curtis," Jackson said as he stood. "One more question. Do you know a man named Paddy?"

Curtis shook his head. "Don't know anyone by that name. Who is he?"

"I'm not sure. But I think he may be the man I'm looking for," he said as he walked to the door.

"I still say you're chasing rainbows with your theory that Morgan is innocent," Curtis called after him. "But I'll ask around about this Paddy person."

Jackson turned to face him.

"Like you said, Ray was my friend," Curtis said. "And I don't take kindly to women being shot."

"You're a good man, Curtis. People on this mountain look up to you. If anyone has information, they'll be more likely to give it to you."

Jackson rode home, lost in his thoughts. Was it possible Curtis had made Morgan so angry he'd killed Ray Wendell? After Ray's best friend's wife ran off with a peddler, Jackson could understand Ray's dislike for peddlers. Ray could have fought with Morgan about it.

He shook his head. His gut told him no. Randal Morgan was not a murderer. Jackson was certain of it. But another peddler? Possibly. Corine had seen a man on a big black horse. The same man Andy had described. And the fire at the Rhodes's house? True, the man Jacob saw the day before the fire wasn't the man in the original sketch, but that changed nothing.

There could be two men involved for all Jackson knew. Partners in crime. Unlikely, but possible. Jackson's mood darkened at the thought. He couldn't seem to get his hands on one killer, let alone two.

* * * *

Jackson had just reached the outskirts of Misty Lake when he spotted Felice Pettington's purple carriage on the side of the road. His instinct to danger propelled his pace as he moved. Something was wrong. His pulse steadied as he neared.

Felice stood next to the disabled carriage under a pink parasol, waving wildly as he approached. Her friend Gertrude stood at her side.

"Good afternoon," she called up to him. She primped at the blond curls beneath the brim of her ridiculous hat, then flashed him a smile. "We're experiencing a bit of trouble with the carriage."

Jackson dismounted, offering assistance to her driver, who was in the midst of repairing the front wheel. After being assured the driver had the matter well in hand, Jackson turned back to Felice. As usual, her faithful maid stood in her shadow.

"How are you, ladies?" he said with a tip of his hat.

"We're much better now that you're here." Felice's flirtatious tone was so blatant, even Gertrude looked embarrassed by it. "Would you be so kind as to escort us back to Twin Bears?" she asked.

Jackson knew the place well. The owner, Eunice Middleton, was the sister of Dannion's deceased wife, Olivia, though there was little contact between them anymore. It dawned on Jackson that there was more to this small town and the people who filled it than he'd ever imagined. Strangely, over time, he'd found himself missing the city less and less.

Whether year-round residents like his brother's family or summer residents like the Elmsworths, they all had their intrigues and troubles. Olivia had drowned in the lake years ago, and just last summer, a guest of the Elmsworths was killed when he'd fallen from a cliff behind their estate. Ray Wendell was murdered, and Mrs. Shaw had run off on her husband. No wonder these people were hardly fazed by Daisy being shot.

"I'd be happy to escort you," he said with as much sincerity as he could muster.

"Oh, thank you," Felice said. "This dreadful sun is so strong, and who knows how long it will take for that imbecile to repair that wheel."

Jackson glanced at the frowning driver. "Of course," he said. Just his luck he'd run into Felice in the midst of what she considered a crisis. "But I'd like to get back to my wife as soon as possible, so we should be on our way."

"Wonderful." Felice turned to Myrtle. "Get our things," she told the woman as she reached for Jackson's arm and latched on tight. "How is your wife?" Felice pursed her lips. "I attempted to pay her a visit, but that beastly servant of hers would not allow it."

"She's recovering nicely," Jackson replied. "And Kotterman was acting on my instructions. Daisy is not yet up to receiving visitors."

"Standing so long in the sun had me thinking of her," she said, nestling closer. "Those nasty freckles of hers might fade with a daily application of a lemon juice poultice," she said. "It worked wonders for Gert's sister, Dolly, and now she's a beauty."

"I don't know that she's a beauty," Gertrude muttered.

Felice shrugged. "Well she's no longer hideous. You must admit that."

To Jackson's surprise, Gertrude made no attempt to defend her sister. She merely nodded in agreement to Felice's insult. Jackson determined the pair were fated to be friends. It still amazed him how birds of a feather truly did flock together. Even vultures adorned in ridiculous hats.

"It's a lemon juice poultice," Felice repeated. "You'll be sure to pass along my suggestion?"

Jackson frowned. "I rather like my wife the way she is," he said. "Freckles and all."

She gauged his sincerity through batting lashes. "Well, of course you do," she said with a smile that didn't quite reach her eyes. "How do you like my new hat?"

The subject of Daisy was dropped so suddenly it took Jackson a moment to reply. "It suits you perfectly," he said of the gaudy creation.

To his relief, a harried Myrtle returned with their things. Jackson relieved her of the parcels she carried. He led the horse by the reins, and they all began walking.

"With your wife incapacitated, I don't suppose you'll be attending the Westcott Ball on Saturday?" Felice asked.

Daisy had been shot, and this woman was talking about attending a ball? Did no one spare a moment to consider there was a killer in the vicinity of their quaint little town? "No, we will not be attending."

"What a pity." She smiled. "My new gown just arrived from Albany, and it's the loveliest shade of blue."

He rubbed his brow to keep from scoffing outright. Increasing his pace, he escorted the women toward town. Felice and Gertrude babbled on about one trifling thing after another. Myrtle didn't utter a word.

It was barely a quarter mile to Twin Bears, where Felice was staying. These women obviously weren't frightened by Daisy getting shot. So intent were they with enjoying their summer they saw little beyond the pretty views and pleasant weather.

A simple broken wheel had left them stranded because they hadn't the wherewithal to walk to their destination without the aid of a man. The helplessness of some women gave him a sudden appreciation for Daisy's fierce independence. The women's gossip and tedious conversation also gave him an appreciation for Daisy's intelligence and compassion for others.

He'd spent a lifetime in the company of women like Felice and Gertrude, gravitated toward women like Edna Easterly and Betty Swootz back in Troy. He'd tolerated their pettiness and endured superficial conversations in his lust for what lay beneath their skirts. The mere memory of it left him feeling hollow inside.

Felice gazed up at him with a well-practiced smile. She batted her lashes again, and he grinned back a snort of laughter in response. Once again, he thought about Daisy and the first time he'd met her.

Daisy's effortless charm was as natural as the waves in her golden hair, the kiss of freckles on the bridge of her nose. Daisy didn't know how truly beautiful she was, which made her all the more beautiful. Jackson couldn't help smiling like a fool.

Running into these frivolous women today had made his muddled feelings for Daisy perfectly clear.

Dannion was right. Jackson was in love with his wife.

Chapter 21

Daisy was elated that Curtis had agreed to ask around about Paddy.

"You're getting close, Jax, I know it. And now with Curtis asking around about Paddy, who knows what else will turn up."

That Jackson had managed to acquire Curtis's assistance filled her with pride. It couldn't have been easy for Jackson to ask for the man's help, but he'd done it for the sake of the case. He'd put his search for the truth above his ego, and the sacrifice showed her so much. Jackson was capable of achieving anything when he set his mind to it. No matter his motive, he was fighting tooth and nail for Randal Morgan. Anyone would be lucky to have Jackson defending them, and he deserved that position in St. Louis for his tenaciousness alone. If nothing else, she hoped his hard work would open his eyes to this.

"I hope you're right," he said.

She smiled, prompting a nod and a smile from him too. In the wake of their heated argument the other day, things had changed between them. The words they'd spoken to each other lingered in the air like a bad odor. While they carried on politely, pretending not to notice, the underlying tension remained.

Daisy hadn't meant to be so blunt with Jackson, but he'd angered her with his dominant behavior. Her independence was all she had; she'd not relinquish it to any one—for any reason. Why was Jackson so obviously surprised by this? Did the man not know her at all?

She sighed. Or perhaps, he knew her too well. While it was true they were using each other, hearing the words from his mouth had cut to the bone.

"You'll be in St. Louis by autumn," she uttered.

His eyes met hers, but there was no anger inside them. "I haven't solved the case yet," he said. "And don't forget, we still have a matter to settle between us," he reminded her.

Jackson's impending departure was like an anvil on her chest. She could barely breathe with the weight of it. She knew now that she couldn't have Jackson's child and then bid him farewell. She wouldn't be able to look at the child without thinking of Jackson, without clinging to the one piece of him she'd have left, like some forlorn lover clinging hopelessly to a token of a broken love affair.

Their relationship was not a love affair, though. It was a union of necessity. And it would not be fair to a child, or to her, to pretend this marriage was something other than that.

"What if that matter were already settled?" she asked.

His blue eyes flashed wide. The start of a smile played on his lips, but he held it in check. "I know what we discussed, but if that is the case, and the matter is settled, as you say, then I don't have to leave right away."

Her heart stopped. Was he saying he would stay? This was so unexpected. Her spirit soared with possibilities she hadn't considered. Her thoughts floated on visions of raising a family with him, building a life together. Endless nights of passion, mornings spent snuggled in his arms. Such a lovely dream.

But it was her dream alone. While the novelty of a child might appeal to him now, it wouldn't for long. Jackson had other plans for his future, and she couldn't live with herself if she forced him to relinquish them. He'd grow to resent her for it, and she couldn't bear the thought of that, either. Jackson did not belong here. She'd overheard him from the balcony, admitting as much. He would wither away in the tedium of life in the country, and eventually, he would leave anyway, taking more of her heart.

Jackson had to go. She needed him to go.

"Daise?" he asked, breaking the long silence. "I can stay."

She shook her head against the stark sincerity of his offer. As tempting as the fantasy of a future with him was, she had to face reality. He was who he was, and she'd not force him to be anything other than the man she fell in love with.

The carefree rake who had charmed her by allowing her to be herself. The man who'd made her feel special, who had shown her true passion and acceptance. She loved him with all of her heart. Because of this, she would let him go. And forfeit her dream for a family in the process. *Please give me strength.* "No, Jackson, you can't."

He blinked hard, looking stricken.

"Be sensible," she said. "You would never be satisfied here in Misty Lake. You know that as well as I do."

"But this is my child and—"

"I'm not pregnant."

His brows knit in confusion. Disappointment.

She steeled her heart against her own conflicting emotions. "I was simply posing a question," she said.

He frowned. "You led me to think you were—"

"That was not my intention," she said, though she couldn't be sure.

His lips thinned with anger. "What exactly was your intention?"

"To release you from our bargain."

He stared, slumping back in his seat. The relief she'd expected to see in his eyes never appeared.

She took a fortified breath and plowed through her surprise. "I've come to realize that my feelings about having a child have changed."

He tilted his head. "You no longer want a child?"

She shook her head. "No."

"Bullshit."

She winced against the anger in his eyes. She'd assumed he'd respond as he had when she'd first offered him his freedom in exchange for a child. With reluctance but relief.

Her change of heart about a child had resulted in quite the opposite, and she scrambled to explain.

"For almost two months, I've watched you work on this case," she said. "And you will succeed in solving it; I don't doubt it for a minute. You've been driven by your goal to get to St. Louis, and I believe you will have a bright future there. I cannot let you sacrifice what you want out of some sense of duty to me."

He eyed her with harsh skepticism. "So you're doing this for me?"

She lowered her gaze, and he had his answer.

"I didn't think so," he said.

She glanced up. "Jackson—"

"You are doing this for you." Anger weighted his words, but she heard pain in them too. "You don't want a child fathered by a *man like me*. A *carouser*."

He tossed back her own words, and she cringed from the brunt of them.

"You want a child, but you don't want *my* child."

The sharp edge of his voice pierced through her soul "That's not true." Not for the reasons he thought, anyway.

"Isn't it?" He shot to his feet. "I am unworthy of fathering your child. Unworthy of giving you the one thing you are desperate for." His reproachful eyes bore down on her. "Unlike your former husband, who was so worthy you risked his life for it."

The cruel remark hit as intended. Devastating and exact. She'd wounded his pride, and he'd fired back with the bullets she'd provided. Confiding in him had been a mistake. She braced herself against the impact of this painful discovery and forced herself to breathe.

Her lungs filled with air, and tears stung her eyes. "My reason for releasing you from our bargain was for your sake." Her voice trembled. "For the man I'd thought you'd become."

"That's a lie, and you know it. But know this as well." He gave a thud to his chest. "This man has not caroused any farther than the Lake Tavern. And he's not so much as looked at another woman since the day he married you."

She blinked at his declaration, which seemed to anger him more.

"The hell with this." He tossed up his hands, turning away. "I quit."

The two words were the worst she could hear. "You can't quit. You promised Randal Morgan."

He turned to face her. "That is not what I meant. I have no intention of quitting this case, but it's telling that you'd thought so."

She had no defense. How had things gotten so mixed up? So twisted around? "Do not presume to know what I think," she said. "I've had faith in you all along."

"Because you were desperate! You had no other choice!"

She shook her head. "You are the one who's afraid you will fail, Jackson. Not me. You are the one who believes you're not good enough. And you can run all the way to St. Louis—all over the world—but you can't run from yourself."

The clench of his jaw slackened as he took in her words. He looked strangely serene. "That may be true," he said with a nod. "I might run from myself. I might run from the mistakes of my past." He pointed an accusatory finger. "But you wallow in yours."

Her stomach dropped to her feet.

"You fester in guilt, blaming yourself for everything. You spend your life trying to atone for things that weren't even your fault. Trying to prove your worth to the world because your parents didn't want you."

She choked back her tears but said nothing. There was a fine line between love and hate, and she teetered on the cusp of it.

Averting his eyes, he took a deep breath. "I am far from perfect, but I was willing to stay." He shrugged in surrender. "Since your plan has now changed, and you don't want my child, I will move into a room downstairs." He turned and started away, looking more defeated than angry. He stopped at the door. "I will solve this case, and then, rest assured, I will go. And you can proceed with the life you have planned."

* * * *

Jackson's pulse pounded in his ears as he charged down the hall. He'd offered to stay—he'd wanted to stay—and the woman he loved had rejected him.

The fact pained him physically, but it was the truth behind her rejection that hurt most. Daisy wanted a child, and there was no way on this earth she would give up the chance to be a mother if she deemed him the least bit worthy of fathering it.

A few short weeks ago, he'd have been relieved to be discharged from this part of their deal. Today he felt crushed. But most of all he felt angry. Clenching his trembling fists, he stomped down the stairs.

While he'd been trying to solve the case for Morgan, he realized he was solving it for Daisy, as well. To prove himself to her, not for some job in St. Louis. But Daisy's support was meant only to hasten his departure. She had her money, and she'd get her day home. He'd hoped she would come to see there was more to him than his corrupt reputation. He'd tried to make her happy, to be everything she deserved, but he'd been fooling himself on that score as well.

When he'd thought she was pregnant, he'd swelled with joy. His reaction had surprised him. In that moment, he'd seen their future together, something honest and real, and he'd never wanted anything more.

In defense of his shattered pride, he'd aimed to hurt her as she had hurt him. Armed with her innermost fears, he'd struck back with a cruelty he hadn't known he possessed. The memory of her pained face filled him with shame. Another rare emotion she seemed to invoke in him, although it changed nothing.

Daisy had confirmed what he'd known all along. He was not good enough for her. Truth be told, he couldn't imagine a man who was.

With a curse, Jackson ran a hand through his hair. He would close this case. He would honor his promise to Randal Morgan. He'd finish what he'd started—what he'd come here to do—but he would do it for himself.

Daisy wasn't the only one who had plans.

Chapter 22

Daisy sat in her room, staring out the window at Jackson outside. He stood by the shore, tossing crumbs to the geese. Apparently, he hosted supper for his feathered friends as well as breakfast. He swiped his empty hands before shooing the geese toward the water, and wherever they'd settle in for the night.

Jackson turned to walk back toward the house, and she ducked from window until he disappeared inside. In stony misery, she returned to the view of the lake and the sun sinking behind the tall pines. Dusk settled over the day like a soft gray blanket, growing denser as the minutes passed. A single star winked in the desolate sky, the sight filling her with a bleak loneliness that spurred her to tears.

He'd offered to stay, and she'd turned him down.

Daisy had been so intent on protecting herself from her feelings for him, she'd never considered the possibility that she might hurt him. She longed to tell him she loved him, that she wanted his child. He would never believe her now, or worse, he wouldn't care. He was so angry.

While it had hurt to hear it, what he'd said about her was true. Her guilt had become a part of her, a force as powerful as her entranced drawing. She'd let guilt control her. Jackson had seen this in her when no one else had. He'd looked, and he'd listened. He'd cared.

How strange that only one night before, they'd slept in their bed, their naked bodies entwined, with no intimation it would be the last time they touched—that they'd shared their last kiss.

Clasping her hand to her mouth, she fought to stifle the anguish of living without him. She'd done her best to prepare herself for his eventual departure, but she'd never expected so hostile an ending to their time together. But with one irrevocable conversation, she'd managed to destroy everything between them, including any chance for a civil good-bye.

She wiped angrily at her tears. She still had access to her money and her independence. What more could any sensible woman want? Her thoughts were interrupted by a knock on the door.

Jackson.

She shot to her feet.

"Mrs. Gallway," Kotterman called through the door. "I have your supper."

She exhaled in disappointment. Jackson had sent Kotterman in his stead. Collecting herself, she said, "Yes, Kotterman, come in." She returned to her seat.

The man stepped inside and placed her supper tray on the table in front of her. "Do you need anything else before I leave for Troy?" he asked.

She stared, puzzled. "You're heading to the city at this hour?"

"I'm to deliver an urgent message for your husband."

The mere reference of Jackson as her husband filled her with sorrow. "Is that so?" she asked, trying hard to sound nonchalant. She gave a stiff shake to her napkin, then placed it on her lap. "To whom is this message addressed?"

Kotterman fished into his pocket. "Miss Ida Remsen," he read.

At Daisy's reaction, he looked suddenly sheepish.

"I'm to wait for a reply."

She inhaled a deep breath to summon her voice. The pungent scent of onions drifted from the bowl of beef stew, turning her already queasy stomach. "Where is Mr. Gallway?"

"He's resting in the library," Kotterman said. "He asked me to wake him before I leave."

"I see. Well, I need nothing from the city, so by all means, deliver my husband's message."

Kotterman exited with a nod.

Daisy slumped back in her seat. So much for her worry she'd hurt him. The throb in her shoulder intensified with the throb in her heart. It certainly hadn't taken Jackson long to solicit a *diversion.*

The memory of interrupting his tryst with Miss Swootz played through Daisy's mind. Her eyes filled with the picture of Jackson's stark look of panic that night—the night Daisy had ended his bachelorhood and forced his world crashing down on his ears.

Frowning, she pushed away the steaming bowl of stew. She glanced to the vial of laudanum she hadn't touched all day, spurning the temptation to take a small dose.

She'd made it clear to Jackson that she wanted him to leave Misty Lake, and he'd made it clear that he would. He was a rake at heart, and he was proving it now.

"Miss Ida Remsen, indeed," she mumbled. Had she really expected anything less of him? She wiped at her tears, because the sad truth was, she had.

* * * *

Jackson woke to a cramp in his neck and the dread of reality. For a moment, he'd thought it all a bad dream. He glanced at the clock. He'd been sleeping for less than an hour, but if felt more like days. The whiskey and ensuing nap had done nothing to ease his troubled mind, and the ugly scene with Daisy came painfully into focus. His head hurt from drinking and thinking, and his chest ached. While Daisy's past was haunted by ghosts, his was haunted by living, breathing reminders to the people he'd hurt. Reminders like Buchanan, who appeared out of nowhere.

Jackson sighed, slumping in shame. He realized now the damage he'd caused to Easterly. As a husband in love with his wife, Jackson could now relate to the pain of a wife's betrayal. The fury toward any man who'd dare touch her....

The urge to give up on it all was overwhelming. In the wake of the maelstrom with Daisy, the thought of packing his bags and leaving her and the case behind became more appealing as the moments passed.

But he wouldn't succumb to the instinct to run. Not this time. Not yet. He would finish what he'd started and prove Morgan's innocence. He would earn that damn reference for St. Louis, then continue his life as it was before he'd met the beautiful widow who'd turned his world upside down.

The woman who'd taken his heart, then handed it back to him.

Even now, in the hellfire of his emotions, he could not bring himself to regret the past six weeks with her. How could he, when he'd never been happier?

Marriage to Daisy had given him something he'd never had before, something he'd never known he'd wanted or needed. Faith in himself. The belief that he could succeed and had something to offer.

Daisy helped open his mind and his heart, and for the first time in his life, he'd allowed something to matter.

He strode to the sideboard and poured himself a cup of coffee. After settling down on the sofa, he opened his files and spread them on the cushion beside him. He needed to finish this case. The sooner he was on his way, the better.

Jackson tried to focus on the files, but it was difficult to concentrate. Although Kotterman had just departed for Troy, Jackson was anxious for his return and Ida's reply. Information garnered in the city could prove critical. He'd have preferred to attain it himself, but he couldn't leave Daisy unprotected. Even with Kotterman watching over her yesterday, Jackson had worried for her while he was in Barston. The trip to Troy was far too long to be away.

He supposed he could have arranged for Dannion and Tessa to come stay with her, but with things the way they were between him and Daisy, he thought better of involving them now. They'd find out soon enough about their impending separation. Why hasten the inevitable?

Instead, he'd scribbled a note to Ida, one of the clerks at the post office, instructing her to pore through the wanted notices looking for someone named Paddy. Ida had a fondness for Jackson and would help him any way she could.

The city seemed so distant, not in a measure of miles but memories. Pursuits he'd once enjoyed no longer enticed him as they had, and strangely his pining for the city had waned.

He'd grown accustomed to waking each morning in the country, found stimulation in the view of the pristine lake, chirping birds, crisp country air.

Any plans of returning to Troy had consisted of spending a night on the town with Daisy, but it was evident now that this was no longer in the cards.

He pushed rueful thoughts from his head and concentrated on the present. With Kotterman personally delivering the note to Ida in Troy, Jackson was able to remain here with Daisy, not that he was ready to face her.

After all that had been spoken between them, what more could he say?

He shuffled through the pages of his notes. He would start at the beginning, and work his way through the case. *You and Paddy are the only ones who believe I'm innocent.*

If this Paddy person was a friend of Morgan's, perhaps he had visited him in jail. Jackson slumped back in his seat. The chance the killer would stroll into the jailhouse to visit the man he'd set up as a patsy was preposterous. Even so, Jackson was suddenly curious to know who'd visited Morgan.

If Jackson's hunch was right, the real killer had disguised himself as a friend of Morgan's. A trusty pal. Something sparked in Jackson's mind. Disguise? He sat straighter as the possibility materialized in his mind.

He dug to the bottom of the stack of papers for the list of Morgan's visitors at the jailhouse. He hadn't so much as glanced at the page since he'd first acquired it two months ago. Cursing, he intensified his fruitless search. He finally located the blasted thing and propped it on top of the stack.

He scanned the page, and his eyes fixed on the third name on the short list. His heart stopped. Then it pounded so hard he thought it might burst through his chest. He sifted through the papers for the sketch of the man Andy had described. He studied it closely, amazed by what he now saw.

"My God," he uttered, as all the pieces of the puzzle snapped firmly into place. He bolted from the sofa, sketch in hand.

He took the stairs to their room two at a time. He flung open the door, then turned up the lamp. The room came alive with amber light. "Wake up, Daisy." He shook her more roughly than he meant to. "Wake up."

"What is it?" she asked, struggling to get up. He helped her to a sitting position as she swiped the disheveled hair from her face.

"I need you to draw for me."

"What? Right now?"

"Yes, now." He held up the sketch, then shoved it at her. "I think I know who the killer is, but I need your help to be sure."

Her sleepy eyes gleamed with surprise. "Hand me my sketch pad," she said with a nod.

He reached for the pad, positioning it next to the sketch on her lap.

Containing his excitement, he handed her a pencil and sat on the bed beside her. "I need you to listen carefully," he said. "And do exactly as I say."

* * * *

Daisy stared at the face she'd just drawn, unable to believe her own eyes. "Dear Lord," she uttered in amazement. "But how—"

"He's one clever son-of-a-bitch, that's how," Jackson said. "I have to notify the sheriff. I've already sent Kotterman to Troy for information on the wanted notices, which I predict will confirm everything. In the meantime, I can't leave you here alone." He helped her from the bed, then began gathering her things. "While I get the sheriff, I want you to go next door to the Wyman's and wait for me there."

After helping her dress, he wrapped her in her shawl. With a glance around the room, he located the vial of laudanum. "It always hurts worse in the evening," he reminded her. "It could be hours before it's safe for you to return home."

His concern for her comfort at so critical a time surprised her. She swallowed hard, stuffing the vial into her skirt pocket along with a fresh handkerchief and the spare house key. "I'll be fine," she said. "Go alert the sheriff."

She handed him the sketch, glancing once more at the face staring back at her. She still couldn't believe it.

They hurried downstairs, and Jackson led Daisy to the door. "Stay with the Wymans until I return for you," he repeated.

"I will." She gazed into his face, and every moment they'd shared, all her love for him, heightened her fear. "Be careful, Jax."

With a nod he ran toward the stable for his horse, disappearing into the darkness. Daisy turned and bolted across the lawn toward the Wyman house. Her pounding pulse quickened with each shadowy movement of the shrubs in the breeze. The fear someone might jump out at any moment made it difficult to breathe.

With only one arm for balance, running on the dew-covered grass proved dangerous. The fate of a broken neck as she fled toward safety was too ironic to tempt. She treaded carefully, slowing the pace of her slippered feet as best she could. Never had she been so eager for the company of the nosy Wymans.

When she finally reached the house, she knocked on the door. Nothing. She knocked and knocked again, before it dawned on her. The Westcott Ball. The Wymans weren't answering because they weren't home.

She turned toward the deserted road. Jackson was long gone in his urgency to get to the sheriff. Her heart plummeted. The majority of the town's population would be attending the public ball this evening. The sheriff would be there too.

Daisy sighed, heading for home. She'd have to wait for Jackson there. She reassured herself that she would be fine. She'd arm herself with the gun he kept in the parlor.

Hurrying toward the glowing porch lamps, she fumbled in her pocket for her key. She stepped inside the house and had just locked the door behind her, when she heard a scuffle outside. She peeked through the curtains, but no one appeared. Her eyes scanned the stone walk and the darkness beyond. An emerging form on the side lawn sent chills up her spine.

A black horse with white stockings.

Chapter 23

A bang on the door sent Daisy spinning from the window. She pressed her back to the wall, her heart pounding in her throat.

"I see you in there. Open the door!"

The familiar voice held a menacing tone she hadn't thought possible. The cold truth made her shiver in fear.

"Open up!" The banging grew louder.

Daisy's thoughts scattered. Closing her eyes against the echo in her head, she tried not to panic. The gun. She considered warning him she was armed, but if he called her bluff by shooting through the door, she refused to die empty-handed. She pushed herself from the wall, preparing to bolt for the gun in the parlor.

"You've got three seconds before I blow this boy's head off."

Daisy froze.

"Please, Mrs. Gallway, open the door!"

Andy!

Her hand shot to her mouth. She gulped back a sob, the panic surging in her throat.

"One. Two…"

"All right!" She had no choice; the man was insane. With trembling fingers, she unlatched the lock. The door flung open, sending her flying. She gasped, stumbling backward.

Jacob Squires shoved Andy into the room. The boy flailed, falling to his knees at her feet.

"Andy!" She bent to help him from the floor. Wrapping his arms around her waist, he held on tight. She cradled his head, whirling to shield his body with hers as he buried his face in her skirts.

"Now then," Jacob said behind her. "Where the hell is your husband?"

Her first instinct was to tell him Jackson was on his way home with the sheriff. But Jacob's drastic actions tonight proved how desperate he was. His imminent arrest would leave him with nothing to lose. He'd kill her and Andy on the spot.

No. She'd have to let Jacob believe he had the upper hand, that Jackson had no clue he was the killer. Her only hope was to buy them some time. She shuddered at the fearful premonition Jacob would wait until Jackson returned, and then kill them all.

She glanced over her shoulder to see Jacob looming closer.

She spun to face him, keeping Andy at her back. Observing the wooly man now, she saw clearly the face Andy had described—the killer inside the disguise. Behind the bushy mask of mustache and beard, she saw the structure of his nose, the squinting eyes distorted by the thick spectacles. How on earth had she missed it?

The long, straggly hair beneath the straw hat, combined with the absence of the forty or so pounds he'd shed, did nothing to conceal his identity now.

"Answer me, damn it. Where is he?"

She mustered her voice. "My husband is at the Lake Tavern." She lifted her chin, finding strength in the falsehood. "As usual."

Jacob tilted his head. His eyes honed in on her, scrutinizing her honesty, seeking signs of deceit. His gaze darted around the room.

"Surely you've heard of my husband's reputation for carousing," she said in mock frustration. "He's neither faithful nor dependable. He won't be home for hours, so you may as well make yourself comfortable."

Jacob's shoulders relaxed a bit. Hers did too. Her lies were working. She glanced toward the desk where the gun was hidden, contemplating a plan. She'd never get to it before Jacob put a bullet in her back. With one arm in a sling, she had a definite disadvantage. Her grip on Andy's shoulder tightened.

She needed to delay Jacob, somehow, until help arrived. If the sheriff was attending the ball, it would take at least an hour for Jackson to retrieve him at the Westcott's house on the other side of Misty Lake. She had to keep Andy alive until then.

"I could do with some coffee while we wait." If she could manage to stall Jacob, they'd at least stand a chance. "May I make some?"

He considered her request, then tossed his hat on the table. "Such hospitality." His shallow smile turned to a sneer, and she wondered again how she'd not seen through his evil façade. "Make it strong. We're in for a long night, and I wouldn't want to be dozing off."

And then it struck her. The laudanum. She still had the vial in her pocket. A plan hatched in her head, and she prayed for the fortitude to execute it. Hope lifted her spirit as Jacob herded them into the kitchen.

The scent of the flowers the odious man had given her a mere three days before made her feel sick. Her fear gave way to anger. She stared at the vase on the table, fighting the urge to smash it over his head.

He had been in her home. In the room where she slept.

The sketch he'd helped her create was intended to throw Jackson off course. This man's propensity for deception was shockingly terrifying.

He pointed a stiff finger at Andy. "Sit."

Andy huddled into a chair at the table. Jacob plopped down, resting his elbows on the table across from the boy. "You try anything funny, and I'll kill him," he said.

Andy stared at the gun in Jacob's hand. The fear on his tear-stained face filled her with guilt. She swallowed hard. She'd failed to protect him; she should have done more. Her hand shook as she struck a match and lit the stove. Placing the coffee canister on the table in front of Jacob, she asked, "Would you mind opening it for me?"

He lifted the cover from the canister. She snatched it up, turning back to her task. The strong aroma of ground coffee filled her nostrils as she fumbled to measure the desired amount and scoop it into the pot. While the coffee brewed, she retrieved the cups and the saucers from the cupboard. She moved slowly as she gathered the creamer, sugar bowl, and spoons. Steadying her hands, she arranged them on the table in front of Jacob.

"Why did you do it, Jacob?" she asked.

"The name's Paddy." He gave a firm nod. "Paddy O'Boyle."

She turned back to the stove, her body blocking his view. "Why did you do it?" she repeated, unable to bring herself to utter the name. If she could only keep him talking to distract him from what she was doing. She slipped her hand into her pocket and clutched the vial in her palm.

"We all have to follow the path that's set out for us," he said. "The path we were raised on. My daddy taught me real good."

She winced at the cryptic explanation. Was committing murder his legacy? His birthright? The man was truly insane. Daisy poured the entire bottle of laudanum into one of the cups. She quickly poured the coffee on top of it, hoping the drug wouldn't discolor the contents. She winced, swirling her finger in the steaming brew.

"Here." She placed the cup in front of the man and held her breath while he raised it to his lips.

He blew on the coffee, then took a good swallow. She exhaled, sliding into the chair at Andy's side. She sipped from the cup she'd poured for herself, while Andy stared at his cup of untouched milk.

"I had to kill this boy's daddy," Jacob announced. "Once he noticed I had Marty Shaw's watch, I had no choice."

"Marty Shaw?"

"I wanted that farm."

Something in the way he said it filled her with dread.

"So I did what I had to do to get it," he said. "Just like my daddy."

She braced herself against the unthinkable. "Marty Shaw is dead?"

Nodding, he leaned across the table. "Him and his whole damn family."

The blood drained from her face. *He'd killed them all.*

Jacob leaned back in his seat, enjoying her horror. Looking as proud as Lucifer, he said, "After I got rid of the family, I took over the farm." He slurped some more coffee. "But Ray Wendell didn't believe the Shaws had left town. He came poking around the farm and caught me there. I told him the place was mine, right and legal, but when he saw I had Marty Shaw's watch, I knew he'd figure out what I'd done. So I followed him home and took care of him too."

Andy stiffened beside her, head hung low. She could barely tolerate the repugnance of what Jacob was saying; she couldn't fathom how painful it was for the poor boy to hear.

He waved the gun toward Andy. "Course I didn't know at the time that the boy had witnessed his daddy's killing. I learned of your sketch after I became Jacob Squires." He patted his belly. "Lost my tub-of-lard gut, dabbed some boot polish on my hair, and even I didn't recognize myself. Except for learning to see through these spectacles, it was easy."

His blatant confession was made more disturbing by the sheer delight he was taking in revealing his grisly crimes. He was bragging. She sensed he'd been looking forward to the opportunity to flaunt his cleverness for a very long time. In that moment, she was certain she and Andy would be his next victims.

The pride on Jacob's face turned to anger. "But your lawyer husband wasn't letting things rest." He pointed to her sling. "You have him to thank for the bullet you took." He shook his head. "Can't say I'm sorry for that, though. That damn sketch you drew started it all."

She straightened in her seat. How dare he shrug the blame on to her? This man was a cold-hearted killer, deranged in his purpose. Nothing Daisy had or had not done could have changed that.

"After I killed the family, I forged a farewell letter from Marty Shaw, explaining his reasons for leaving town so suddenly," he continued. "I concocted a story that Marty's wife ran off with a peddler, and Marty was heading west. Then I wrote that he'd sold the farm to a man named Jacob Squires."

Her knees trembled beneath the table, and she tightened her grip on her cup to steady her quaking nerves. "Please, Jacob, think of your wife. What will become of her—"

"The name's Paddy. And I have no wife." He smiled. "Fooled them all with that too."

She couldn't bear to hear any more. Glancing at Andy, she bit back the screams she was forced to contain. *Jackson, where are you?* Her control was shattering to pieces, and she held back her tears. How long would it take for the laudanum to take effect? Surely, she'd used enough.

Jacob continued to ramble, but a few minutes later, she noticed his speech was getting slower. His words were slurring, and he yawned several times.

He noticed too.

He blinked hard. "What did you do?"

Daisy stood slowly. "I don't know what you're—"

"Bitch!" He slammed his fist on the table. Andy jumped to his feet, shrinking behind her.

Jacob kept blinking, trying to focus. His lips gnarled with fury. Reaching for the gun, he moved to get up. His chair toppled over.

"Andy, run!"

Daisy flung her hot coffee into Jacob's face.

"Run!"

The boy took off like a shot. Daisy turned to follow, but Jacob grabbed her. After snatching a fistful of her hair, he yanked her against his chest. He was unsteady on his feet, and they both crashed to the floor. The gun flew from his grip, sliding into the baseboard.

Pain tore through Daisy's shoulder, leaving her immobile where she'd sprawled. With a grunt, Jacob flipped her to her back and straddled her in place. His glassy eyes kept blinking; coffee dripped from his angry face.

Kicking her feet, she pounded him with her free hand. His spectacles went flying. She poked at his eyes, striking her target, and he spit out a curse. He pinned her arm to her side, leaving her helpless. He grappled for the gun, but it lay out of reach. She struggled frantically beneath him, kicking some more.

With another vile curse, he gave up on the gun and went for her throat. His hands clamped her windpipe. Tears flooded her bulging eyes. She sputtered and struggled for air. Squeezing harder, he choked off her gasps. Dark spots filled her vision as she faded away.

"I'm taking care of it, Daddy," she heard him say through the din. "Just like you would."

His rambling assurances to the demons in his mind drove him onward, and she knew she would die.

Chapter 24

Jackson spotted the black horse tied to the gate post right away. His chest constricted, tightening his muscles with every terrifying scenario that had flashed through his head during the frantic ride home.

He'd left Daisy alone....

The sight of the horse's white stockings confirmed his sick fear. He dismounted, sliding from the saddle as quickly as he could. Sheriff Coons slogged behind him somewhere, but there was no time to wait. Jackson ran up the sidewalk to the house, passing Andy, who bolted right by him.

Jackson raced into the house, heard the sound of a man's voice in the kitchen. He charged into the room to see Jacob on top of Daisy. Her body lay rigid beneath the man, whose ramblings grew louder. Jackson's rage overwhelmed him, and he became someone else.

"Paddy!"

Jacob looked up. His crazed eyes flashed wide as Jackson pointed his gun and fired a bullet through his head.

Jackson's heart pounded as the man fell backward to the floor. He raced to Daisy, heaving Paddy off her legs. He scooped her into his arms.

She clutched her throat, gulping desperately for air.

She was alive.

He exhaled in relief, blinking back tears. Forcing himself to loosen his embrace, he allowed her some space to catch her breath.

He held her in his trembling arms as her lungs filled with air. He kissed her temple, the top of her head, while the frantic rhythm of her breathing subsided to a more normal pace.

Unable to restrain his emotions a moment longer, he drew her against his chest, rocking her gently. "I'm sorry," he murmured against her ear. "I forgot about the Westcott Ball. I never should have left you alone. I'm so sorry."

She gazed up at him, tears streaming down her cheeks. Her parted lips trembled, her voice a raspy whisper. "Andy?"

"He's safe," he assured her.

She slumped in relief, and he loved her all the more for risking her life for the boy. He choked down the lump of emotion that caught in his throat.

Reflections of the traumatic horror she'd endured shone in her bloodshot eyes. Jackson saw his whole world in her eyes, in the pale face staring up at him. His rage at almost losing her returned full force, roaring inside his chest like a violent storm. It took all the strength he possessed to restrain himself from plugging another bullet into Paddy's dead body for trying to murder the woman he loved.

* * * *

The remainder of the night and following morning passed in a dizzying blur. Jackson's body ran on taut nerves and coffee. He sat next to Daisy in the library, holding her hand as Sheriff Coons and his deputies assisted the coroner in removing Paddy's body from the house.

To spare Andy from the gruesome aftermath, Jackson had asked the Wymans to take the boy back to Barston. Daisy had agreed that Curtis and his family were probably frantic in their worries for the missing boy, and the Wymans had been happy to help.

Jackson could hardly wait for the questioning to be over so he could concentrate on Daisy. She'd been through so much. Bruises covered her throat, and it pained her to speak. The wound on her shoulder had torn open, but she insisted she was fine. But she was still digesting the ordeal, and Jackson would feel better after the doctor examined her.

Sheriff Coons and his deputies returned to the library, then listened intently as Jackson relayed the chain of events that had led to the death of the man who'd killed five people in this county alone.

"According to the wanted notices Kotterman retrieved, Paddy O'Boyle is wanted for murder in two other states," Jackson said.

Sheriff Coons leaned forward. "I've just been informed that they've discovered four graves in the field at the Shaw farm." He turned his grim focus to Daisy. "He admitted murdering the family?"

Daisy nodded. "And writing letters in Mr. Shaw's name to explain their disappearance."

"Devious son-of-a-bitch," the sheriff mumbled.

"Since Paddy had been holed up at the farm for weeks, he had ample time to study Marty's handwriting," Jackson said. "During that time, he altered his appearance as well. It wasn't until Andy showed up after the fire that he emerged as Jacob Squires. He'd pretended he'd just arrived from Pennsylvania, but he'd been in Barston for months, hiding at the Shaw place."

"O'Boyle set the fire," the sheriff clarified to the deputy who was scribbling the details in a notebook. "He's also the one who placed advertisements in the papers, under Marty's name, stating his wife had run off, and he wasn't responsible for her debts."

Jackson nodded. "Word of the scandal spread through town, and everyone accepted the family's departure—and Jacob Squires as their newest resident."

"Unbelievable," the sheriff muttered.

"When Ray Wendell questioned Paddy about Marty Shaw's watch, Paddy killed him too," Jackson added. "Then he stashed some items he'd stolen from the Wendell house in Randal Morgan's wagon."

"And Morgan never suspected a thing," the sheriff said with a shake of his head.

"But Paddy's confidence that his crimes had died with Morgan must have faltered when he learned Andy had witnessed his father's murder. Paddy visited Morgan at the jailhouse to gather information on the status of his case and the evidence against him," Jackson said. "But on the last visit, he slipped up. He used his new identity when he signed the jailhouse visitor log, which is how I tied it all together."

Sheriff Coons heaved himself from the chair. Shoving his hat on his head, he gazed down at Jackson and said, "Congratulations, young man. You've managed to find a killer we didn't believe existed. And you cleared an innocent man's name in the process."

Jackson swallowed hard at the man's newfound admiration. "The real credit goes to my wife." Jackson glanced to Daisy. "I couldn't have done it without her."

The sheriff nodded. "The authorities from Troy are on their way to Misty Lake to take statements from you all. Reporters from the papers are waiting for me outside as we speak. I suspect you're about to become a public hero," he said. "Let me be the first to say that the publicity is well deserved." The deputies followed as he trudged toward the door. He tossed a wave behind him. "I'll be in touch."

Jackson exhaled, turning to Daisy. "Are you all right?"

Her silent nod was no comfort. The aftermath of her trauma shone in her somber eyes, leaving him helpless. "Andy is fine," he assured her. "None of this was your fault."

"I know," she said.

He smiled, relieved by her certainty, and then she smiled too.

"You did it, Jackson."

Her face beamed with pride, and he basked in the thrill of it.

"You really did it."

While her words should have played like music to his ears, all he heard was the underlying chorus. His heart sank.

And now you may go.

* * * *

Daisy sipped another cup of hot tea, as Doctor Gregory had prescribed. The warm brew soothed her raw throat. The sweet scent of chamomile offered a calm in the lull of activity in the parlor. People had been dropping by all morning, gathering on the porch outside to offer congratulations to Jackson for revealing the killer who'd been living among them.

Overnight, Jackson's status had risen from that of disreputable rake to revered hero. Despite her inner misery that he'd be leaving soon, she couldn't be prouder.

The telegram Jackson had received earlier from Randal Morgan's children, expressing their undying gratitude for proving their father's innocence, had brought them both to tears.

For the rest of her days, she would cling to the reminder that this one simple telegram had made everything worth it.

A man and a promise redeemed. Two names restored.

She glanced up as Jackson entered the room.

Despite his palpable nervous energy, he looked exhausted. "How are you feeling?" he asked as he sat beside her on the settee.

"My shoulder still hurts, but I'm feeling much better."

"That's good." He inhaled a quick breath. "I'll be leaving tomorrow," he said.

The words hurt more than the bullet she'd taken, and she pursed her lips to stave off her pain. This might be the last time she saw him. She studied him closely, preserving his image in her heart and her mind. His broad frame and shoulders. His strong arms and kind eyes.

"But I can't go without telling you something first." He inched closer, grasping her hand between his. He stared into her eyes, and she hung on each word.

"I know you have your own plans," he said. "But I have a plan too."

She blinked in surprise.

"I don't want to leave."

Her breath hitched. "But what about St. Louis?"

"I don't want St. Louis," he said. "Solving this case has almost cost me everything I never knew I wanted."

Daisy furrowed her brow in confusion.

"It's cost me you, Daisy. I want you as my wife. I love you."

The candid words rushed through her like a warm stream of light. Shadows lifted from her heart.

"I no longer care about that position in St. Louis," he said. "I want to settle here—with you." He smiled. "And the geese."

She smiled, emotions bursting inside.

"I can start my own investigation agency in Misty Lake. I believe I'm a good investigator, and with my background in law, who knows. I suspect there are a lot of people out there like Randal Morgan. People who've been wrongly accused of crimes they didn't commit. People whose names and reputations have been destroyed. I want to help them get the justice they deserve and reclaim their lives."

She took in his words, her pulse racing.

"I may have to do some traveling from time to time," he said. "But I've always enjoyed traveling." He smiled. "Of course, I will need a partner. Someone smart, someone who's good with people. Someone with a talent for sketching, perhaps."

"You really mean it, don't you?"

He gazed into her face, nodding slowly. "Yes."

She saw in his glistening eyes it was true. Felt it in the depth of her soul. "Oh, Jackson." She flung herself into his arms. "I love you."

He stiffened against her. "You do?"

She drew back from him, nodding at his honest surprise. "Yes, I do. I was afraid you couldn't be happy here. That you would leave me eventually. I was so determined to safeguard my heart. I was breaking it by letting you go."

She smiled through her tears, and then he smiled too.

He blinked, and his eyes filled with sorrow. "I'm sorry for the hurtful things I said to you. I was afraid too. You were right about me. I thought I wasn't good enough."

"You were right about me too. I was wallowing in my past. It just took someone else to point it out. To help me pull myself through it."

He kissed her temple, smoothing her hair. "You told me once that every sinner has a future," he said. "Mine is with you."

"Yes it is."

"I love you." He brushed a tear from her cheek. "And I will not—I cannot—live my life without you."

Her heart swelled with joy. She kissed his smiling lips. "If that is the case, I will promise you'll never have to."

Epilogue

With the hectic activity of the past week behind them, Daisy and Jackson were falling into an easy routine that included little more than spending every possible moment together. Aside from a few errands, Jackson hadn't left her side, and the arrangement suited Daisy fine.

A lifetime of mornings like this, with Jackson reading the papers over breakfast, the view of the lake sparkling in the distance, filled her with such happiness she feared it a dream.

She turned toward the sound of the door creaking open. Kotterman stepped out to the patio with another seemingly endless delivery of cards and notes. The town would be buzzing for weeks, and the pile of cards on the tray Kotterman placed on the table proved it.

Jackson doled out the cards addressed to Daisy, then began scanning through those meant for him.

Daisy opened the first card, smiling as she read. "I've been invited to tea," she said. "Gianna Elmsworth writes that her dearest friend will be visiting from Saratoga next week, and she'd like for us to meet."

Jackson nodded. "Landen mentioned she'd be writing you when he stopped by to see me last week."

"I'm sure they're as curious for the details about what happened as everyone else so obviously is," Daisy said.

"That's what I thought at first. But from Landen's pointed questions about you, I got the impression they're more curious about your entranced drawing than anything else."

"Really?"

"He seemed quite intrigued."

Daisy shrugged. "Well, I'm not ashamed of my ability anymore. I'll not hide it. Besides, I like Gianna. I'm sure I'll like her friend, Madeline Merrick too."

"You can never have too many friends."

She smiled. "I love Tessa dearly, but it would be nice to have more than one."

He reached for her hand, then gave it a squeeze. "Are you up for taking a ride today?"

"To visit Andy?" She set down the card.

Jackson shook his head. "Not to visit him, no. To bring him back here to stay with us."

Her heart leaped. "Curtis agreed?"

Jackson gave a nod toward the note on the table. "He's answered my appeal. Curtis wants Andy to have a real home. A real family—with a mother and father. We'll see how Andy likes it here with us before making the arrangement permanent." He smiled. "You know what this means, of course." He leaned back in his chair. "I promised you a child, and now you have one."

She rushed to his side, then hugged him tight.

He stood to accommodate, returning her embrace. "Since I've now fulfilled my end of our deal, I believe, we are unobjectionably even."

She swallowed back her tears, hugging him tighter. "I suppose we are." She stood on tiptoes to whisper in his ear. "But just because we have one child, doesn't mean we can't enjoy trying for more."

"Every night." Grinning, he pressed his forehead to hers. "Let's make it our plan."

THE END

In case you missed it, keep reading for an excerpt from the first book in the Sole Survivor series,

The Lady Who Lived Again

Madeline Sutter was once the belle of the ball at the popular resort town of Misty Lake, New York. But as the sole survivor of the community's worst tragedy, she's come under suspicion. Longing for the life she once enjoyed, she accepts a rare social invitation to the event of the season. Now she will be able to show everyone she's the same woman they'd always admired—with just one hidden exception: she awoke from the accident with the ability to heal.

Doctor Jace Merrick has fled the failures and futility of city life to start anew in rural Misty Lake. A man of science, he rejects the superstitious chatter surrounding Maddie and finds himself drawn to her confidence and beauty. And when she seduces him into a sham engagement, he agrees to be her ticket back into society, if she supports his new practice—and reveals the details of her remarkable recovery. But when his patients begin to heal miraculously, Jace may have to abandon logic, accept the inexplicable—and surrender to a love beyond reason…

A Lyrical e-book on sale now.

Learn more about Thomasine at
http://www.kensingtonbooks.com/author.aspx/31713

Chapter 1

Misty Lake, New York, 1882

Everyone wished she had died with the others. Maddie Sutter had accepted this truth long ago. But much to the small town's dismay, she insisted on living and breathing despite it.

Straightening her shoulders, she lifted her chin against the barrage of eyes watching her every move as she forged down Main Street. After three years of suffering this unwelcome attention each time she ventured to town, one would think she'd have grown used to the assault.

Maddie had resigned herself to many things since the accident, but she'd never adapt to the dread her presence induced in those she had known all her life—those who had once loved and cared for her.

With a fortifying breath, she approached a cluster of young boys on the corner. The same wretched imps had greeted her earlier when they'd spied her arrival in downtown Misty Lake. She braced herself for a repeat performance of the cruel rhyme they'd composed in her honor.

"Four dead girls on the slab, on the twelfth day of May. On Friday the thirteenth, one girl walked away."

Refusing to alter her course, Maddie strode straight toward them. Her lungs swelled with triumph as the alarmed little brats scattered like mice. With another fractional lift of her chin, she swept onward and rounded the corner.

She entered the general mercantile, the jingling bell on the door her only greeting as she stepped inside. Along with a handful of patrons, the store housed a hodgepodge of scents. Aromas of charcoal and beeswax mingled with the sweet smell of cinnamon and apples. Renewed by the boon to her senses, she enjoyed the whiff of fond memories that came with it. She shopped quickly, spurred on by the hushed whispers echoing through the aisles as she browsed the shelves.

Gathering a bag of sugar, a tin of baking powder, and the other items on her list, she headed to the front of the store, then placed them on the polished counter.

"Good morning, Mr. Piedmont," she said with a smile.

He wiped his hands on his bibbed apron and took a step forward.

"Madeline."

With a curt nod, he lowered his somber eyes to the items on the counter and began to tally her purchases.

Maddie's smile faded, her mind drifting back to the days when Mr. Piedmont's face would light up to see her and her friends bounding into the mercantile. The Fair Five, as they were known back then, had charmed everyone. The girls had hardly put away their pinafores when they first learned to use their collective wit and beauty to full advantage. The Five always left Mr. Piedmont's store lapping at complimentary peppermint sticks, pressed upon them by the kindly merchant with a playful wink.

Maddie took a deep breath, forcing away thoughts of the past and the accident that had snatched her friends from this world. At twenty-four-years old, Maddie was a living reminder and the sole survivor of the worst tragedy in Misty Lake's history. People could barely stand to look at her. And Maddie couldn't blame them. She could barely stand to look at herself.

Mr. Piedmont worked swiftly, the sound of crumpling paper filling the awkward silence as he wrapped her purchases and bound the tidy parcel with string. By rote, his freckled hand reached to the nearby jar of candy. Placing a single peppermint stick on top of the bundle, he slid it toward her, then turned to face the shelves lining the wall behind him.

Tears blurred Maddie's vision as she stared down at the red-striped treat, the simple reminder of who she once was—who she still was, if only one of her neighbors could manage to look her in the eye long enough to see it. She swallowed hard.

"Thank you," she murmured to the shopkeeper's back before he walked away.

Maddie left the store and proceeded to her final errand. As she'd anticipated, a letter from Amelia awaited her at the post office. Maddie would wait until later to open it. Their recent correspondence had rattled her to the bone, and she knew any public display of emotion would be ripe fruit for hungry local gossips.

Not that maintaining decorum could help her cause now. People already believed the worst about her. These rare trips to town only served to remind her that nothing had changed.

Shoving the letter into her skirt pocket, she headed south on Main Street. To her relief, the band of young hooligans that had taunted her earlier was nowhere to be seen. She hurried out of town nonetheless. Each dreaded trip was a tax on her nerves, and when added to the anxiety of what awaited in Amelia's letter, Maddie yearned for the comfort of home.

When she reached the outskirts of town, she took the path through the woods that opened to a large field. She welcomed the sound of chirping crickets and birds. As always after she exerted herself with a lengthy walk, her leg was beginning to ache. She slowed her pace, then stopped to rest at her favorite spot on her grandfather's sprawling property. Sitting on a felled birch log in the broad clearing, she stretched out her leg. The cramped muscles unfurled as she enjoyed the serenity of the surrounding forest, the gentle spring breeze through the swaying trees. The sun felt heavenly, and she lifted her face to bask in its glow.

She'd avoided town all winter, hibernating like a bear in a cave. She'd emerged from seclusion renewed by foolish hopes, but the first outing of the new season had been just like the last. A bear would be better received.

Maddie sighed in defeat, dug out the letter that was fairly vibrating in her pocket, and unfolded its pages. The bold strokes on the delicate cream sheets conveyed Amelia's confident tone and dramatic style.

My dearest Mads,

I received your response denying my request, but I refuse to take no for an answer. I simply cannot get married without you!

You swore an oath to one day serve as my bridesmaid, and it is time for you to honor it. My deep love and concern for you force me to hold you to your promise.

The past is the past, my dear friend, and you must lay it to rest. Eventually, the town will follow suit. Consider attending my wedding as your first step toward getting on with your life.

We arrive in Misty Lake in three weeks. I look forward to seeing you then.
Forever yours,
Amelia

Maddie's breakfast turned in her stomach. How on earth could she attend? No one, save Amelia, wanted her there. Certainly not Daniel. The mere thought of facing her former fiancé and all the others who'd blamed and abandoned her…no. Maddie hadn't the courage. Amelia didn't understand. How could she? She was not present when it happened. Nor was she here for the aftermath.

Something rustled in the woods across the field. Squinting against the sun, Maddie scanned the trees. A deer hobbled into the clearing, took one final step, then collapsed to the ground. Maddie gasped at the arrow protruding from its shoulder.

Without a thought, she ran to the deer and dropped to her knees at its side. Blood flowed, a crimson stream from the gaping hole around the arrow. The trembling doe stared up at her, eyes wide with pain and terror.

Maddie glanced around to ensure she was alone. The arrow was a direct hit to the vitals, and the poor creature couldn't have traveled far. Someone might be tracking it. Glancing into the deer's desperate eyes again, Maddie tossed caution to the wind.

She grasped the arrow, clenching it as hard as she could. The blasted thing was in deep. Mustering her strength, she pulled, grunting as the arrow ripped through the torn muscle and flesh in which it was lodged. She fell backward, arrow in hand. Blood gushed everywhere. Tossing aside the arrow, she leaned over the deer and pressed her hands to the wound. Blood oozed between her fingers. Life drained from the deer, the warm flow filling her nose with the acrid scent of looming death.

She squeezed her eyes shut, swallowing against the bile rising in her throat. Behind her closed lids, pictures flashed in the darkness. The wagon careening out of control. The approaching tree. The bodies hurling through the air. Sounds of terrified screams filled her ears. Tears poured down her face as she opened her soul. All the pain, all the guilt, manifested inside her, raging through her veins. Heat radiated to her hands, transferring everything onto the dying deer.

Her hands grew hotter and hotter. Her heart pounded and she could barely breathe. She opened her eyes, watching through her scalding fingers as the stream of blood slowed and the torn hide around the wound began to close. The deer stirred, and Maddie sat back on her haunches, panting for air.

The deer sprang to its hooves. Its wide eyes met hers before it darted across the field, white tail raised like a flag as it hurdled the birch log, then disappeared into the forest. Maddie exhaled a shaky breath. The thrum of her pulse waned in relief. Once again, she felt worthy, if only for a moment, of surviving when no one else had.

She'd awakened after the accident with the ability to heal, and the absolution implied by this power helped her cling to her sanity. The mysterious gift was her only justification for living now, a token she'd smuggled back from some place between heaven and earth. One she had to keep hidden if she hoped ever to regain any semblance of a normal life.

"Hey, there!"

Maddie spun toward the voice in the trees. A man charged into the clearing, a large bow in his hands. With a curse, she pushed to her feet and turned her back to him as she gathered her wits. Wringing her bloody hands furiously between the folds of her beige skirt, she fought for composure, concocting her lies.

She inhaled a sharp breath and turned to face him. He stopped, startled by the sight of her. "Are you all right?" He rushed toward her. "Did it hurt you?"

"I'm fine," she said, backing away from the tall stranger.

He glanced down at the pool of bright blood at his boots, then looked around for the deer. "What the devil happened? Where is it?"

Maddie pointed toward the trees. "It ran into the woods."

"It's still running?" His blue eyes narrowed. "Impossible. I struck a kill shot."

"Unfortunately for the deer, your aim was not so precise." She gauged his wary reaction. "Nor is your eyesight if you thought you struck the vitals," she added, pinning her lies firmly in place with an angry nod. "Your clumsy shot to the gut will prolong the poor animal's misery. I dislodged the arrow to lessen its suffering."

His brows shot up. "You dislodged... Are you addled?" He stared in disbelief. "What possessed you—?"

"Senseless torment possessed me," she shot back. "And I assure you, my mind is quite sound."

The man was not convinced. Lowering his chin, he yanked off his hat and scratched his dark head. "I could have sworn I hit the..." Tousled black hair gleamed in the sunlight as he bent for the arrow. "You dislodged it, you say?"

He analyzed the bloody hair on the arrow, clearly distracted. She could see the questions forming in his bewildered eyes. She had to get rid of him.

"Your deer bolted, but it won't get far." She gave a nod toward the trees. "You should hurry."

Ignoring her suggestion, he took a step forward. "What's your name?" He dropped the arrow, his gaze fixing on her bloody hands. Reaching into his coat, he pulled out a handkerchief. He grabbed her wrist and attempted to wipe at the blood.

Maddie yanked back her hand. "My name is Madeline Sutter, and I can do that myself."

With a frown, he relinquished the cloth and let her proceed with the task.

"I'm Jace Merrick, Miss Sutter. I've taken over Doctor Filmore's practice in town now that he's retired."

The news surprised her. Doctor Filmore was eighty years old, if he was a day, and she'd always assumed he would die wearing his stethoscope. She was equally surprised by the youthful mien of Filmore's replacement. And by this new physician's obvious appetite for hunting. Weren't doctors supposed to be devoted to preserving life? Not that Doctor Filmore had gone out of his way to preserve hers. He'd pronounced her dead for God's sake. She slapped the cloth between her palms.

"It's about time that old fool retired," she muttered.

Pushing her disdain for the elderly doctor aside, she focused on the man before her. Jace Merrick possessed a palpable confidence, but dressed as he was, he didn't look like a doctor. His brown trousers were tucked into large boots, and a green flannel shirt peeked out from his open tweed coat.

And yet, even in his casual hunter's uniform, the man was impressive. The words ruggedly appealing sprang to mind. He stood taller than most, surely taller than Daniel. Doctor Merrick's build was broader than Daniel's as well. A twinge of longing fluttered in the pit of her belly.

The queer sensation took Maddie aback. She straightened her spine, steeling herself against her attraction to the handsome stranger. As she knew only too well, a man in the medical profession could destroy her. The doctor's stern voice snapped Maddie out of her reverie.

"Wild animals can be dangerous, Miss Sutter. Especially when they're wounded. You were fortunate in this instance, but I'd advise you against taking such risks in the future."

"I appreciate your advice, Doctor Merrick, and I have some for you." She took a step toward him. "There is no hunting allowed on Sutter land, so please do your murdering elsewhere." She finished wiping her hands, then handed him back the bloodstained handkerchief. "Now take your belongings and get off my property."

* * * *

Jace blinked, staring at the woman. Whatever he'd done to earn her hostility, he'd obviously done it well.

"This is your property?"

"My family owns twelve acres. Hunting is restricted on all of it." Her spine stiffened like a broomstick. Beneath her simple straw bonnet, wisps of dark hair fringed her pretty face. Specks of hazel and gold sparked in her brown eyes, along with an annoying tinge of righteous indignation. "My grandfather makes exceptions in cases of necessity only." She eyed him from head to toe. "Since there are several eating establishments in town, and you're clearly not starving, you can pursue your sport elsewhere."

"In my defense, Miss Sutter, this hunt *was* necessary."

"Is that so?"

His business was none of her concern, but the challenge in her skeptical tone got the best of him. "Your elderly neighbor, Mrs. Tremont, is a patient of mine. Her weight has dropped drastically, and her appetite continues to wane."

Her smug tone faded. "I'm sorry to hear that," she muttered, looking genuinely distressed.

"The woman has a craving for fresh venison. I apologize for trespassing, but I intend to provide it."

She lowered her eyes, and Jace couldn't help enjoying her contrite response.

"Had you not intervened with my deer, I'd have no reason to dally here. On *your* property," he added, just for the hell of it.

"Well, don't let me keep you," she snapped. "Good luck with Mrs. Tremont." Her hard look softened again, as did the harshness in her voice. "Please send her my regards."

With a lift of her chin, she collected her market basket from where it sat beside a log, then hurried away. Jace stared after her, absorbing the view. She held her head high, her stance rigid and aloof. Her frame was small but curvaceous, possessing the perfect measure of female proportions. Ample breasts, narrow waist, pleasing backside.

Of course, one had to get past the bloodstained dress to appreciate what lay beneath, but as a doctor who'd seduced dozens of nurses whose aprons were soaked with far worse, this posed no problem for Jace. Her slender form moved swiftly as she made her way down the path through the field, but her pace was slowing. He detected a slight limp in her gait, though from this distance, he couldn't be sure.

"Madeline Sutter," he mumbled, shaking his head. What kind of woman went about pulling arrows from dying deer?

Jace had met some odd people during the month since he'd arrived in town, but he'd yet to meet anyone like Miss Sutter. Dragging his gaze from the fading view of her, he squatted before the patch of blood in the grass where his deer had fallen.

From the amount of blood and crimson color, Jace agreed with Miss Sutter's assessment of the situation. The animal was certain to bleed to death before getting far. It had to be dead on its feet to have allowed her anywhere near it, let alone remove the arrow. How it summoned the stamina to move on, Jace hadn't a clue, but he knew it would bed down in dense cover as soon as it could. Like any diligent hunter, Jace was obligated to recover it.

He reexamined the arrow. The hair attached was coarse, dark gray with dark tips, and two or so inches long. This evidence indicated a perfect kill shot behind the shoulder, not in the gut, as the girl had claimed.

With a shake of his head, Jace stood, preparing to track the deer. He would find out the truth soon enough, though with a wounded deer, one could never be certain as to how soon that might be. Mrs. Tremont was in dire need of protein. Since the old woman had no husband or sons, Jace would do what he must to provide it.

It had taken only one house call to discover that the duties of the country doctor entailed catering to each patient on a more personal level than was possible with the human wreckage he'd treated at Pittsburgh Hospital. Although his office had yet to open officially, he already knew the hell of the emergency ward—and the endless misery that flowed through its wide double doors—was a stark contrast to a small-town practice. He could make a real difference in Misty Lake, and not just to the wealthy summer visitors. Here he'd have the time to focus on each patient case without the patch-them-up-and-ship-them-out approach of the hospital. The change would be just what he needed to replenish his spirit from the toll of the daily tragedy that had sucked him dry.

Inhaling deeply, he forged past the memory of his internship in the city and the suffocating despair that came along with it. The pine-scented breeze coursed through his senses, anchoring him back to the present. The beauty of his current surroundings lifted his mood. There was nothing like a walk in the woods and reconnecting with nature to remind him that he was alive.

Perhaps if he'd found some comparable diversion from his rote existence in the city, he might have fared better there. Not that it mattered now. He'd made a decision to build a practice in the country, and he intended to succeed come hell or high water. Even so, he knew that, as a stranger, he should expect some initial hostility and skepticism from Misty Lake's residents. Miss Sutter had merely acted upon the resentment that a lot of her neighbors were nursing privately.

Swatting at a horsefly, he took a few steps in the direction in which the deer had bolted, searching the ground for the blood trail that would lead to his prey. Bloody hoof prints led from the scene. Hunching down for a closer look, he followed the tracks to a birch log, scanning the ground as he moved. "What the...?"

Not a single droplet of blood lay anywhere in the vicinity of the tracks. Had the deer's wound simply stopped bleeding? He scratched his head, glancing around. The blood flow might have ebbed somewhat, but to cut off entirely without leaving a trace? Preposterous. There had to be a logical explanation. There always was. As a man of science, Jace was curious to know what the devil that explanation was.

He inspected the peeling bark on the decaying log, then saw something flutter on the ground behind it. He reached for the discarded leaf of paper trapped in the weeds. Miss Sutter's? He collected the thing, then read with interest the letter that was, indeed, addressed to Madeline Sutter.

The past is the past, my dear friend, and you must lay it to rest. Eventually, the town will follow suit.

Who was this strange woman he'd encountered in the middle of nowhere? The woman who refused to attend her friend's wedding, but had no qualms about dislodging an arrow from a wild animal or ordering a man twice her size off her property?

Madeline Sutter intrigued him, and few women accomplished that feat. Jace looked forward to meeting her again. He glanced toward the path through the field. Locating her residence wouldn't be difficult. And her dropped letter gave him the perfect excuse to pay her a visit. For the moment, though, he had a deer to track in the opposite direction.

He gathered his things, then headed into the woods. When he returned to town, he would ask around about his latest acquaintance. Whoever she was, he couldn't wait to find out more.

Meet the Author

A three-time RWA Golden Heart® nominee, Thomasine Rappold writes historical romance and historical romance with paranormal elements. She lives with her husband in the small town in upstate New York that inspired her current series. When she's not spinning tales of passion and angst, she enjoys spending time with her family, fishing on one of the nearby lakes, and basking on the beach in Cape Cod. Thomasine is a member of Romance Writers of America and the Capital Region Romance Writers. Readers can find her on Facebook and follow her on Twitter: @ThomRappold.